TERROR NOVA
THE THIRTEENTH EXHIBIT

Published in Canada by Engen Books, Chapel Arm, NL.

A CIP catalogue record for this book is available from Library and Archives Canada.

ISBN-13 print: 978-1-77478-173-9
ISBN-13 eBook: 978-1-77478-174-6

Distributed by:
Engen Books
www.engenbooks.com
submissions@engenbooks.com

First mass market paperback printing: February 2025
Cover Image: Mike Hickey

TERROR NOVA
THE THIRTEENTH EXHIBIT

ENGEN BOOKS

1

"You know it's the thirteenth."

Sophia looked up from her coffee, making eye contact with Erin for the first time today.

There had not been enough coffee in the pot this morning. No matter how much had been in it, it had not been enough.

Not enough to clean the building, not enough to deal with people, and certainly not enough to suffer Erin and her bullshit.

Sophia and Erin Valentine were not related despite the relatively uncommon surname. The genealogical study Sophia had conducted while working on her history degree revealed that "Valentine" wasn't her family's actual name, but an anglicized version of Valenzuela adopted when they migrated to Newfoundland from Spain several generations back. Erin's family was just Scottish, and Sophia took some solace bordering on pride that even her ancestry seemed more interesting than her co-worker's.

That same last name, despite not technically being the same last name, was about the only thing the women had in common other than their duties as the weekday caretakers of the museum.

The museum wasn't open on weekends, not in the last four years anyway. In the last three years it hadn't been open on Thursdays. It started closing on Tuesdays two years ago, and a year ago, the government announced that funding had been cut once again, and as a result, the museum would be closed every other Monday moving forward.

That left Wednesdays, Fridays, and every other Monday for Sophia to put in hours and earn her living. Still, she took the bad with the good—the good being that the substantial cut in hours also meant a substantial cut to the amount of time that she had to spend with Erin and listen to her vocalize this exact dilemma.

Erin fiddled with a salt packet, flapping it back and forth with her middle finger, trying to get as much from it as she could onto the day-old fries she brought from home. She was eating them at room temperature, which was preferable to reheating them in the microwave.

The museum had no commercial kitchen, no kitchen at all, actually. What it did have was what would be generously described as a "kitchenette" that featured a kettle, a microwave, and a coffee perk. So, reheating her fries in the oven, or the far superior option of the air fryer (which she had tried at her brother's one time), weren't available to Erin so she would just drown the leftovers in salt and bemoan the experience, whining to Sophia about her plight as though Sophia wasn't in the exact same position.

There wasn't even a fridge, not since it had died on them last year, grossly limiting the things they could keep. They'd asked for a new unit, professing that even a minifridge would suffice, but time and time again were told no in the same way a parent tells a child no when they know something worse is coming down the pipe anyway. "No, you can't have that toy," *and soon you're losing all your toys so this won't seem so bad.*

And the limited hours gave neither of the Valentines the disposable income required to go out of pocket for such an extravagance as a minifridge, even for a Facebook Marketplace find.

"It's the thirteenth of the month," Erin said again, hissing the words from between clenched teeth. She leaned in when she said it, as though to stop anyone else from hearing.

As Sophia was about to turn to broadly gesture to the empty room and dramatically inquire for whom Erin was whispering, her eye caught a little old man on a bench in the corner. Large, thick glasses made him look all the smaller, and they made his sunken eyes look huge. Scant wisps of hair clung to his scalp like dried hay, and he wore a bowtie that was bright pink with green splotches that might have been polka-dots.

There was a juice box next to him, the sort the museum gave out when a child demanded a drink but refused water. It was grape; they were all grape. They'd been in the back of the kitchenette's sole cupboard so long that Sophia had joked they might soon be wine.

The old man picked it up and fought to catch the small straw with dry lips. When he finally caught it, he turned and watched them over his shoulder as he suckled.

With a shudder, Sophia turned back away from him to Erin, escaping the gaze.

"They shouldn't have this place open on the thirteenth," Erin hissed again. She finished, finally, with the salt packet she had been garnishing her fries with and laid it aside with three others she had procured.

"Jesus Christ, girl. How much salt do you need?"

Erin frowned at her then reached to the basket between them on the table, fiddling and fussing, and produced a sugar packet. She fought with it to tear it, and when she did, she held it tear-side down over her coffee and started the process of beating it with her fingers all over again. The rhythm was the same even though the condiment was different. Fwap-fwap-fwap-fwap, back and forth, hit first with the knuckle and then with the pad of the finger, and then again, so fast that it was a blur.

When she was done with that packet, she placed its empty carcass atop the bested salt packets and reached for another, rustling through them to find real sugar, nothing synthetic.

Sophia did not question the sugar the way she did the salt. The coffee *needed* the sugar to be palatable, and there was no milk. The lack of refrigeration meant it would have gone bad almost instantly and the tar-like coffee black was still better than using powdered creamer.

"We're already down to ten days a month, I can't lose another day when one of those happens to fall on the thirteenth," Sophia said, taking another sip of her coffee. "What are we supposed to do? Cancel when there's rain, but also too much sun? Cancel if the snow's been plowed but also if it hasn't? There's only so many days you can cancel before you have to shrug your shoulders and lock the doors for good."

Erin frowned at her. She sipped on the black drink that even Tim Horton's would feel guilty calling coffee, curled her lip at it, then fished for more sugar.

"I'm not sayin' it should close every time anything bad happens, I'm sayin' it should close on the thirteenth. I'd gladly give another day for it to do so. They can take the Lord's Day back if they like, every last one of them in the year if it means I don't have to work another thirteenth. That and every Friday too, Good or not. They can even take Christmas, if they wants it, and everything that comes with it under my tree. That's how much I'd rather not work another thirteenth, 'Phia. They can make me work every other day of the year and on into the night. Frig, they can make me sleep in the storage shed and have me forage the grounds for food like my great-grandfadder said he had to, if that makes 'em happy. Just so long as they don't make me work another thirteenth of the month."

Sophia rolled her eyes. "You can always just call in sick."

She'd attempted to poke holes in her co-worker's logic before, giving her facts about the calendar, about just how many days had gone missing, lost to history, since we started using it. How there was no way to know *exactly* what day it was, only what day we all *agreed* it was, and so it didn't make sense to be superstitious of the day one way or the other. She'd had this debate so often that it had boiled over into an argument a few times, and into a fight once, and since then she had resigned herself to the fate of having to hear this speech, periodically, for the rest of her adult life.

Now, whenever it was brought up, Sophia tried her best to keep her argument to a frown, and maybe one or two snide retorts.

"You seem to be forgetting the rest of it." Erin gestured around the place, the same way Sophia had before spotting the old man, only Erin was sincere. "*Thirteen* exhibits, maid. Thirteen of them, each with thirteen things in them. And the whole thing on the *thirteenth* building of 13th Street."

She stopped, catching her breath. "There's too much, Sophia. There's too much for the world to take all of it. That's why this place should be closed on this day. That's why it's the place and not the day. It wouldn't happen at home, and it wouldn't happen nowhere else in this town."

Sophia opened her mouth then closed it again.

It was on the tip of her tongue to say that when it had been constructed, the museum had not been the thirteenth building, nor had it been on 13th Street. The street had only been 13th Street for a couple years, a recent development after modern sensibilities pointed out that the people the streets in town were named to honour (usually dead white men) were guilty of historical atrocities ranging from sexual misconduct to genocide, resulting in a more straightforward numbered street system that was put in place until new names could be properly vetted.

It occurred to her to explain these things, but she stopped herself, knowing that it was as fruitless as it was to explain the inaccuracies of the Gregorian calendar to her.

But to Erin, the names of things mattered. You could

say a hotel had thirteen floors all you wanted 'til the cows came home, but as long as the managers called it the four-teenth instead, some would be assuaged. As though you could fool the devil with pig Latin, or by just calling the right thing by the wrong name.

The bell chimed before she could engage further, and the three of them—Sophia, Erin, and the old man in the corner—all looked up. The chime meant the front door was open and, given how long it was before it chimed again, had been open for a long time. A group had just arrived for a tour, and it was a large one.

Sophia got up, wiped the remnants of schmutz from her face, and pressed down the wrinkles of her blazer.

Erin took one last sip of her coffee and found it, still, too bitter by half. She abandoned it, leaving it on the table to be cleaned later. There was no harm in leaving it since the person she was leaving garbage for was herself.

Behind them, by the window, the pale little man in the bow tie arose from his seat as well. He pressed his hands down over his suit as though they were irons, but it did not straighten. He started at the top, pressed firm, then slid his hands down. When he released them to let the tension up, the suit wrinkled back into place, as though stuck like that.

Sophia and Erin watched him do this three times and on the last, he turned his head up and looked at them, small eyes almost invisible under his thick brow. He shrugged.

Sophia turned to Erin and Erin to Sophia, and without a word, they left for the main foyer.

Thirteen people were waiting for them.

It was enough that the amount of them took both Erin and Sophia by surprise when they came into the room, both stuttering their gait for a moment.

When Erin counted, which took a moment as the heads moved from one place to another, the crowd oblivious to how difficult it made the simple task, she turned and looked at Sophia.

Sophia had completed her head count sooner and was standing, teeth clenched, as she fought from turning to meet Erin's gaze and giving her the satisfaction of acknowledging the ominous coincidence.

The thirteen stared back at them, waiting, expectant.

Sophia and Erin stood frozen until the little old man brushed past them and stepped into the corner. He stood like a butler, wrinkled suit and all, waiting to be given a command. His passing broke the attention of those gathered, their eyes following him for a moment.

"Hello everyone!" The accent Erin spoke with in private conversation disappeared when she affected her public speaking voice. "I'm Erin and along with…"

"Sophia," the other Valentine said with a small salute to the crowd.

"And Barry," the old man chimed in. Erin and Sophia shot each other a glance before Erin continued the introduction.

"We'll be leading you through things today," she said. "But first, we'll start with documenting the fine souls who have joined us for this journey."

Erin moved to the podium in the centre back of the room. It was triangular with a hollow body kept behind glass and supported a broad, thick table on the top. Behind the glass was a section of a door that had been cut out, preserved. At first glance, it might have been mistaken for just discarded wood, but the number on it—a golden, emblazoned thirteen—marked it as a door. Further, just above the space between the one and the three was a small hole with a glass lens on it, a peephole.

More than a door, a specific door. A hotel door.

Erin opened the large leather guestbook that sat on the podium. It creaked and crackled as the dry spine on it bent and stretched over the pages inside. She licked her fingers and turned the pages until she found the most recent entry then dipped a quill pen in ink.

For a moment, she hesitated and gulped before she scrawled a florid number thirteen into the top corner of it.

She took another pause to regain herself, and, when she was ready, she looked at the tall, burly man in front of all the rest and beaconed him forward with nothing but her gaze, asked him his name, his town, and his occupation.

"David Hunter," he said. "From the northern coast, Snook's Arm. Politician."

The next was Clive Burr of Aaron's Cove, who worked with paper.

Then John Barker of Harbour Buffett, Freeda Smith of Bear Cove, and Alphonsus Buck of Bear Cove, but not the same Bear Cove, who were all fishers.

Gary Linehan of Oderin Island, unemployed. Creed

Dunford, Rencontre West, fisher. Derek Rose, King's Cove, District of Fortune Bay and Hermitage, fisher. Bernice Fletcher, Little Harbour Deep, postmaster.

Sarah Childs, Tickles, student. Bruce Goodard, Three Arms, unemployed.

Charles Henry, Mosquito. He refused to state his employment.

And, finally, Rowe Saunders, Current Island, first-year carpenter.

"Now then, that's done," Erin said, blowing on the ink to dry it. "I've kept you all waiting long enough, I'm sure."

David, still at the front, had let his gaze linger off to the side until it had fallen on the old man in the bowtie and rested there.

"Well," Sophia clapped and that pulled David's attention back. She put on a broad customer-service smile. "Let's get going. If you'll follow me, I'll bring you to the first artifacts."

"Pardon me," came a hoarse, low voice from the corner. All eyes turned to Barry. He straightened his bowtie, and, unlike his clothes, it stayed straight. "But that's not the first artifact."

"Ignore him," Sophia smiled, stepping toward the hall. "Right this way."

David raised a hand. "Oh no, no. No, I'd like to hear what he has to say."

Sophia pursed her lips into a small thin line.

Barry smiled and, suddenly, he wasn't small. Now he was a carnival barker, only missing the top hat, and when he stepped over to the podium, he splayed his hands out towards it like Vanna White revealing a prize.

After the big reveal, his gestures shrunk as he delicately promoted the section of the hotel door inside the glass case of the podium. "They always miss this. This is the first one. And let me, if I may, tell you about it."

OVERNIGHTING
Mike Fardy

The radio blared to life, briefly filling the car with a stutter of static-soaked classic rock. Ana jumped in her seat and swerved the car back into her lane as her sluggish mind rushed to catch up with her body. She had nodded off at the wheel. She could feel her pulse in her neck as she slowed her breathing, climbing down from the panic. Harris was sound asleep in the passenger seat, oblivious to the whole event.

How long had Ana been asleep? She imagined the car drifting from lane to lane, teasing the woods on either side of the highway while she slept. Tom Cochrane sputtered a last "All night long!" before returning to the steady hiss of central Newfoundland's favourite radio station: No Signal. Ana clicked the radio off before the white noise could put her back to sleep. She looked to Harris again, blissfully unaware with his head lolling forward, big arms crossed over his chest, chin resting on his collarbone. If they'd hit a tree and the airbags deployed…the angle of his head…that sharp curve through his neck…Ana winced the thought out of her head.

She wouldn't tell him about this. He'd never know

that he owed his life to Tom Cochrane; she'd bear that fact alone. Harris was a worrier, he'd never let her drive again if he found out, and Ana couldn't bear the extra hours that would be added to every trip by his white-knuckled, ten-under-the-limit, nan driving. She checked the clock — 11 pm on the dot. The road stretched ahead, a narrow two-lane highway lit by the old Corolla's candle-tinted head-light beam. Most people avoided highway driving at night. The roads were narrow and dark, and wet snow weighed down the branches of the malnourished firs causing them to lean even closer to the narrow shoulder. A night drive on Newfoundland's highways could never be truly serene with the ever-present risk of a moose stepping from those tightly packed trees like a living slab of granite sent to remind us that our thin lines of asphalt shouldn't make us feel safe or welcome. Ana slowed the car and looked for somewhere safe to pull off the road, she needed a break to clear the morbid thoughts.

She stepped out of the car and lit a cigarette. Nicotine and cold night air would give her enough energy for the next hump of the trip back to St. John's. They'd stayed in Buchans overnight after finishing repairs on the community's water treatment plant and woke up to a dead car battery, which delayed them from getting back on the road until well after dark. Standing on the side of the road, free from the humming of the tires, the forest was so silent Ana could hear the cigarette's satisfying crackle as she took a long draw. This was the stillness that only came with windless winter nights.

She looked at Harris through the car window, still asleep. He made the long weeks on the road easier. This would be their eighth year working together. There was a charming mismatch between his nervous personality and pre-hibernation grizzly bear build. With tired eyes and a lazy smile, his red hair and beard were starting to grow unruly at the end of their week. Ana put him in the category of sleepy-sexy. Not her type but she could see the appeal. Anyway, he was happily married, and most nights Ana could hear the occasional excited word or booming guffaw through the walls of their motel rooms when he called home. She was staring. She let out a long exhale and watched the smoke and vapour of her breath mingle and rise into the trees above. It wasn't attraction, just proximity.

Ana closed her eyes and let the winter air cool her cheeks. She flinched as the silence was broken by a crunch of snow from the woods behind her. She wheeled around but saw only thin tree trunks and the dark between them. She froze in place, her fear replaced with curiosity. Whatever animal was tromping in the snow had woken her up much more than her cigarette had. She squinted into the dark and strained her ears for another clue of what was hiding in the treeline but saw nothing and heard only her breath and the ringing in her ears that she only noticed in dead silence. Just one sound then nothing, maybe some ice falling from a tree, even the collapse of a mouse tunnel under the snow would stand out with no noise to compete with. Her breath caught in her throat. From behind a small group of trees, less than fifteen feet away, there was a silvery cloud dispersing into the air. Then another appeared; a jet of steam from slow, hot breath. Something was standing just out of sight behind the trees. She leaned

to the side, trying to get a peek at whatever was hiding
back there. Not a moose—the trees were too thin to hide
something that big so completely—but the height that the
haze appeared from would put the animal's face a foot
above Ana's head. How could an animal that tall get so
close while hardly making a sound? She took a step to the
left, and, as the snow crunched underfoot, the breathing
stopped. Ana held her breath, willing her pupils to dilate
further as she stared into the dark. No sound, no movement, but Ana was certain that the unseen thing standing
behind the trees was looking right back at her, muscles
coiled tight and ready to chase her down. She took a careful step backward, trying not to break the hardened upper layer of the snow. Another step and her foot found
the pavement again. She scurried back to the driver's side
door, keeping her eyes on the woods until she was in her
seat with the door closed behind her.

Harris woke as Ana started the car.

"Where are we?" he asked. Ana looked past him towards the trees, nothing running towards the car or peering out at her from the darkness.

"Nothing," she said.

"We're at nothing?" Harris was blinking sleep from
his eyes. "Never heard of a town called Nothing. Pretty
metal name. Jesus, it's late, we almost there?"

Ana tore her eyes from the woods, Harris's voice dragging her out of fight or flight. "No, sorry, no. Just had to
pull over for a smoke." She took a last look towards the
trees and then turned to pull back onto the highway.

"Look out!" Harris grabbed the wheel and jerked it
back towards the shoulder as a pickup swerved around

them, horn blaring. Ana slammed on the brakes and the two of them watched the truck round the corner ahead. Harris let go of the wheel and let out a relieved laugh. "We're good," he said. "All good. Awake now"

"Sorry, I was...haven't seen another car in over an hour." Ana took a deep breath through her tightening throat, trying to bring her nervous system down from high alert. Tears burned at the corners of her eyes.

Harris undid his seat belt. "Let me take a turn driving, I slept while you were doing all the work." Ana wanted to argue but thought her voice might crack if she spoke, so instead she nodded and took the opportunity to wipe her eyes as she opened her door and stepped back onto the road. She didn't meet Harris's eyes as they switched sides, feeling foolish for her shame at being scared. What a mess. As Harris pulled the car back onto the highway, Ana looked out the passenger window at the dark woods, so mundane now from inside the car with Harris's company. Maybe that hot-breathed animal was watching them drive away, considering running into the road to chase down its skittish prey. She almost hoped it would, just to see what it was. Almost.

As they rounded the bend their headlights washed over the truck they had nearly hit. It was pulled over on the side of the road, headlights on, and a steady trail of exhaust rising from the tailpipe. Harris slowed down as they approached.

"What, does he want to air his grievances?" Harris asked, but as they pulled closer Ana could see there was no one in the cab.

"Maybe he needed a smoke too."

"Or we scared the piss out of him, and he had to change his drawers and bury the evidence," Harris said, shooting her a teasing smile.

"Pretty specific, man, are you speaking from—" Ana stopped mid-jab and squinted into the woods. The lights from the two vehicles lit up a few rows of the snowy trees and sitting just at the edge of that light was the driver. She couldn't make out much detail, the light only revealed his work boots and jeans, but she could see he was sitting in the snow, leaning against a small birch.

"Experience? Obviously. You gonna lie to me and say you never had too much faith in your ability to hold it? I've left my fair share of unmarked graves along the road if you know what I mean." Ana barely heard Harris. Someone else was in the trees with the driver, standing over him, just out of the light. Tall and thin and featureless in the dark, the brume of their breath swirled in the light. Harris glanced her way as the car picked up speed. Ana faced forward again, finally processing Harris's admission.

"That's rotten. You're an animal," she said.

"You're not wrong. I prefer the term beast though."

The truck disappeared as they rounded the next bend and soon the monotonous routine of Ana and Harris's "road time" returned and the strangeness of their pit-stop drifted to the back of Ana's mind. Long-haul truckers often refer to "windshield time," long hours of staring straight ahead with nothing but your thoughts to keep you company, for better or worse. She had heard many truckers describe this time as therapeutic, a sort of forced meditation. A few years back they had ended up trapped in a conversation with a trucker from Utah in a small community's restaurant (small enough that the restaurant was just called Restaurant) who made a bold comparison between truckers and religious prophets, wandering the desert, forest, or in this case highway, in search of inner peace and enlightenment. "You might not find God staring through the windshield but you're sure as hell gonna face some demons," he had said. Ana spent the rest of that trip imagining what world religions would have looked like if their founders had been popping caffeine pills and pissing in bottles during their search for divinity. Ana and Harris didn't travel alone often enough to experience the introspective therapy of windshield time but instead altered the title to driving time. This involved time split between commiseration, attempts at deep philosophy, companionable silence, and trying to make the other laugh, rage, or occasionally throw up. This stretch of driving time started with a tired conversation about what they were looking forward to or dreading when they got home. For Harris, it was excitement for his wife Gerry's birthday. For Ana, some forced time off to even out her timesheet. She didn't specify that this fell into the dread category. Conversation soon faded to silence as the car meandered forward under Harris's cautious watch. He was hunched forward with hands clenched at ten and two, eyes glued to the road, Ana could almost hear the tension in his jaw. She stole a look at the speedometer—fifteen under the limit—held back a sigh, and turned back to the window.

The trees opened up to the barrens, rolling hills of white snow spotted with erratics and guarded by the enormous transmission towers that marched electricity across the island in orderly lines. Ana rested her forehead against the window and let her eyelids droop as the cold seeped through the glass into her skin. What felt like a moment later she woke with a dull pain in her neck as the car pulled off the road and into a parking lot. Her eyes adjusted to see the illuminated sign of a Quality Inn.

"Hey, sorry, I'm droppin here," Harris said as Ana squinted and stretched. "Let's just see if they've got space here tonight, and we'll get back at it fresh tomorrow morning."

Ana was about to say no and offer to drive the rest of the way, but the mild nausea of exhaustion and the dull pain behind her eyes changed her mind.

"Yeah, sure. Good call."

There were two rooms available, Harris paid for both of them. They headed towards the stairs with their overnight bags but Harris paused.

"I'm starving. There's a bar attached to the back of this place, might have some chips or something. Want to go?"

"I could go for a beer," she said. "Something to settle my stomach."

The room was dim and dirty with a small tube TV over the bar with a screen so yellowed and fuzzy Ana could barely see the CSI rerun playing on it. It was almost empty, just a couple of skippers at the bar and a woman sitting alone, finishing her drink at a locked-out VLT. The bartender had his sleeves rolled up just past his hairy forearms and was wiping down the bar.

"When's last call?" asked Harris.

The bartender glanced at a branded Becks clock hanging over the register. "Ten minutes ago, but if you're quiet about it..."

Ana ordered four beers and six mini bags of Hickory Sticks. "We won't hold you up, just kick us out when you're sick of us."

They found a table near the window and tucked into their drinks and snacks. The salt and alcohol did its magic, and the haze of the road drifted to relaxation. They chatted and listened to the grainy country songs playing from the bar's blown-out speakers. Soon their bottles were empty, and Harris was smiling at his phone as he texted Gerry. Ana tried not to peer over his shoulder but started to feel like a third wheel despite being the only other person at the table.

"I'm gonna call it a night," she said. Harris looked up as if he'd forgotten she was there.

"Yeah, good call. I'm done for." They stood and Harris grabbed their empties to carry them back to the bar. "Just gonna hit the washroom then I'll be up, you got a key?"

Ana flashed him the keycard as she made her way to the door.

She stepped into the parking lot. The air had gone frigid and dry in the early hours. Ana shivered and started to jog back to the hotel entrance. The parking lot was silent but for her sneakers on the salted pavement and the hum and squeak of the hotel's air system pushing plumes of steam through an exterior vent. Ana glanced back to see if Harris was trying to catch up but stopped as she noticed a red truck parked across multiple spaces in the center of the parking lot, the same truck she'd almost run off the road earlier that night. It was still running and the driver's side door hung open, but she didn't see anyone inside.

She started towards the hotel entrance but paused again, looking at the exhaust spewing out of the tailpipe. Idling trucks irked Ana. It was a self-centred "the world revolves around me" kind of statement or a way to bait strangers into a political argument about pollution and the liberal Illuminati. She looked again for any sign of a driver and, not seeing anyone, walked over to the truck to turn off the engine. It had been an interest in environmental sciences that led to her career in water treatment after all.

As she approached the truck she was hit with a smell that made her gag. Fish and seawater and something sour. An opaque liquid ran from the truck's floor before freezing into gelatinous icicles in the winter air. Ana held her breath and reached into the truck. The air conditioning was on blast, full cold, but the seats were soaked through. Her eyes watered as she quickly killed the engine then stepped away retching. She pulled the collar of her sweater over her nose and mouth and stared in confusion at the cab of the truck. The driver must have been carrying something foul that had spilled. No wonder he had abandoned ship so carelessly. But where was he? She took a few more steps away from the truck and noticed a set of footprints on the dry, salted pavement. Just a few steps straight out of the truck and then two prints side-by-side right in front of her. If the one who made those prints had been standing there now they would be nose to nose. Stranger still, there was no boot tread. They didn't look quite like they were made by bare feet but something close. Maybe he had run off in his socks? This guy was having the worst night of his life, and Ana wanted no further part in it. She hurried her pace back to the hotel entrance. The lobby and front desk were empty. Ana rang the bell on the counter hoping the clerk was somewhere within earshot but there was no answer. She spun around as the lobby doors hissed open and Harris stepped inside, shaking off the cold with two more bottles of beer in his hands. She must have looked upset because concern spread across his features.

"What's up?" he asked. "Key didn't work?"

She told him about the truck, the smell, the mess. He stepped back outside and squinted across the parking lot.

"Maybe someone came to get him while he airs it out, not a whole lot of options on places to stop this time of night." He gave her a reassuring look and held up the beers. "Charmed the old timer into a couple of road rockets, let's just head up. If you want to tell the desk about the truck we can call from up there, but I bet it's all fine and probably none of our business."

"Sure, yeah, we'll call from upstairs," Ana said as she shouldered her travel bag and started up the stairs. Harris's level-headedness was getting on her nerves. He was always the worrier, and she was the one telling him to relax. This role reversal was exhausting. There was just something about this night that had her on edge.

They had two neighbouring rooms on the third floor, each with a small single bed, a lamp over a squat desk, a sterile bathroom, and even a TV mounted on the wall. It was nothing exceptional, but it felt like a Vegas suite compared to the motels they got stuck in on some of their more isolated trips. There was a knock on the set of inside doors that connected the two rooms. Ana opened her side to find Harris standing in his doorway holding out a bottle of Blue Star as if he were a sommelier.

"A bottle of the house brown for madam?" he asked as he hinged forward to display the label. He'd taken off his sweater and overshirt and draped them over his forearm like a serving towel. He smiled, pleased with his impression, and Ana smiled back, more focused on his snug tank top. She snatched the beer out of his hand.

Ana crossed the room and sat on the bed. "Stupid."

"This is the fanciest spot we've stayed in a while, just trying to bring the class!" Harris made a show of delicately opening the beer, wafting it in front of his nose, and taking a thoughtful sip.

"I think waiters have a stricter dress code, they don't serve wine at garages."

"This is a classic look!" He did a spin to give her the full view. "You're not seeing Marlon Brando here?"

"Maybe if he ate the streetcar."

Harris roared with laughter and Ana couldn't help but join in. Soon they were both red in the face. Harris wiped a tear from his eye and gestured to the TV. "Flip that on, would ya? See if they get the hockey game."

"Doesn't your room have a TV?" Ana replied.

"You gonna make me drink alone?"

Ana rolled her eyes and turned on the TV, which was tuned to the third period of Chicago versus Toronto. Harris sat on the bed as they sipped their drinks. Ana's eyes were heavy but she was enjoying the company, so she didn't try to shoo him away just yet.

Ana woke up to the muted sounds of a post-game recap. She must have nodded off. Harris was fast asleep on the bed next to her. One of his arms was across his belly and the other was extended towards her. His weight made a dip in the mattress that created the slightest slope towards him. She considered just lying back down, going to sleep, and letting gravity decide what came next but instead. Instead, she rolled the other way and quietly walked through the joining doors into the room that was supposed to be Harris's. Just proximity. Don't be stupid. She shut the door on her side then paused and opened it again, just a crack, enough to give them privacy but open enough that Harris would know he could come in. In case he needed something.

Ana took her usual hotel precautions, taking two of the coat hangers from the closet, hooking them together then looping one over the door handle and the other over the catch lock above the deadbolt. She tested the handle, and the hangers successfully stopped it from turning all the way. She'd made a habit of this ever since she saw a video of someone trying to open a locked hotel room by sliding a long wire under the door to jimmy the handle and undo the catch. Feeling secure, she took a shower to wash off the day of driving then climbed into bed. As her body cooled under the hotel sheets she fell effortlessly into a deep sleep.

When Ana woke the room was pitch black. She had a splitting headache and her heart was racing. She rubbed her head and rolled over but as she shut her eyes she felt a cold breeze on her face and realised she was shivering. The room was freezing. She was groggy and disoriented as she patted the nightstand and grabbed her phone. She squinted as its screen lit up, and she flicked on the flashlight. The bedside clock was off, and she saw that there was no light visible under the door to the hallway. There must have been a power outage. She felt the cold breeze again and turned the light in that direction to see the door that joined her room to Harris's was wide open. Did he have his window open? The draft must have pushed her door open as well. He must be froze in there. She swung her legs over the bed to go wake him up or at least close the window to save them both from hypothermia, but before she could stand she heard a thump behind her as something dropped to the floor and the room brightened as the ambient light from the parking lot shone through her window. Something had been blocking it. She turned her light in that direction but saw nothing. Had she laid her bag on the windowsill? She leaned forward to check the ground on the other side of the bed and the flashlight cut back the hard line of shadow, revealing a blur of grey skin. The form disappeared as it pressed itself against the side of the bed, out of sight. Ana screamed and pulled her legs back up onto the bed. Her knee collided with her phone, sending it clattering to the floor. The phone's light was facing up which threw the room into a split of grey darkness and cold, white light.

"Harris?" Ana called, but that couldn't have been him. Why would he be crawling across her floor? And the skin. The skin was wrong. Cold, hairless, shining like wet clay. Harris's room was dark and still. She looked towards the door to the hallway, the coat hangers still securely fastened. "Harris!" This time she yelled, her voice cracking to a panicked high note. Silence. She could make a run for the door, but could she undo the hangers before whoever was lying at the foot of her bed caught up to her? Maybe she could vault the intruder and make it through the open door to Harris's room. She caught movement from across the room and tensed in fear. In the full-length mirror hanging on the wall, she saw herself, pressed up against the bed's headboard, jaw tight, eyes wide. In the reflection, she could see the foot of the bed. Her breathing quickened then stopped altogether as she found another set of eyes staring back at her. The thing had a thin body that was pressed flat to the floor. The skin of its face was smooth and glistening. Long, black hair gathered in pools under its face, smooth strands sticking to the oily skin on its back. It had large, sunken eyes with pupils that shone yellow in the phone's light. Its mouth was small and rounded giving it a look of surprised curiosity as it stared at her in the mirror's reflection. Its long arm was outstretched and slowly moving over the phone. Its gnarled fingers cast stripes of shadow across the ceiling until its palm caused a slow eclipse as the flashlight was covered. Ana's vision began to swoon, and her breath caught in her chest. The thing exhaled a mauzy bloom in the cold air and its hand enveloped the phone. There was a crunch and the light went out, plunging the room into darkness. The creature disappeared except for those two floating discs of pale yellow pupils. Ana found her breath in a stuttering gasp and screamed. She called for Harris, for God, for anyone, until terror took her words and left her only with the primal language of fear. The glowing pupils began to rise and Ana watched helplessly as slim grey arms reached over the foot of the bed one by one as the thing lifted itself up from the floor. As it turned to face her, Ana stopped screaming. Its face was still locked in wide-eyed curiosity, and it didn't make a sound. A calm came over Ana as the thing made her understand. She could feel its perspective. She was standing behind a copse of trees, investigating the snow and the air, she was exploring and everything was new. She was looking at a fallen tree, the wall of exposed roots, and the hole in the earth that it had exposed. Her home. She could smell cigarette smoke, a scent that was alien and hypnotizing. She turned to catch more of the smell and her foot plunged through the snow with a crunch. The cold was exhilarating but even better was this new feeling, an electricity from the direction of the road. Fear, stress, curiosity, lust. While Ana had been peering into the trees this creature was feeling her emotions and drinking them in like liquor. The thing in the trees had followed the sound of the car and found the driver of the red truck. Anger, relief—the feelings were intoxicating. It needed more. It had grabbed the driver. Too hard. The man had crunched and bent in the creature's grip and those exquisite feelings had dispersed. Ana saw herself pass by through the passenger window. She had seen it, and it her. That had been when Ana's life ended; all of this was inevitable after that moment.

The creature had crawled onto the bed and was hovering over Ana's legs. She kicked feebly, some part of her subconscious still believing she could survive. The thing caught one leg in both hands, its eyes still staring into hers, and began to squeeze. Ana felt nothing more than a dull pressure as the creature's long fingers pierced her skin. It broke eye contact to inspect the wounds opening in her calf and the feeling of numb acceptance faded. Ana was detached from the creature's mind. As it opened its mouth and slowly sank its needlepoint teeth into her knee she willed her body to feel it. She wouldn't accept this. This was not inevitable. This was all random chance, and she was not going to submit to the thing's lethal curiosity. The pain rushed up her nerves like a freight train and her mind ignited into wildfire that boiled over into a hateful scream. She kicked hard with her free leg and felt her heel connect with the thing's eye. Its head flung back, and its arms fell limp to its sides, freeing her mangled leg from its grip. Ana rolled out of the bed and stumbled through the open door into Harris's room, spinning and slamming the door behind her. She caught a last glimpse of the thing sliding off the bed and crawling after her. It didn't rush, slithering low to the ground with long limbs keeping a smooth four-legged stride. The door shut and Ana scanned the room frantically. She could hear the whistling of wind blowing through the room's open window. The smell hit her suddenly as her adrenaline-fueled focus widened, a sickly smell of brine like the spill in the red truck. She pulled her shirt over her nose and then felt a swell of relief as she saw Harris sitting up in bed turned away from her and facing the open window. As her eyes adjusted, a moan escaped her clenched jaw. Harris's chest and shoulders were relaxed and facing the window as if he were gathering the willpower to stand up out of bed, but his head was wrenched the wrong way and was hanging limply over his back. Lifeless eyes gazed down at the bloodstained sheets. The moan became a scream. She couldn't focus the sounds into words, she just needed someone to hear her, to take her away from this, but the only one coming for her was the creature in the other room.

The door behind her began to splinter, not from heavy blows, just giving way as two grey arms pushed their way through the heavy composite wood. Its head passed through the hole with shards of wood tangled through its hair. It was as if it didn't understand that the barrier should stop it from entering or even slow it down. This was not its world, here it was like a child playing with paper dolls, unaware of its strength and unbothered by the damage it inflicted. Ana ran for the door to the hallway. Thankfully Harris hadn't watched the same hotel safety videos she had, so he hadn't secured his door. She threw it open and limped into the hall, every step on the battered leg sending white-hot pain through her. She felt nauseous, and her vision became dotted with growing black stars, but her adrenaline had the wheel and its instructions were simple: RUN OR DIE. The hall was dark, no light shone from any of the rooms, and with no windows, she was running blind as she stumbled forward screaming for help. Could they have been the only ones staying here tonight? She threw a look over her shoulder and saw the creature standing in the beam of dim light coming from Harris's room. It stood on two legs, still bent forward to stoop under the door frame, its black hair floating around it as if carried by current, and its eyes followed her movement. The door behind it was swinging closed, and the darkness slowly swallowed the beam of light. The creature sank lower to the ground, and just as the last sliver of light disappeared it began to gallop towards her. Ana collided with the elevator at the end of the hallway and desperately felt her way along the wall until she found the stairwell.

Thankfully the stairs had a window on each floor that lit each landing enough so Ana could continue down the stairs as fast as her bloodied leg would allow. She was halfway down the first set of stairs when the door behind her exploded from its hinges and ricocheted off the wall above her head before crashing to the ground inches behind her. She dared a glance upward and saw the thing leaning over the railing, its hair hanging low enough that Ana had to duck to avoid it. She rounded the next floor as she heard the screech of metal as the grey creature tore through the railing above and dropped to her level, catching the railing behind her. It reached out with its other arm, but with another shriek the railing it was holding bent and gave way, tearing heavy bolts from the concrete floor. It was thin but its weight must have been immense to tear through the heavy rail like it was a bundle of sticks. It fell the last story to the ground level, blocking her escape to the lobby. Ana took the opportunity to dash into the hallway on the second floor. She was plunged into the darkness of the windowless hall once again but saw light coming from around a corner less than fifty feet ahead. Her leg was sticky with drying blood, and the air that moved over the wound stung deep into the muscle. She had no idea how far the thing's claws had dug. She was alternating between moans of pain and screams for help, her raw throat tasting of metal.

She reached the lit area but sobbed as she saw it was just a business center with moonlight streaming through the glass doors into the hall. Looking around helplessly in the dark, she couldn't see another stairwell door, and she couldn't return the way she came, so she opened the door to the suite and slipped inside where she crawled under a desk and curled her knees up to her chest. It was only a matter of time now. This thing had followed her for miles in a car, and now it had a trail of blood to lead it right to her. She stared out through the glass doors and into the hallway, waiting to see the creature crawl into view. She could feel her racing heart behind her eyes, and her breath came in quick gasps. She shut her eyes and tried to relax. There was nothing to be done now. Tears streamed down her cheeks as her shoulders dropped, and she took a long, ragged breath. She turned her thoughts from fear and anger. She thought of home, her bed, her friends. What would they think happened to her? What would the papers say? She squinted these anxious thoughts away. She thought of Harris. She'd been so stupid, holding back how she felt. It would have changed nothing to just let him know. Life really was too short.

She jumped as she heard a voice. Her eyes shot open, and she saw the hallway was now lit up.

"Hello?" the voice said again.

"Here!" Ana replied, although her ruined voice could hardly manage a whisper. She crawled from under the table and towards the door. In the hallway, she saw a man with dark, messy hair dressed in a loose hoodie and pyjama pants. He was holding a flashlight, which he pointed at her as she opened the door to the business centre.

"Oh my god! Jesus, are you alright?" The man lowered the beam and ran to steady her. "What happened? Shit, your leg."

Ana tried to muster up an explanation to put the situation into words that wouldn't make him think she was just insane but gave up. "Run," she said.

"Did someone do this to you?"

"We have to run."

"You're alright, there's no one else here. I'll call an ambulance, come on." He stepped forward to steady her. Ana glanced down at her leg and her vision swooned. The extent of the damage sent her to the edge of shock. The man caught her before she fell and laid her against the wall. He took off his hoodie and pressed it to her calf. "It's clean," he said. "Wrap it around your leg. I'll be right back."

"No, please." Ana tried to go after the man as he jogged back down the hallway.

"I just need my phone," he called over his shoulder. "I'll call an ambulance." Ana let herself feel hope with the thought of flashing lights and painkillers, of being carried far away from here.

The hall dropped to near darkness once again. Ana turned to see that the man had stopped jogging. His arms were limp at his sides and the flashlight pointed at the ground. His face was turned upwards as if enraptured. Her throat grew tight as she saw long, black hair hanging around the man and the grey impression of a form clinging to the ceiling above him. The man didn't move as a thin grey arm reached towards his face, and the creature gently, gracefully let its feet swing down so that it was standing over the man, one hand cradling his face, the other still holding the ceiling above. The flashlight dropped from his hand onto the hotel carpet with a thud. The man stood motionless as the creature enveloped him. Ana remembered its gaze, the feeling of inevitability, the paralysis.

"Fight it," she said. Her voice was weak and she was exhausted, but it was enough to cause the thing to look up at her. The man shuddered and began to scream, falling to the floor, pushing back the induced calm and replacing it with fear. Looking into the creature's curious expression Ana could taste that fear like it did. The man picked up the flashlight and swung it at the creature over and over. The beam of light became a strobe, sending long shadows sprinting across the walls. They had to move. It was blocking the stairway now. Ana stood. How many times could adrenaline kick someone from the brink of unconsciousness? She hoped at least once more.

"This way!" she called behind her as she rushed back to the business center. She tore a screen off one of the windows and forced it open as far as it would go. The icy wind felt as though it opened tiny cuts over her whole body. Her jaw clenched as she turned and swung her injured leg out into the open air. They were still a story up but there was a small ledge just under the window. If she was careful, she could shimmy along the wall and lower herself onto a dumpster below. She groaned as her bare feet touched the icy ledge. She held the window frame as she gathered her balance then looked up just as the man came crashing through the glass door of the business center. He met her gaze with a look of terror. Long gashes stretched across his face from mouth to ear, fresh enough that they hadn't begun to bleed. The monster was already on top of him, dragging him backward with its impossibly strong arms. Ana reached for the man, but he was too far. The creature looked up at her and gathered the man closer to its chest as if shielding him from her. He was brittle in its arms. His torso deflated under the pressure of the thing's embrace, and the man's expression went flat as he coughed a mist of blood. Clasping the window frame, Ana's breath came in heaving bellows as she stared into the thing's enormous black eyes. It clutched the man's lifeless body. A milky tear ran down its face. Ana felt a tear trace a frigid line down her cheek. They stood in mirrored silence breathing in time together as the wind whistled over the hotel's siding. Ana shivered. Her feet ached as the snow clawed the dregs of warmth from her. She forced herself to move, sliding her foot along the ledge. The soles of her feet were so numb she didn't realize she had slipped until the creature disappeared from sight, and she turned to face the parking lot pavement rushing up to meet her.

She lay sprawled in the parking lot under the warm glow of a streetlight. Her back arched as she tried to breathe. Every movement was a burst of pain and the lack of oxygen turned her mind to tar. She rolled over onto her back, letting out strained grunts with every attempted breath. Snowflakes blew in gusts past the streetlight above. Ana could hardly feel the cold. She looked up at the window she had fallen from, expecting to see the grey-skinned creature leaping down to finish her off. Instead, it was there, just out of the light, its eyes once again a glossy yellow catching the light from the parking lot. It watched her, strands of its hair whipping in the wind. Ana's head swam and darkness rushed over her.

She woke in an ambulance, oxygen mask over her face, a young paramedic looking pale as he dressed her leg. The back door was open, and she could see red and blue lights flashing from a police car. Another paramedic was wheeling someone out the front door of the hotel on a gurney. Next, she was in the hospital, a police officer was speaking to her, asking her questions until a nurse forced him out of the room. She woke again in a different hospital room. Her eyelids were heavy. She was hooked up to IVs, which must have been responsible for the euphoric calm she felt. One of her arms was in cast and her leg was wrapped in dressings with spots of blood dotting through the white bandages. There was a call button next to her bed but when she reached to push it her arm came up short. She was handcuffed to the bedrail. Ana called out for a nurse, but it was a police officer who entered the room.

"Glad to see you awake. You were in quite the state when we found you." The officer pulled a chair up next to her bed. He placed his hat on a table and gave her a warm smile.

"Didju getit?" Ana's words were slurred, and her tongue felt swollen and slow.

"Get it? What do you mean by that?" The officer's smile left his eyes, and he took out a notebook.

"That thing. The grey thing. It killed…" The image of Harris sitting lifeless on his bed with his head turned the wrong way came rushing back. Ana couldn't hold back a sob. The officer watched her eyes closely as he jotted something down.

"So it was a… grey thing that kicked in the door and killed Mark Harris?"

"It was after me. I saw it in the woods. I think it killed that man…in the red truck."

"Did… *it* get anyone else?" There was no trace of a

smile left on the cop's face. Ana nodded as tears stung her eyes.

"Another man. On the second floor, right before I fell. He tried to help me, but it got him too."

"Anyone else?" He asked. Ana shook her head no. The cop paused as if waiting for her to say more then said. "I'll chalk this up to the drugs ma'am. If you want to tell me what happened I'll be right outside those doors. Now you're awake we'll get someone to come check on you."

"What do you mean? Didn't you find it?"

"We didn't find anything but you and four dead bodies." The cop took his hat from the table and walked back into the hallway. Soon after, a nurse entered to give her another injection of morphine to help her sleep until morning. As the nurse left Ana began to drift into a heavy sleep. She let her head fall to one side of her pillow and looked to the window. Crouched in the snow on the other side of the glass was a thin, grey form. Its eyes were no longer wide with surprise, it looked focused. It had found her again, following the trail of her misery. It was drunk on her morphine-ridden mind. She knew now she couldn't be rid of it. As her eyes closed she saw herself through its eyes. It had been too eager with the others; they had broken too quickly. It would keep its distance as much as it could and drink in Ana's despair and terror until it was bored with her. It liked this world and there was so much yet to see.

2

David stared at Barry, even after he finished the story.

The last of it came with a gleeful flourish that implied the old man's joy in the tale's stark terror.

They had moved, as a group, into the museum proper, past a large display of birds on stone that must have been brought in when the place had been nothing but foundations.

"That's real stone covered in fake shit," Barry said as they stepped past.

He explained that it had been made from toothpaste mixed with water and squirted from a syringe to look just like gull shit splattered on rock upon impact.

"The fluoride in the Colgate makes it last forever," he said. "We rarely even have to touch it up."

He turned and wriggled his fingers inches from the face of a young girl near the front of the line, no more than twenty years old. "Imagine what that does to your insides, hey?"

She'd cowered back, more from the man than from the statement, and he had continued on with his tale.

Now the entire caravan of tourists was in a large open

part of the museum. There were hardwood floors that, should the funding completely dry up and they find the museum closed a full seven days a week, would have been reclaimed by someone with a plucky entrepreneurial spirit. Assuming, of course, the entire building wasn't reclaimed as a craft brewery.

Throughout the room and along the walls, spaced equally apart, were square glass cases, each atop their own small podium. The podiums were hand-carved from cedar that would likely join the floorboards in the future project driven by the imagined entrepreneurial spirit before the government could lay claim to them.

Under each glass was a carving, some of wood, some of stone, some of soapstone. They all glistened in the bright tungsten spotlights angled specifically to distinguish them from the dull fluorescent glow emanating through the rest of the hall. There were little wooden men rowing little wooden boats and small recreations of menhirs held together with tape and glue, but more than anything else, there were *animals*. Animals in wood, animals in stone, animals in soapstone.

Clive Burr, John Barker, and Freeda Smith stood around a sculpture of a seal in glass and its mate. It was intricate, the first seal's head and shoulders above the water, lower half below. The water was represented by a wafer-thin segment of glass that had been blown perfectly straight, and for the life of them, John Barker could not fathom how they'd done it. The addition of the second seal beneath, as though it had been caught mid-dive, sold the illusion of the water's edge all the more.

To their side, Alphonsus Buck, Gary Linehan, and

Creed Dunford stood around a large display that showed a bear with a fish next to it. It was made of porous stone, like a sponge, and looked as though, had it not been in a glass case, it would have been a devil to clean. The bear was looking down, below its base, to some hidden region below the wood of its display. Its base was porous as well with an oval around it, but of a different colour stone. While the bear was a cappuccino brown, the base was grey and cold.

"It's an ice flow," Creed said after a long silence. He said it as it had just come to him, vocalizing the realization the moment it hit him

The brown of the bear's stone had thrown him off and it took him too long to realize it was intended to be a polar bear. Now, with that knowledge, the colour and the texture of it made it look *dirty*. It made it look weak, and it made it look *hungry*. The fish next to it on the flow was not enough to sate its appetite, it looked like little more than an appetizer next to the beast. It stared past the wood of its display into an ocean the artist imagined was devoid of sustenance: stuck on a shrinking island in the middle of nowhere, waiting for food or death to present itself, whichever came first. The piece was called "The Slow Death of the Cod Fishery."

"What do you think that means?" Creed asked, his voice a hushed whisper. Gary Linehan shook his head at him.

To their left, Derek Rose, Bernice Fletcher, Charles Henry, and Rowe Saunders huddled around a wide display. There were a dozen or more soapstone carvings on display, each one that lush lime green that characterized so much of Inuit art, swirls of white and black running through it in rich veins.

From a distance, it was hard to decipher the little green figures, but when you were close enough it was obvious; they were men, or more aptly, they were a community.

There were men with their dogs, the two held together by real string that looked stiff and brittle after years of display. There were fishers with a rod and reel dangling over a hole in the ice carved beneath them. There were women with children, one on the hip, one at the side, and another within. There were men with spears along the outer edge, looking out at the tourists staring at them with distorted faces from beyond the glass display as if to say, try something, we dare you.

Around that same edge, protected by those men with spears, were rudimentary houses. Cubes carved in stone with doors and the feint visages of families within that were only seen properly when the light shone on them just right, making the figures with the shadows.

Charles Henry squinted as he looked at it. "What's this one called again?"

Bernice adjusted her glasses and bent down. "'Island Life,' I think."

Charles Henry wondered how the museum's caretakers looked after it—if they had to wear special gloves.

He wondered if they deigned to touch it at all.

This was what he was thinking when he discovered it.

"Come look at this."

They crowded around to his point of view on the display.

There, behind the houses, peering from a hidden vantage point at the men and women who went about their days, was a small figure watching the goings on of the town.

The figure was small and grey. Not small as in short, small as in thin. He looked even thinner compared to the other soapstone men, who were all quite boxy. But this thing was made so you could see its little soapstone *ribs*. Its hand—*his* hand—was on a windowsill, gaining purchase as it stared out at those hunting, fishing, tending to flock.

It had large eyes. And it had small, sharp teeth that looked as though they would slice the skin of anyone who picked up the stone.

"Why would that be there?" Bernice asked, hushed.

"Island life," Derek said, as though that were enough.

Sarah Childs peeked over their shoulders at what they were seeing, took note of it, then moved on, looking at one display and then another. She went to a display with no one else at it, regarded it, and kept moving through the room.

There was one piece, a long spiral that looked as though it had been made by nature, contrasting all the other things made by man. That opposition transfixed her for a moment, such that she didn't feel anyone stepping up behind her until there was a cold hand on her shoulder.

"Lovely, isn't it?"

She jumped and turned, and suddenly Barry was inches from her.

"You scared me," she swallowed.

"It's the closest a human artist has come to a perfect spiral. You know those perfect spirals? Where each segment gets larger, adding itself to the previous two widths? Fibonacci spirals?"

She shook her head, no.

"Well, they found this, and it's the closest they've found to a human achieving it. They thought for years that it was natural. It took years to refine the tooling to examine these things, so fine as it is."

"That's…that's amazing."

"It is," he agreed.

They stared at it together for a moment, both equally lost in its spin. Then he straightened, as if remembering himself, and turned, gesturing. There was another case, apart from the others, tucked into one corner near a back exit to the exhibit. "Come, I must show you this."

At once, there was a hand on Barry's shoulder, just as a moment ago his had been on hers. There was a turn but not a jump, and David was behind them both. "Show the both of us, why don't you?"

Barry stared for a long moment then nodded, slowly, and the three of them made their way to the case he had gestured to.

Behind the glass was a carving of an animal. It looked to have been done in driftwood. The wood was old and cracked, but it had not affected the shape of the beast.

The wooden face looking through the glass at the tourists was small and triangular, pointed with sharp ears. Its head was tilted, curious, yet a mouth that was opened only a fraction revealed sharp teeth. There was no placard, but even the most rudimentary grasp of the island's wildlife would allow you to identify it as a pine marten.

"It's amazing," Sarah said, voice hushed. She tilted

her head this way then that. "What's it called? There's no title."

"Ahhh!" Barry exclaimed, mouth spreading wide and wrinkles pushing up and around his eyes. "But why have a name when you can have a tale, yes?"

THE IMMOVABLE
Ali House

The rapid clicking of the camera's shutter burst through the air, shattering the silence before stomping on it for good measure. It lasted for about six seconds before ending as abruptly as it had started. Peace returned, but it didn't last long before the clicking started up again. Jack tried his best to ignore the sound, but it was so out of place in the quiet, isolated cemetery that he couldn't help jumping every time.

The noise didn't bother Lee, who was moving around the graves with the camera in front of his face, as if he didn't trust his own eyes. He'd take a few photos of something then wander around, waiting for inspiration to strike again. The abandoned plot was overgrown with tall grass, concealing fallen branches and broken headstones, and Jack considered it a small miracle that Lee hadn't yet tripped and faceplanted. Still, the sight of his roommate stomping over the graves, sometimes leaping over headstones, made him uncomfortable. Since finding the graveyard, Jack had stayed off to the side, leaning against a tree. He felt that the dead should be allowed to rest in peace and not have to put up with some photography student treading all over their final resting place.

When Lee initially asked John to help him with this trip, he implied that he'd done his research and knew where the best spots were located. However, the first two sites had offered nothing except a long, boring hike in the woods with no trail to follow, no cell reception, and no graves to be found. At least this cemetery existed. Lee could get his photos and then they could finally go back to the city. Jack didn't consider himself a fan of hiking, and after today he doubted he'd ever become one.

"That should be enough," Lee commented. Lowering his camera, he stepped over a low headstone, his sneakers sinking slightly into the ground.

Jack tried not to flinch at the thought of Lee standing over the bones of someone who'd been buried decades ago and instead turned to start the hike back to the car. There was no path, but Lee had been smart enough to mark their journey in, so all they had to do was follow the clues. It was easy—especially since the entire area looked like it hadn't seen a living human being in at least fifty years.

Lee scrolled through the photos on his camera's screen as Jack started up the car. "With all this effort, I'd better get an A."

"Your effort?" Jack laughed as he put the car into drive. "I'm the one chauffeuring your butt all over the island." So far this trip had eaten up nearly four hours, driving down barely-used roads and searching for signs of relocated communities that Lee had researched online.

"Hey, it's not my fault the prof loves this resettlement stuff. I'd rather be downtown, but I want a good mark on this project, and the only way to do that is to pander to the prof." Lee put his camera in its bag. "As much as I like photography, I fucking hate this course."

Jack nodded and began the drive back home. He'd been lucky enough not to have any profs like that for his courses, but he'd heard horror stories from friends — especially those who hadn't been able to work out the "magical winning formula" before the end of the year, much to their grade's detriment.

"And I did offer to pay for gas and buy you pizza and beer," Lee added, pointing an accusatory finger. "You're coming out pretty good on this, especially since you're out in the fresh air and not sitting on your butt playing games or watching TV all day."

"If you want to lecture me, I'll let you out here and you can walk back."

Lee put up his hands in surrender and they drove for a few minutes in silence.

"Hey, stop the car!" Lee suddenly exclaimed, grabbing Jack's shoulder with one hand and pointing out the window with the other.

"What? Why?"

"I saw a cross back there. There might be another cemetery."

Jack groaned, but he obediently pulled the car over and put it in park. "Haven't you got enough photos?"

"There's no such thing as 'enough photos.'" Lee leaned closer to the window. "There were a bunch of communities in this area, but some have no information, not even a name. This could be one of those places lost to history."

Jack looked around but couldn't see anything other than trees and rocks. "Are you sure you saw a cross?"

"Definitely." Lee took out his phone and pulled up Google Maps. After a bit of messing around, he smiled triumphantly and showed the screen to Jack. "There should be a small road just behind us. If we go down here," he pointed at a spot on the screen, "it should get us closer."

"Can't we just go home?" Jack asked, aware that he was dangerously close to whining. Even though they weren't going back very far, he didn't want to turn around. He wanted to be in the apartment watching TV and eating chips. That's what normal people did on their weekends when they wanted to unwind from a long week of classes. Not drive their roommate around the island for a project you had nothing to do with.

"Look, someone else is bound to have this idea, but if they're doing the same research as me, they won't know about this place. If eight other people show up with similar photographs, I'll at least have something different."

Jack hesitated.

"Dude, my last project got a C. I worked so damn hard on it, getting the lighting and the blur just right, but the prof thought that pictures of people in clubs was 'pedestrian' and 'low brow.' I need a good mark on this so I don't blow my GPA."

Sympathy took over and Jack nodded. "All right. But it's the last one. I'm getting hungry."

He turned the car around, being careful not to accidentally fall into the ditch on either side of the road. As the car moved, he kept an eye out for the turn-off, which was little more than a dirt path. Driving down it, Jack tried not to think about how much these roads were messing with his car's suspension.

It wasn't long before the dense trees opened into a large clearing and Lee told him to stop. Looking around, Jack doubted that there was a cemetery nearby. The area looked like a place that would have been ideal for setting up a small community, with wide spaces for houses and farming, and close to the wharf for fishing, but there was nothing here. There were no decaying buildings or half-standing houses or broken piers, like at the other sites. If people had lived here, then something must have wiped away their entire existence.

After ten minutes of hiking through the forest in the direction that Lee had seen the cross, Lee let out a triumphant whoop at the sight of a small clearing. Among the long grass were weather-beaten wooden crosses and mossy headstones. Lee took out his camera and snapped some photos before trudging straight into it.

A cold shiver ran down Jack's spine as he hung back at the edge of the clearing. Something about the place made his skin crawl, even more so than the last cemetery. This place looked even older and more abandoned than the last one, with grass so tall that he could barely see half the headstones. He didn't understand why this would be here when there was nothing else. Had there been a community nearby? Why was there nothing left of them, but the cemetery remained?

He had a feeling that they shouldn't be here. He should have kept driving.

"Hey! Check this out!" Lee called to him.

Jack snapped out of his thoughts and looked over to see Lee bending over one of the graves. "What's up?"

"There's something buried here."

"No duh," Jack remarked.

"No, idiot," Lee laughed. "There's something poking out of the dirt."

Jack frowned, hoping that his roommate wasn't about to dig up someone's bones. "Maybe you should leave it—"

"It's a carving!" Lee said, standing up. He had something in his hands and was brushing the dirt off of it. "Some kind of animal."

"Whatever it is, you should leave it here. Didn't your parents teach you not to muck around with the dead and their belongings?"

Lee rolled his eyes and made his way over to Jack. When he was only a few feet away, he threw the carving at Jack, whose reflexes made him catch it so that it wouldn't fall on the ground. As soon as his hands made contact with the item, he saw an image of a building engulfed in flames, but as soon as it appeared it was gone, and he was left blinking in the bright sunlight.

"It's some kind of ferret or something," Lee said.

Jack blinked a few more times, the memory of the flames quickly evaporating from his mind, making him wonder if it had even been there. He looked at the item in his hands, which was about three inches long and two inches high. The small, long animal had been carved out of a single piece of wood, which looked burned, but most likely had just been charred. Looking closer at the dark animal, he could see that its mouth was open and its teeth were bared in anger. "It's a pine marten. And you should definitely put this back where you found it."

"No way," Lee snatched the item from him. "Finders

keepers. Not like they can use it now that they're dead."

Jack frowned but said nothing.

"I'm calling it *Immovable*," Lee said, taking a swig of beer. "The government moved all the people, but didn't want to move their dead." He laughed. "It'd be kinda awkward. People showing up in new towns, carrying their dead kin on their back."

"And your prof likes that kind of stuff?" Jack asked, taking another slice of pizza from the open box in front of them. There was an action movie playing on the TV, but both of them had already seen it.

"Yeah. He's hardcore into old-timey history stuff. Hates anything modern. Even cameras, but at least he can't mark us low for that," Lee laughed bitterly. "As soon as this semester's over, I'm not taking another course with him. I'd learn more from online tutorials."

"You're probably right about that."

"I wonder if I could bring in that animal thing for extra credit," Lee said, looking at the carving that he'd placed on the side of the coffee table.

Jack avoided looking at it. It still gave him the heebie-jeebies to think about where it had come from. "I doubt it would help," he remarked. "Probably wouldn't make your *Immovable* project look good if you *moved* something from the area."

"I guess not." Lee picked up the carving. "The prof would definitely pick up on that kinda symbolism and mark me down. Hey, catch!"

Jack flinched but obediently caught the carving, cursing his reflexes as the wooden animal landed in his hands again. Everything went black and then there was a flash of flames, growing bigger as they consumed the large building in front of him, hungrily eating the wooden structure until everything and everyone was fire.

"Dude!"

Jack's vision suddenly went back to normal. When he realized that he was still holding the carving, he quickly tossed it across the couch to Lee.

"What was that?" Lee asked. "You zoned out super hard. I only tossed it to you for a joke 'cause you seemed so spooked about it. Are you so afraid of that thing that your spirit is leaving your body?"

"Shut up," Jack replied, reaching for his bottle of beer. He considered telling Lee about the vision but quickly decided against it. Lee obviously wasn't seeing the same thing, and Jack didn't want to sound like a weirdo. "I don't want to touch something that's been in a grave. It's weird."

"It's not weird, it's cool."

"You should bring it back."

"Pussy," Lee muttered. He picked up the carving, placed it on the coffee table, and turned his attention to the movie.

Jack was tired, but he wasn't able to sleep. Every time he closed his eyes, he saw that large building on fire. He had no idea what that had to do with a carving of a pine marten buried in a grave, but he had half a mind to get up, steal the carving, and drive all the way back to that cemetery.

Closing his eyes, he tried to think about giant robots and monsters and ordinary people saving the world. Anything but that damn burning building.

In front of him was the church. The same church that had been here long before he'd been born. He was standing outside, looking at it, waiting. After a few minutes, he saw the smoke, and then the bright flicker of flames in the windows. The flames began to eat through the wood of the church, devouring the structure from the inside out. He watched as the flames engulfed the church. One person shoved the door open and ran out, the stranger's face a mask of fear as flames licked at his clothing.

The stranger didn't notice where he'd been hiding, and he barely paid the stranger any attention. More than anything, he wanted to be in the church with the others, but he had a job to do.

When the stranger was gone and the church was fully engulfed, he picked up a burlap sack and began the work that had been tasked to him. Going from house to house, he set everything alight and then turned his attention to the wharf and boats. It was a clear, sunny day, and he knew that the fires would burn until there was nothing left of the town but ash and bones.

Soon it was time for the final task. He took the small path through the woods, heading to the cemetery where past generations had been buried. The graves were marked with stones, wooden crosses, whatever they could find or thought worked best for the person lying below.

He knelt down on top of the grave where his great-grandfather had been buried. Placing a hand on the stone, he took a deep breath. Then he opened the sack and withdrew a small carving of a pine marten that had been in his family for generations. It was made of wood and had been charred to help protect it from the elements. Digging a small hole in the grave, he placed the carving inside, covering it up with the same earth.

Wiping his hands on his pants, he placed a hand on the stone again. "Let the outsiders who disturb our bones get what's coming to them."

Taking the box of matches out of his pocket, he lit a match and held it to the bottom of his shirt. As the flames began to grow, he looked towards the burning town and smiled.

Jack woke up drenched in sweat, the bedsheet twisted around his body. The dream felt so real that for a moment he thought he could see flames on his skin.

Taking a few deep breaths, he managed to calm his heartbeat, but his skin still felt like it was on fire. Getting up, he decided to go to the kitchen and get a cold glass of water. Damn Lee and his stupid cemetery project. Damn Lee's stupid prof for making him have to go to such lengths.

When he touched the doorknob, he heard a sizzle as the hot metal scorched his skin. Leaping backwards, Jack suddenly realized that the heat wasn't his imagination. His bedroom was much hotter than normal, and he could hear the crackling of flames within the apartment. Swearing under his breath, he grabbed a sweater and wrapped it around his uninjured hand before opening the bedroom door.

An inferno greeted him. Flames had filled the living

room and kitchen area, devouring the furniture and kitchen cabinets. Dark, acrid smoke billowed inside the room, gathering along the ceiling. Jack pressed the sweater to his mouth and nose and ducked low, hoping to keep from inhaling too much smoke. He turned to Lee's room, but the door was fully engulfed in flames, and he knew it'd be dangerous to get any closer.

"Lee!" he yelled, coughing because of the smoke. "Wake up and get out!"

The hot smoke burned his eyes. For a moment he considered going back to his room and jumping out the window, but he was on the second floor, and below him was the parking lot of the physio clinic on the first floor. Keeping that idea as Plan B, he ducked even lower and moved toward the front door. Despite the fire's rage, only the bottom of the front door was on fire, so Jack quickly used the sweater to grab the handle and wrench open the door. He raced down the stairs, coughing the entire time, until he finally spilled out into the cool night air.

A few minutes later, he heard the wailing of sirens in the distance, but he didn't look towards them. Instead, as the top floor of the building continued to burn, he looked for any sign that Lee had made it out alive.

After the firefighters and cops and ambulance were done, and the building was declared safe enough, Jack was finally allowed back into the apartment to gather any belongings. Because his door had been closed for most of it, his stuff wasn't too badly damaged by the fire, but a lot of it would have water damage. The landlord was in hot trouble because the fire alarm never went off. It was luck that Jack had woken up before the fire got him.

Standing in front of the burned apartment door with caution tape spread across it in a flimsy X, Jack hesitated. He didn't want to go inside, but the practical part of him knew that it'd be best to go through his stuff before it all got tossed. Taking a deep breath— the smell of damp, burnt wood still in the air—he opened the door and ducked under the tape.

The apartment was a mess of burned, soggy furniture. The walls had scorch marks at least halfway up, and the ceiling was blackened with soot. Plastics and electronics had melted into Daliesque lumps, and windows had shattered from the heat. Ignoring most of the damage, Jack focused on the path to his bedroom. However, he'd only taken a few steps before his eyes turned to Lee's bedroom door. Lee's remains had been found after the fire was out. He'd never even made it out of bed, and the official cause of death was smoke inhalation.

The half-opened door was blackened and charred, as was the wall around it. He remembered hearing that the fire had started in there, although nobody was sure what had caused it. Their best guess was an electrical short.

Jack suddenly found himself walking towards the door, as if in a trance. Pushing the door open, he saw that the entire room had been destroyed by the fire. There wasn't a single part of the room that wasn't burned to a blackened crisp. Jack's bedroom shared a wall with this room, but somehow the fire hadn't burned all the way through. He tried not to think about how terrifying it would have been to wake up in the middle of all of this. Maybe Lee was lucky that the smoke had done him in before he'd burned to a crisp.

A shiver ran down his spine and Jack started to turn away, but then his eyes fell on the burned reminds of the nightstand. At first, he wasn't sure what had caught his eye, but then he noticed it. The dark wood blended in with the rest of the fire damage, and others might have thought it had been charred by the fire, but Jack knew the truth. The carving was exactly the same as when it had been taken from the grave by Lee. Everything else in the room had burned, but the carving was untouched.

Let the outsiders who disturb our bones get what's coming to them.

Another shiver ran down Jack's spine.

3

"That's not how that story goes," Erin said, even as the group made its way to the next room.

Barry turned, arms still splayed out, in the position they had been in when he had completed the tale, which his audience began to recognize as a performance trait, the gesture of how he ended each story. "No?"

"No. It was never fire. There's never been a fire in that story before."

Barry turned to her and smiled. The smile travelled, up his face, *too far* up his face. It curled at the corners, pushed his cheeks into his eyes, and obscured his ears. "No fire, you say? No fire in that story?"

David gingerly stepped forward between them, his hands out in front of him, the way one would do when trying to calm a particularly large animal.

"That's not the way it *goes*," Erin said again with emphasis, her teeth bared. She stepped forward, indignant. "It started, let me tell you, it started when my mother was twelve, actually."

David touched her shoulder, leaned in, and spoke something into her ear. She turned to face him when he pulled back, as though surprised he'd been there. As though she had been so focused on Barry that she hadn't even seen him there, hadn't even felt his touch on her shoulder until his words had registered. She looked at him, surprised, and his hand on her shoulder became an arm around it and he guided her off to one side.

Barry clapped his hands together, producing a sound so loud and sudden that it made the two visitors from the two different Bear Coves raise their shoulders in fright, whole bodies constricting and clenching.

"Now then," he said, smile widening past where it should've reasonably stopped. "Speaking of fire..."

He stepped past Barker and Linehan. The young girl, Sarah Childs, had been there speaking to them. Just as David had done with Sophia, Barry put his hand on her shoulder in one smooth motion, bony fingers wrapping around the exposed skin and guiding her away without her even realizing that she was *being* guided.

The pair of them stepped past Creed Dunford, Charles Henry, and Rowe Saunders. They stepped into a room apart from the one they'd been in, a room that even now smelled of soot. Even after the years that might have come since the flames had made them, the area around these artifacts of fire still smelled of soot and coal.

Barry, with Sarah in tow, stepped past Derek Rose of King's Cove and Bernice Fletcher of Little Harbour Deep, nodding to both. Bernice hadn't even seen who Sarah had been with, she was so focused on Sarah's face, that when she nodded, it was with a smile that matched Barry's.

One unnaturally wide smile was creepy, and Derek unknowingly wished he had the same focus on one or the other that Bernice had because seeing it on the both of them was absolutely unnerving.

. The image of an old house projected against a large sheet of plexiglass hung from the ceiling in the centre of the room.

The effect, known as Pepper's Ghost, was commonly used in haunted house attractions to create an eerie, partially transparent image.

More than a house, the projection featured a home. There were signs that it had been lived in, even in a photo as old as it was. It had been taken on a camera so old that even attempts to clean the image and improve upon it digitally could not hide the fact that it was not of this century, nor the last.

As she watched the guests mill about the room, Sophia walked closer to the projected home. She and Erin had argued over it with Erin insisting that one of those AI programs she kept seeing people posting about on Facebook could do the restoration work on the image that previous, human-made attempts couldn't adequately perform. Sophia's stance had been that the house—the home—was the last remnant of an otherwise forgotten place and using AI to try to remove the dust and cracks would remove the last strands of humanity that clung to the memory of the place.

Erin didn't seem to think that mattered, which made her outburst all the more curious to Sophia.

She sighed, and the responding inhale brought the smell of burn alight in her nostrils and she became more aware than ever of the display's immersive morbidity.

Arranged around the room at the feet of the projected

home was preserved burnt wood. Hundreds of pieces, some great and some small. Some were barely charred at all, some were blackened beyond recognition. Some were clearly pieces of not wood but... something.

You walked among the charred remains while in this exhibit, encouraged not to touch but to otherwise get close, to truly experience it.

There were subtle lines on the floor that glowed faintly purple. Sarah noticed it and looked around the top of the room, finding a glowing purple rod in a far corner. It was a black light to illuminate the lines in the otherwise low light required to make the projection effective. She followed the lines and stopped near a chunk of charred wood the size of her forearm and bent down to be near it, then read the inscription alongside it, also glowing from the black light: "Living Room, Northern Wall."

She realized, starkly, that these charred bits of frame were the only parts that remained of the home in the projection. That they were the same, and that the artifacts were arranged in such a way to show the vaguest of outlines of the house as it had been with the purple guides providing the blueprints to further aid in visualizing the space. They had been arranged to try and show from where in the frame they had come from: pantry, kitchen, stairs. She looked up, and the ceiling also had subtle lines outlining the second story's room. They were here to be a reminder. This is the home as it had been, and this was all that was left.

For a moment the projection shimmered, and with a swoop, the picture of the home was suddenly projected onto the floor and onto the remains of the home themselves, and each showed up where they would have been, like the image of a ghost projected over a corpse. It only lasted a moment, a jump-scare to any who were transfixed, before the image ratcheted back up onto the glass.

While all of this was happening, Barry was chuckling to himself. "No fire, she says," the chuckle broke into a laugh as he spoke up to the crowd, beginning to wind them into the next tale. "Newfoundland knows fire, is what I say. Newfoundland and her people know fire better than most others. We know the swell of fire, the fear of fire, the hell-on-earth that fire brings. Like a man caught in the flame, we bear the scars of fire for eons after."

He turned to face Sarah and took her by both shoulders. When he did, he saw that the rest of them, David included, had followed them into that next exhibit. They had not just walked past the others, they had been hitching followers with each one, continuing until they were all there behind.

He made a sound with his cheek that no one was meant to hear but did. He gestured to the charred piece the size of Sarah's forearm that she had read the inscription of. He bent down and picked it up by two joints that were deemed safe.

"Fire, I think, holds a lot of Newfoundland history," he said, holding the pieces forward for all to see.

"I think this island…" he paused, uncharacteristically taking a moment to compose himself before continuing. "I think it lives in contrast between the fire and the sea. If the water don't get ya, the fire will. I think this is an island prison for fire, and that every so often, by the lord, it riots."

THE GREAT FIRE
Jon Dobbin

"My son, St. John's is up to its ankles in blood," Mark said.

"You're drunk." I walked at his shoulder, kept him to my left, the road to my right. This had become a bit of a routine for us. Mark drank to get drunk; I didn't so that Mark wouldn't kill himself.

"No, b'y," Mark stumbled over the sidewalk, cursing it. "The ocean…" He said it as though he were the first to discover it and waved a hand towards the harbour, dismissing it and including it in one motion. "More bodies in there than in the ground, more than what lives on this wretched island."

"Fish don't count," I said and dodged a poorly aimed kick then pivoted to keep the drunken Mark from falling on his ass. "And you're most definitely drunk."

"Maybe." He straightened and pulled up his pants. "But I ain't wrong. Think about that sealing bunch that Cassie Brown wrote about—"

"That was on the ice." I remembered reading the book in high school. The cover little more than a sketch of men terribly underdressed for their frozen surroundings. The red sky made by their attempt to construct a hasty signal.

Fire in the sky. They all froze to death.

"What…fuck off. Ice on *the* ocean, you bastard." He raised his fist and belched. I bowed away, hands up, palms out. Surrender. "Fine, what about the *Titanic*? The iceberg that took out that bitch was just off the coast. More than 1500 people died that day."

"Everyone knows that," I said and stepped into the street to make way for a woman who had been walking towards us. She was tall, her hair long and purple. She was incredibly pale, and she was afraid. Of us? Probably. I wanted to reach out and grab her hand, tell her we weren't the bad ones. Well, I wasn't anyway. Who knows about Mark. When she passed between us, the strong scent of incense burned my nostrils. It reminded me of church on Ash Wednesday.

"I'm the king of the world," I said and shouldered Mark gently.

"That Leo, b'y," Mark stopped, leaned against a brick wall, and plugged a smoke into his mouth. "Hell, in the ole Dubya-Dubya-two, a German submarine snuck over this way and sunk some boats out by Bell Island. Few good Newfies died that day."

"That's nothing but an old myth. No submarines made it this far."

"Tell that to me fadder and he'll skull ya. Besides, it's a fact that they sunk the *SS Caribou*. 137 dead from that."

"Don't forget about the *Titan* submarine," I said, hoping to move the conversation along. I hadn't known Mark long, but in the short time I had made his acquaintance, I found out that once he got started on something, it was hard to get him to stop. In truth, I had no idea how to stop Mark's onslaught of morbid factoids. Bringing up the much-memed submarine was the best I could do. A joke. A distraction.

"The *Titan*." Mark blew out a stream of smoke. "Fucked up way to die."

The corners of my mouth felt cramped all of a sudden. I dropped my smile and fought the urge to massage my cheeks.

Mark bent at the waist and spat on the sidewalk. "Don't forget about the *Ocean Ranger* disaster. My mudder still isn't over that one. 'Shocking,' she says. 'So many young people dead.'" Mark's voice raised to a breathy falsetto when he imitated his mother. The sound he made grated on my nerves. Like chewing on aluminum foil. My skin crawled and a creeping sensation flittered across my shoulder blades. Mark must have noticed my reaction, he smiled around his smoke.

"That's only what happened out on the ocean, then you got all the shit that happens on land. People gone missing, bodies found in the woods, young fellas killing themselves. Buddy, if you don't think *that* caused a wound, you're more foolish than I thought."

"A wound," I said, wondering what the fuck he was on about.

"Yep. People don't think about it. Fuck, why would they? But a wound is kind of like…a door. Nah, a path. Yeah, that's it, that's what he said."

"Who, your father?"

"A path, an opening. Doctors use scalpels to make a path and they fix you up, right? That's a good path. But there is the opposite too. Some young fella high off fentanyl might stab you in the guts, wiggle the blade around for good measure. Now, that wound, er…path, that ain't a good one. Jagged, my son. Sloppy. That's what *this* wound is like." He waved his hand vaguely. "Ugly. Puckered." Mark shook his head to express the shame in it all.

He stopped and nodded at me, signalling me to move closer. When I did, he whispered nearly too low to hear: "That's not the worst part, these paths."

"Wounds."

"Whatever. They go two ways. Once you force your way *in*, other things can come *out*. Whether it started with a doctor's scalpel or some skeet's stolen kitchen knife, you get stuck by something sharp, the door opens for something on the other side to get out. Blood, guts. You turn inside out. Same thing with all these deaths. A wound opens the path. What's waiting on the other side?"

"Jesus, Mark, what's got you so worked up?" I could see him working up an answer, moving his mouth around behind his closed lips. Chewing it over. Finally, he shrugged and gave me a sheepish smile.

"It's nothing, b'y. Just the booze talking," he said and tossed his smoke. "Come on, we goes. I got something to show ya."

Mark staggered forward, his hands in his pockets. I followed. I thought about standing at his shoulder again, blocking him from the road, but I couldn't do it. Mark still wavered, still swayed close to the edge of the road, but something kept me back. I wanted the space.

The night bore down. Fog crept over the harbour blotting out the stars and making a hazy outline of the crescent moon. The rotten scent of the ocean, the garbage and human waste spilled inside of it, threatened to turn my stomach. The little booze that I had consumed curdled in my guts. It burned and gurgled. I had the urge to stop walking. To let Mark walk off into the night, while I snuck the other way to go home out of it. I looked behind me, saw the woman who'd passed earlier and imagined I caught up with her and tried some small talk. Maybe she wouldn't be completely creeped out by the strange guy running up behind her. It could have worked, but not likely.

Mark had gotten further away than I'd expected. His silhouette faded in and out of the fog as he swayed into the streetlights. With one last look at the woman with the purple hair, I ran to catch up with the drunkard I'd kept company with.

We walked in silence for some time, passing by the retro candy shop that called a small brick building its home, and then the glass monolith called Atlantic Place, dark and empty at that time of night, peering down upon us from on high beyond the ceiling of fog. The whole time Mark remained quiet, his hands jammed into the pockets of his tight jeans, bulging there as he made them into fists.

At Prescott Street, we ascended the small hill and stopped by the old Tim Hortons. The shop stood empty, a big "For Lease" sign on its front window. We stopped long enough for Mark to light a smoke.

"Never understood why they shut this place down," he said and stuffed his old Bic lighter back into his pants. "Figured they did well enough. The place was packed half the time, sure."

"No drive-thru."

Mark pointed at me and winked. "You might have it there, my son. Fadder says we're all lazy arses nowadays. Says we can't walk the length of ourselves without a phone in our hand or a boot to the hole. Imagine having a problem walking in to buy your coffee and donut. Just imagine." He huffed and shook his head. "I'm telling ya now, I don't know if he's wrong." He took a long drag from his smoke, straightened his jacket and started walking again, this time towards Signal Hill. He motioned for me to follow. I did.

"Don't you find it strange that there were three 'Great Fires' in this city?" Mark asked. From behind I could see that his shoulders were hunched up so high that they nearly touched his ears. A plume of smoke rose from what I assumed was his mouth and melded with the wispy fog that surrounded us.

"Three?" I hadn't known there had been that many. Though, admittedly, my knowledge of local history wasn't up to snuff.

"Yes, my son," Mark said and twisted his head to look at me. "Half the city was destroyed in each of 'em. 1819, 1846, and the best-known of 'em all, 1892." He counted them off on his fingers.

"That's not the weirdest thing either, right? Ya see, while all kinds of buildings were destroyed and hundreds of people were left without homes, only three people died." He held up his three fingers again. "Three deaths each time. Strange, eh?"

It was strange. "Maybe you should start a podcast, buddy. Talk about all these things online, make a bit of cash."

"Three fires, three deaths in each fire. Threes. That's a pattern if there ever was one."

I swallowed hard. Coughed. Thought about the woman with the purple hair who'd passed us on the street and wondered how far away she'd gotten. Wondered if I ran back would I still see her walking away or would the fog have taken her and left no trace.

I didn't want to talk to Mark anymore. I didn't want to hear his crazy stories, his conspiracy theories. If only he'd drunkenly babble about something else. Hockey, his quad, hell, even work. Anything. But no, he kept on. And so, I kept on. "What kind of pattern?"

"Magic numbers, my son. Scientifically speaking, we meat sacks like patterns. Three? That's a basic pattern. We see three things in a row, we remember it. 'Easy to recognize and recall,' as he said. But that's not the interesting part. Not at all. Threes are in all the big parts of life. Past, present, future. Birth, life, death. Let's not forget the Father, Son, and Holy Ghost. Jesus, Mary, and Joesph. The world is maggoty with threes. You find an occurrence of three, that's an omen."

"Omen of what?" I said and kicked at an empty fast-food cup.

"I don't know, man. But, in this case, three fires, three deaths. I don't think it's anything good."

Duckworth was quiet. The businesses had shut down hours before, and the street was lined with dark and empty buildings. There were some other stragglers from George Street, but there weren't many. Those who were around kept their distance. From time to time, we'd hear a laugh or belch from out of the fog, but that was it. Thankfully, even Mark decided to keep his mouth shut. At least for the time being.

"Hold up a minute," Mark said once we got to the war memorial. He took out another smoke and bent down. "Look at this," he said holding up another takeout drink cup. He shook it from side to side and sloshed the remnants around inside of it. It sounded almost full.

"Wasteful," I said and made my way around the memorial. A place of reverence, memorializing all those who lost their lives at war. Its five bronze statues, old and green, stood out from the pavement they were placed on. The Spirit of Newfoundland was the topmost statue on the memorial, her arm held aloft with a torch. The Statue of Liberty in miniature.

As I made my way around it, I looked towards the road that'd bring you to Signal Hill and caught sight of the Sheraton Hotel, formerly known as The Newfoundland Hotel. I wondered if Mark knew anything about that place. Who had died there? Was it someone from one of the Great Fires?

The scent of something familiar brought my thoughts back to where I was, what I was doing. I sniffed the air to try and identify it, casually moving my head back and forth in front of the memorial. Not the ocean with its rotting innards and dead bodies. Not incense like the perfume of the woman with the purple hair. Not smoke from a fire burning its way through the city. Not fire, but something adjacent to it. What was that smell?

"The good thing about those wounds," Mark said behind me, "those pathways. They can be healed. Cleansed with fire."

Cold liquid splashed over my head and ran down my face and neck. I had enough time to imagine being baptized in a dark lake, maybe the ocean, before I heard the flick of a lighter. Then the world disappeared into flame and heat.

4

When the story was done, Sarah took a quick sharp breath.

She wasn't where she remembered being at the start of it. Close geographically, but far situationally. She was alone now, she realized, alone in the dark. There was a window in front of her, large and shaded like polarized glass. Through it, she could see the other patrons of the tour.

David, John, and Rowe were looking at a stuffed fox. She watched them watch it. Watching its eyes, or more accurately, the glassy marbles that had been placed where its eyes had been. Rowe was tapping them with his finger, in defiance of the sign he was looming over that warned people not to do exactly that. He was saying something, inaudible to Sarah through the glass, and looking back at the other two, making comments.

They were talking about the eyes, Sarah decided, how they followed you.

The room Sarah was in was dark. There were exhibits in there, in the dark. They were there but they were not ready for the public; they were covered in white sheets and looked like the ghosts in old television shows. There was something so haunting about them still, she thought, as she saw their reflection in the glass, recreating the haunting effect of Pepper's Ghost in a way much closer to the trick's original intention.

She watched through the glass as the other tour patrons moved through the room and the reflections of the weird white inhuman shapes of the exhibits she currently shared a space with. They would occasionally cross paths and line up perfectly, not unlike when the house's projection overlayed the remnants of the house itself.

Alphonsus Buck, Gary Linehan, and Charles Henry were looking through a large book.

It was a sign-in log, tracking the sailors aboard a boat that hadn't touched water in over a century. Each man who got aboard the ship had to show his name and place of origin with some space to write a message. While the intention was for notes on health, family, or any other pertinent information, the sailors proved that men were capable of expressing short messages of vitriol long before the internet gave them 140 characters to do it.

Crude, lewd, and hateful comments filled the logbook's column, and the exhibit was going out of its way to remind us not to paint the past in too rose-coloured a lens.

Sarah watched them read it, chuckling over the notes, and she suddenly remembered stepping away from those people during the story of the fire.

She had been reading those same names, places, and comments (many of them awful given retrospect, many of them awful even for the time, further reinforcing her mental comparison to Twitter) and had stepped away, as though in a trance. There had been a door—no, not a door, only a hall—and it had led to here. With the white-sheet ghosts and the polarized glass that she could see out of, but that they could not see in through.

Creed Dunford and Derek Rose stepped in front of the glass and looked in at her, as though they could see her.

They scrunched their faces, touched their lower lip to their nose if they could, could not, and looked ridiculous trying. They motioned and Bernice Fletcher came over, adjusted her glasses, and looked at the book displayed before their side of the glass.

As Sarah watched them, she screwed up her face, too.

"It's about genetic traits," came a small, wormy voice from behind her.

Sarah's shoulders tensed. From the right of her periphery, an arm not her own extended past her and pointed a bony finger at the three of them: Creed, Derek, and Bernice, all of them holding their ears now, waggling them, like they were mocking her.

Her memory began to clear, and more details came into focus. She had not walked down this hallway in a trance and found herself among the silken ghosts of classic television, she had been *led* there.

She could remember how silky his voice had become towards the end of that tale, how those same bony fingers, skin with no elasticity, clasping at her shoulder, led her away.

She could still feel his icy grip, first thinking it was just the lingering sensation of memory, but when she looked, she realized that it was because his hand *was* still there.

One hand held her in place, while the other extended past her to show her where to look.

Breath, hot on the back of her neck.

"It's only half the exhibit," he continued, still pointing at her three compatriots and the faces they made. "You come to this mirror and there's a sign in front of it showing traits from the Old World. Red hair. Freckles. Dimpled chins. And it gets you to look in that mirror and examine yourself for that genetic history."

His grip, she thought, tightened. His breath on her back seemed hotter, closer, more intense. He smelled of capelin, that salt and brine.

"And then it goes on to other traits. People who can touch their tongues to their noses. People who can waggle their ears. People who can cross one eye. And it encourages you to test these things out. When the exhibit is done, it will lead you back to here next, and you'll see that that mirror was a one-way glass, and that people were watching you make all those silly faces at them."

He pointed, now, to the edges of the glass.

"The soundproofing was the hardest. They had to make it so that when the witnesses laughed, it would not tip off the people making the faces."

His grip on her shoulder tightened even more and he pushed her gently forward, toward the glass. "Nobody can see us, and nobody can hear us."

"I should go," she said, voice hushed, and took a step back toward the hall. "We're supposed to stay together as a group."

His grip on her shoulder intensified, suddenly, urgently. His free hand, the one he'd been gesturing with, snapped to her right shoulder, close to her neck. Cupping her neck, like a threat.

Wait and watch, it said. Try it and see.

"You can't." He said, his voice heated like the fire from his story, like the air from a beach bonfire fuelled with more than just wood. "You *mustn't*." His breath stank of gasoline and capelin. Fuel and rotting fish. "Please... I *hunger*."

He said it with such gravitas, such need, that she wanted nothing more than to get away. Her need to escape was equalled only by his own. Equal and opposing forces, a tug-of-war with her flesh as the rope.

Her muscles tensed.

She was focused on the benign gaze of Bernice Fletcher, the Postmaster of Little Harbour Deep, coiling her limbs and getting ready to push off from him and run for the hall when his voice dropped, again, and became deeper. Lower.

Hypnotic.

It dropped the same way it had when he'd told her the last story, and some part of her, somewhere, was compelled to listen. "Let me tell you another..."

ALLURE
Alex McIntosh

The eggs benedict at the Bagel Café in St. John's was an absolute must-have. It was one of those culinary delights I used to rave about to my friends back in Central. I'd spent most of my life going through social circles and having laughs with my usual gathering of chums that I'd forgotten the joy of just sitting alone in a mostly empty restaurant enjoying my own company. I savoured every bite, gave the waiter a kind word and a generous cash tip, and had plenty of time to check into the hotel early. People in a city come and go in waves. You feel as though you recognize everyone and yet none, like images in a videogame. It's easy to feel lonely when you're by yourself.

It was a little after 3 pm when my large rolling suitcases and I arrived at the black wooden door of the room I had specifically requested. The key turned in the lock with a grinding effort because the room was rarely booked. Still, there was a comfort to this, the same kind I solicited in house viewings with clients, that sense of ownership. I pushed open the door to that scent of worn carpet and mildew. Untouched yet strangely inviting. That homely familiarity. Oversized merlot red drapes covered the wall to disguise the fact there was no window.

Earlier this year, the hotel ended up cancelling my reservation by mistake and everywhere else in the city was fully booked. After profusely apologizing that there was nothing they could do, one of the housekeeping staff overheard and suggested this room on the first floor—room 102.

"I don't care what it looks like, I'll take it," I said, pleading and grabbing my wallet so they could see the credit card. "As long as it isn't haunted."

The manager, stoic-faced, replied: "No, Mr. Bradley. It's just that there's no window, it's small, the air conditioning doesn't work, and it smells damp. We don't use it. It's basically the worst room in the hotel. I wouldn't stay there."

I could tell she loved her job.

I told her I'd be fine. I would always tell myself it would be luxurious compared to sleeping in a tent in a hot Iraqi desert co-habited by wild dogs and camel spiders . My younger days of serving in the military had indeed humbled me. The manager had the receptionist credit me with two free nights in future. I only wished I could have seen her face when I called back and requested the same room all these months later.

The room was like a box and not the kind you'd wrap a gift in. I guess the coziness was all part of its charm. The bubbled ceiling felt lower than most rooms, and I was amazed they managed to fit a full-size bed in such a tiny space. Elsewhere, the writing desk with a large mirror, chair, mini fridge, and tea and coffee-making amenities came complete with century-old camomile tea bags probably six years past their expiry date.

No ghosts.

Just a room you'd likely complain about if you were asked to complete an online survey asking, "How was your stay?"

So, why did I request it?

I kicked off my shoes and peeked in the bathroom to satisfy my curiosity and there it was, that old alcove bathtub, complete with that glass mason jar of rose petals and dahlias, untouched since the last time I stayed here. The bathroom's faux wooden vinyl floor had curled up in the corners, and the beige toilet and vanity looked severely outdated. I pulled down gently on the brass handle of the tub and after a few splutters of trapped air, the water rolled out hot. I snapped the mason jar open and generously sprinkled in some of the floral mixture. I knew underneath the old façade, there was still a coziness to this space that was unparalleled. I'd missed it.

I removed all my clothes and laid them neatly inside one of my suitcases and there I was, standing still, checking myself in the mirror and listening to the rippling flow of the faucet. I'd often been complimented on my tidy hair and defined jawline, my body itself quite broad and toned. I never liked my stomach; the dad bod with no kids, a side effect of being a craft beer connoisseur. My girlfriends never seemed to mind, God love them. My legs were a staple: firm, muscled, and with a Sean Connery amount of hair. I was proud of never missing leg day at the gym, and what was between them, I'd never had any complaints there either. There I was, James Bradley, the same conventionally attractive professional I'd seen staring back at me for most of my young adult life.

Steam had filled the confined space until it clouded out into the main room and resembled a Turkish bath house. As the manager had mentioned months ago, the vent in the room did not work. I walked in and turned off the faucet where the beautiful aroma of those flowers had woken up like a rainy garden first thing in the morning. I eased myself gently into the hot luxury of this familiar tranquillity. As soon as my shoulders disappeared under the surface, every ache from my body seemed to evaporate with the steam. I filled my stomach with a deep breath and submerged my head to feel that glowing throb of heat. I was up again to let out a breath brimming with new life, and that's immediately when the smell of blood filled the air, as metallic and fragrant as the flowers. It was the same incense as the last time. I was expecting it.

The porcelain mould had quickly turned into a hot bubbling pot of flesh soup. My skin floated in strips with exposed muscle fibres coming off in stringy chunks leaving a layer of film on the water like fat in a homemade stew. The loosened nails on my fingers peeled right off. I could only begin to imagine what the pain of this experience would truly feel like, as my own body pumped with what I could only describe as a feeling of pure euphoria and revitalization, like the energy you get after an orgasm. Underneath the old flesh, a layer of new skin had developed, softer than before, a retraction in my body in some places, and yet growth in others.

A completely different shape.

A completely different person.

I had transformed.

I itched when I stepped out of the bathroom, as if I felt every particle in the air land on my skin at the same time. My bare feet were warm against the carpet, my nipples erect and sore, and the feeling on my shoulders was very different. Beads of water trickled down my exposed body. I turned to face the mirror in the room.

The woman staring back at me was excited, elevated, beautiful—the same as she was before. It was like staring into the eyes of an old friend with the same characteristics. I looked down at my dainty fingers wrapped between strands of long auburn hair as I moved it behind my neckline and away from my new chest. I felt a tear roll down my cheek. I was happy to see you again, my love.

I grabbed my phone from the nightstand and took several minutes to just photograph myself. A new pose, a new facial expression, a new angle, a different me. It wasn't long before the excitement got the better of me, and my new hands were left to their own devices.

The early check-in was key. Whereas my own girlfriends had been adept at getting dolled up before a night out, it had taken me seemingly forever to scroll through the videos online to teach myself even a beginner's course in makeup application. Once I found a couple of starting points, I unzipped my second large suitcase and retrieved the dusty leather makeup bag I had packed. I wasn't taking any chances. Whatever frightening magic was in that bath mixture had worked again, and I was back to being a goddess. This time, I wasn't panicking, I felt very much at home with the gender change.

I was prepped.

I was ready.

I wanted to be stunning.

The foundation, mascara, highlights, lip gloss, and eyeliner, then allowing it to bake, contouring, and re-applying over the mistakes I had made took *time*. This was like painting a pure work of art only my face was the canvas. The girls I knew made this operation look easy, but then they had also practised and fine-tuned over the years. Every time I watched them applying makeup in the mirror, I'd always say, "You don't need that, you look beautiful without it." Seeing them in makeup didn't matter to me, but it *mattered* to them, and here I could see why. After gazing back at myself, after nearly three hours of perfecting everything those videos had taught me, I could *see* why it mattered so much.

I looked *sensational*. That feeling of excitement also brought empowerment. I felt as though I could go out now and own this city and know every eye in each room was laid on *me*. My perfect symmetry, dusky eyes and smoky visage—everything beautiful about my feminine self was highlighted so there would be no question; *all* eyes would be on *me*. *I* wanted to fuck me. Bringing a man back who'd wish to do the same would be easy.

Underneath the neon green lights that polluted the air as much as the rattling exhaust manifolds on the cabs, Medusa's Lounge offered a glitzy night out with a high-class restaurant in the front and a dark dance club in the back. A nice yin and yang of personalities befitting the name of the place. The irony wasn't lost on me either.

Inside the bar was a gorgeous backdrop of crystallized glass and amber colours flicked by the soft glow of the ceiling pot lights. There, stood a goddess in a long copper dress that flowed down to her ankles. That was me, all business. If it wasn't for the smoking ban, I would have rested a cigarette between my fingers to complete the look of old-timey Hollywood bombshell glamour, that fair glow of my cobra green eyes waiting for a kind gentleman to offer a light.

Meh.

That's all it was, old Hollywood glamour. Those charming chivalrous men didn't exist anymore. I was probably too old school for my own good in that respect. Mind you, I knew why I was there, and it *wasn't* to be romanced or to look for a relationship. I was out to *play*.

I sat down and sipped on my Long Island iced tea and surveyed the room; I was ready to lock eyes and not let go.

"Oh, hey!"

My perusal was interrupted by a deeply familiar voice. I turned to see Jillian, an ex-girlfriend. The anxiety in my stomach hit me like a gunshot.

"Hey, what's up?" I replied, playing it cool.

Of all the scenarios I had run through my head preparing for this careful night of animalistic coursing, this hadn't come up. How could it? I was no longer James Bradley.

How?

I knew my smile was sparkling. I'd *worked* on it.

Her own facial expression was a strange one. Jillian and I had only dated for a few months on purely amicable terms, but I knew she was fiercely perceptive. Her eyes peeked as though she were trying to solve some sort of puzzle just by staring at me, trying to focus on something that was there, and yet at the same time, was not. Like trying to define and confirm that recognition, yet her mind was drawing a blank. Almost on autopilot, I asked: "I'm sorry, do we know each other?"

Jillian appeared quizzically disappointed, then embarrassed, and the anxious pit in my stomach turned to guilt from my deception. I also yearned to hear how she was doing. I wanted to ask for her opinions on the latest season of *Drag Race*, if she was still teaching Boxfit, and if she ever did get to travel to Vallon-Pont-d'Arc in the sunny south of France. I'd never felt anything like this before, it was a position I'd never been in. It was as though James Bradley were a ghost and he was helpless to reach out to her.

"Oh, I'm sorry, I thought I recognized you from somewhere," Jillian said before she swiftly left with her gal pals.

I had gone back to sipping my cocktail and noticed my blood moon lipstick on the straw; a sight that was new to me. I was using my smartphone camera to check on my makeup as I'd forgotten to pack my compact mirror. It didn't take my feet long to physically complain to me about wearing these heels, it also didn't take me long to notice I should have worn earrings. And from the way I was sitting on that barstool, it didn't take long before my dress started to ride up and bunch itself up into the curves I wasn't used to owning.

At least I remembered to tie my hair back.

After a moment of fixing myself, the smell of liquor and artificial fog gasped into the room from the club door and three guys strode over to the bar. One of them caught my eye immediately. He looked exactly like Jason Momoa.

"Double spiced rum and whatever these two dipshits are having," I overheard him tell the server behind the bar before he slapped one of his buddies across the back. His style was embarrassing. I could faintly see a black band T-shirt showing itself through his wrinkled white dress shirt like tracing paper with black jeans and scuffed work boots that had no place being there. Still, he *did* look a lot like Jason Momoa, only shorter. I wasn't sure of his height exactly, my own height being changed had thrown off my sense of perception. He *was* muscular, I'll give the guy that. He had those deep-set eyes too, and once they strayed from the glass of liquor in his hand and caught the bewitching gaze of this honey sitting near him, I knew *my* fun would begin.

"You look just like that movie star. Anyone ever tell you that?" I inescapably locked my eyes on his making sure they never left and gently bit my bottom lip for good measure. His expression was one of interest. I bet he'd never had it so easy from a Venus like *me* before. I always preferred to wine and dine, but these days, if you wanted nothing more than a good fuck, these were the a-holes you got free range of. As I mentioned earlier, I was prepped.

I knew his name was Charlie.

I knew he would be here this very night.

I knew he was married.

I knew he was readily available, and with what I was about to offer, I *knew* he'd be well up for it.

"Are you going to keep staring at me, Charlie?" I asked. His eyes blinked like he'd snapped out of a trance before they proceeded to size me up.

"Do you know me?" he asked with one of those dirty grins before he sat down next to me and cleared his throat of the rum he'd swallowed too quickly.

I extended my hand, hoping he'd notice my pretty nails: "I'm Catherine."

His rough hand enveloped mine, and we shook. My handshake was firm. *Too* firm. I'd grown too accustomed to using a firm handshake when meeting clientele. Not very delicate at all. Shit.

"That's a *firm* grip there, darlin'. I bet *those* hands could do some damage," he said with a wink before he ordered another double rum.

Like, *seriously*? Was I *not* sitting here looking like an enchantress? Everything about me was incredible. What would possess him to make a comment like *that*? Oh my God, did I feel *devalued* over that comment? No, I had to stick to my guns. I wasn't used to it.

"*These* hands can do a *lot* of damage *if* you're in the mood," I said before I winked back at him.

Jesus, I felt downtrodden about that comment. It was also so strange, the feeling I got from the handshake and his much larger hand than mine. Part of me felt emasculated, yet part of me felt...oddly aroused.

He looked me in the eyes again. "I'm not sure where you heard the name Charlie. That *is* my name, but everyone calls me Chucky."

"*Chucky*? Really? You don't look like a Chucky. The only *doll* in here is the one you're talking to right now." I took a sip of my drink and smiled at him while my lips wrapped the straw. *Fuck* him. My self-esteem isn't going anywhere. I want to have fun with this.

"You're right, darlin'. You *are* a doll. You're stunning," His gaze didn't break, even when he took another swig of rum. He was fixated on me, yet his eyes were puzzled. I wondered if I was coming on too strong. "You look *so* familiar. Where do I know you from?"

Jillian had given me the same examination, but then Jillian *knew* James Bradley. I'd never met this guy before. As a man, I knew every inch of myself, yet the first time this had ever happened to me, the first time I'd become Catherine, the first time I calmed after a heart attack of confusion, panic, and shock when I viewed this new person in the mirror, I could see James Bradley's characteristics beyond the new flesh I'd metamorphosed into. I *wore* the same expressions, the same wrinkles, the same gestures, the same smile. I could *tell* it was me. And if *I* could, I guess so could anyone. Maybe he had seen me before.

"Where do I know you from?" He repeated.

"I'd say you probably saw me in your dreams," I replied coolly and gently stroked my forefinger on his leg, "A lot of guys I've met say I look familiar. I must have a doppelganger somewhere. Well, you must know how that feels to get recognized all the time."

I had him in agreement. "Yeah, sure. I get it. Everyone

in St. John's knows who Jason Momoa is, so I get it. I wish I knew who you reminded me of. Where are you from? Why haven't I seen you in here before?"

I'd had plenty of time to rehearse that response.

In between clients, every morning after the gym, in the shower, after getting home from a game of cards with the guys, and mostly from date nights, *every* question asked of me, or that I could think of, I had drafted a response to consummate my Catherine's backstory. Catherine Bloom was named in honour of the scary floral mixture that transformed me, although for anybody I'm likely to converse with, I'd say it was a Norwegian name. I was from St. Anthony originally but moved to the mainland when I was six with my mom. Dad was a fisherman. No siblings. That way they couldn't try to creep them on social media. I'd tell people I didn't use a personal social media page myself because there were so many creeps around. I was a self-employed interior designer. Being a real-life realtor, they went hand in hand.

None of it really mattered anyway.

Even after explaining such a carefully laid out backstory like this to Charlie, it seemed he was only interested in one thing.

"Do you want some of this *dick*?"

I knew I was playing easy to get. This is what I wanted, but the *arrogance*, the *sliminess*—it made me uncomfortable. I wasn't expecting him to hit me up with any of that Jane Austen stuff, but still. I had to remind myself that this was a brand-new experience, with brand-new feelings. A lot of the feelings I was experiencing were not that of James Bradley.

"Oh, Mr. Darcy, I bet you say that to all the girls," I said with a wry smile.

Humour to disguise discomfort was something I had used too often. I got up from the barstool and stood painfully in my heels not knowing if they were too small, too tight, or just too awkward to walk in because it was the only pair I thought to purchase since the last time I "bathed" at the hotel. Charlie stood up and finished his drink. His eyes looked as though they were losing focus with each movement, and judging by the way he rifled each pocket in check of his phone and his wallet, he was feeling some serious aftereffects.

I checked the time again on my phone before we walked outside into the crisp night air filled with the smell of rain on stone mixed with the sounds of puddles slushing underneath fast-moving cabs. We made our way to a taxi. I had my heels taken off and put in my purse. The idea of stepping on a broken bottle in my bare feet seemed way less painful.

I turned the room key with a frustrated force and lost one of my fake nails in the process. I doubt fuck-nuts would have even noticed, but I was sweating profusely from a combination of nerves and body heat since his hands hadn't stopped groping me since we left the club. All new, all alien to me.

"Do all you *sinattny* women be made like you?" he slurred with his breath hot on my earlobe.

I wondered if the actual Saint Anthony had to put up with people saying his name in such a way. I didn't know how to respond to his comment other than a mild fake laugh, and I didn't care to engage knowing he probably wouldn't listen anyway. He was holding himself up against the knobbed door frame with his left hand while his coarse right hand squeezed hold of my right tit through the bra, while he pressed his jeans against my bottom. I threw the door open and hurried inside. My purse thumped against the carpet when I tossed it.

I wanted this to be over and done with. I wanted to enjoy myself, *feel* something, feel some kind of reward and validation for looking the way I was that evening. It took me *so long* to get ready and I looked so damn stunning! I honestly thought this would be different.

Charlie tried taking his boots off before he scuffed sideways and fell against the bed. I heard him laugh from the floor, that same drunken laugh I'd heard myself do on many an inebriated cabin trip with the b'ys. I sat on the small wingback chair in the corner of the room to have a controlled view of the proceedings. I watched his dark hairy hand struggle to bring its body up onto the bed. With some effort, he let out a guttural cough and managed to climb onto the hard mattress enough to sit down and take off his shirt.

His muscular abdomen was on full display.

I was curious to know what kind of core workouts gave him those abs, or whether it was just dietary restraints, another part of me admired it in a different way. I was so *confused*. The longer I spent in this body, the more comfortable I became with these thoughts and expressions of interest.

He clasped the belt around his jeans and threw it to the

floor before he undressed fully. He lurched himself onto the bed and moved backwards with his head resting on the pillow. His eyes were just about gone, his pupils like black mirrors completely at a loss of what was in front of them. I could practically see his head spinning. He turned to look in my general direction. I knew in this state he wouldn't be able to even string together a sentence. He patted the space on the bed next to him and languorously invited me to join him. His penis was totally flaccid. He may have been Aqualad on the streets, but he looked like a dead fish in the sheets.

It was nice to know that the little "extra" cocktail I slipped into his drink at the bar worked a charm, and it didn't take him long before he was sleeping like a rock.

I took my time when I undressed, just to calm myself. I then stood in the room as naked as the day I was born, which was only that evening depending on which way you looked at it. It was difficult *not* to admire myself, puckering my lips at myself in the mirror. I placed my hand on my hip and perceived myself through every angle, every pose, just to see which side was my best, until in all this experimentation, that arousal grew within me again. It fired me up. I'm not sure whether it was just the way I was feeling about myself, or whether it was the attraction to this fine woman flirting with me in the mirror, but I couldn't complain. In a way, I was really feeling *myself*.

Earlier this year, we had our annual work excursion to our boss's luxury cottage in Humber Valley. It always made me laugh, the way she described this eight-bedroom, seven-bathroom, oak-beamed mansion as a cottage. I'm sure the English peasants from back in the day would've been over the moon if they all lived in one of these. The wood stove was fired up with crackling splits, the 80s soundtrack featuring Bonnie Tyler was on, the smell of piping hot sausage rolls was fragrant, and everybody had a drink in their hand. Everybody except Kate.

Kate got her real estate license and started selling houses the same year I did, and we quickly became best friends. With a mutual love of playing darts, trying different craft beers, and watching old-school pro wrestling, we were sold on each other immediately, striking up fun conversations on a whim and laughing at the same stupid jokes. She once got so drunk at a Christmas party she told me she'd screw me harder than Bret Hart in Montreal, and I lost it, laughing so hard I almost cried. Nobody else at the party got the reference, and we were looked upon like two weirdos.

I was involved with another woman at this time, and I was surprised at how badly Kate took the information, like the wind had been taken out of her sails. She never made a move on me again.

Three months after that, Kate was in a relationship, and she didn't tell me. We had talked daily, and I felt blown off that she hadn't mentioned it to me. I loved Kate, but despite our similarities, never fell *in love* with her. I had never fallen *in love* with anyone. I guess I was too scared to make a commitment at this stage of my life. Late twenties, making six figures a year, with no ties, I was having a lot of fun enjoying my freedom, whereas Kate's freedom became nonexistent.

A missed evening of playing darts soon became a frequent absence, then she stopped attending socials with work colleagues, and then out of the blue, she stopped texting me. Her attitude at work had changed. She used to love sharing excitement with her clients, taking selfies with them holding the keys to their new homes, and posting them all over her business page on social media. This stopped entirely. Her personality became barren, like a projected recording just running the same scene on a loop day to day. I asked her if everything was okay, and she'd respond with the same, "Yeah, why wouldn't it be?" I asked her why she'd stopped texting me back, and she'd tell me she accidentally deleted it or just didn't see it because she was getting so many client texts.

I knew there was something going on.

It was only when Kate's sister, Jenn, contacted me secretly that I was about to be clued up on the exact ins and outs of what happened to my friend.

I had a lakeside cabin just outside of town. I invited Jenn over that evening. I didn't know her that well other than her reputation as an RNC officer with zero sense of humour. She stepped inside the dimly lit porch and took off her drenched coat while I poured a glass of IPA for myself and a glass of kettle sour for her at the kitchen bar area.

"Thanks for meeting with me, James," she said sitting down across from me at the table. I handed her the cool pint I just poured up and she took a big swig.

"What's going on with Kate exactly?" I asked matter-of-factly, my stomach in knots. "Your messages were very vague."

"I'm sorry, it's a lot to type, and I really don't *want* to type it." Jenn seemed angry. I knew it wasn't with me. "James, I'm sorry to spring this on you, but I know my sister and you are like *best* friends. She's being abused by her husband, and I don't know what to do."

I paused. I didn't want it to be true. It felt like my heart stopped and followed my stomach as it dropped out of my body. Tears welled up on Jenn's face and my hands started shaking. I'd never felt sheer anger like this before; I wanted to leave and punch something, or just go and scream outside. I immediately felt like a bubbling cauldron of hate and heartbreak.

I conversed with Jenn through the knots and fought back my own tears while Jenn told me everything she knew, filling in the blanks and detailing the chain of events.

Every sordid detail covering the past few months was like a stabbing pain to my soul.

Kate had gotten married in secret to a man who had been regularly beating her, with Kate covering up bruises daily. He was gaslighting her, reading her phone daily and wouldn't allow her to contact her friends, and he was cheating on her every free weekend he had.

I couldn't bring myself to accept it. I stepped away for a moment on shaky legs to go outside. I faced the trees behind my cabin in the thundering torrent, and I screamed until my throat was hoarse, so sharp it felt like swallowing razor blades.

When I returned a few moments later, Jenn's face was

beet red. She had no more emotion left to give. We were both numb. She explained to me that she called the detachment on the guy several times after becoming aware of the abuse. Kate denied everything when the police arrived. She then stopped responding to Jenn's texts. Jenn did some digging through her own resources and found out that the guy was also previously up on charges in Ontario for domestic abuse with another former spouse. God knows how far back into his past this cycle continued.

The more she told me, the worse I felt. The same questions spun cycles in my mind: *How* could I have *corrected* this earlier? *Why* didn't Kate tell me she had gotten married? How could this happen to *Kate*?

I would make sure this wouldn't continue.

"Who is he, Jenn? What's his name?" I asked directly.

"He's not on social media, but his name's Charlie Sawyer, and he looks a lot like Jason Momoa."

I propped his naked body up against the toilet, the back of his neck resting against the base of the bowl awkwardly. Hoisting him, dragging him, maneuvering him, it was tough on my new body. My tits had rubbed and pressed against his clammy skin, and I felt disgusting. My emotions were firing on all cylinders. I stood up and planted my feet on the floor, catching my breath and glaring down at this dogshit excuse for a human being. I thought about *everything* he'd done to Kate.

The punch I delivered to his nose was by far the most perfect shock of orgasmic gluttony I experienced that night. The mild crunch from his vertebrates snapping when his head struck the bowl was music to me. A split-second reaction later and he was waving his arms with a panicked childlike moan spewing from his mouth as if waking from a nightmare.

"Hey, Charlie! These hands can do a *lot* of damage when they want to!" I shouted. The saliva flew out of my mouth like a barking hockey parent to a young volunteer referee.

He could barely register what just happened, let alone see what I'd grasped from the vanity and held in my hand. I wanted him to feel every blow from the claw hammer when I smashed it against his teeth.

The sound was indescribable. I had crumbled away some of his jawbone like a piece of drywall, white beads of spit and bone hung from his face in pieces. My rage was inconsolable, and I brought it up and down repeatedly, huffing and spitting, my own teeth clenched together, my arms stiff and tiring until his own arms stopped flailing. The chipping sounds turned to popping, and the spray of blood and brain matter mixed with other fluids covered the vinyl floor like foam. I was panting like a dog, yet I was energized and invigorated. It seemed effortless when I lifted to place him in the bathtub, and the gore didn't bother me at all, even wearing it.

I had packed a lot of things for this evening. I washed my hands, threw a towel on the floor of the bedroom, and turned on the TV, the mixture of spatter and steam streaming down my legs. Any channel with an action movie would do, the louder the better. After some mindless channel-hopping, I discovered *Terminator 2* was on. Perfect. I put the sound up on blast and took the reciprocating saw from my carry-on case.

In the weeks that followed, I saw clues that Kate was slowly readjusting. She had taken time off work following the receipt of a surprise text from her "husband" informing her that he was leaving to go back to the mainland and that she'd never see him again. Perhaps I was too blunt and straightforward doing that; I didn't know Kate's feelings towards him well enough. It seemed a better option than him just disappearing and not contacting her again.

I also *chose* not to reach out to her.

I was numb. Barely a feeling registered in my physical form; it was like a drunk driver operating a human shell. Every emotion had been stripped from me like the multiple layers of wallpaper in a hundred-year fixer-upper. It felt as though I had grieved and was still trying to process everything. I was living in a husk of who I was, or at least who I felt like I was. I had committed a perfect crime and saved one of my best friends from a life of misery, and I didn't even have the inkling to contact her again. I knew if Charlie's body parts were ever found, they'd just be marked as a cold case under "Jane Doe." The rose petals and dahlias apparently didn't need living subjects to work. Maybe the numbness came from the shock of all this, but to add to that, I didn't know who I was anymore. It was the longest period I'd stayed in female form, and my feelings inside were torn. Emotions wrestled against each other, undecided. Catherine Bloom wanted to take over. The more I thought about her, the more I fell in love with her.

I'd never had a long vacation to myself. As I'd said before, it was always golfing weekends with the guys and a scattered trip to New York City. Besides that, I stayed grounded on the island. Three weeks in Montreal was something that I desperately needed; I yearned to feel real again.

Walking down the delightful cobblestone streets in Old Montreal and listening to the hustle and bustle of busy city life, I could *feel* it coming back. The smell of smoke permeated the air in the mornings. I ate the best poutine I'd ever had in my life at the colourful La Banquise. My senses were sharpening and the good was finally coming back to me, life like a slow seeping of water filling up a bathtub.

I was down front for the Canadiens game at the Bell Centre. The rivalry between Montreal and Toronto during a hockey game was good for the soul. I was a big Habs fan. The memories of watching the games with Pop at the house before he passed away were some of the best days missed, but now it was time to focus on the new best days. The feeling of excitement was back. A vigorous buzz surged through me, and I could feel myself. I was happy.

Once the halftime buzzer sounded, I made my way to one of the bars where the cacophony of flavourful snacks was fragrant in the air. The smile on my face was infectious, and it didn't take long before a conversation was struck up with Nathalie, a forty-year-old bookstore owner with the most amazing head of wavy red hair I'd ever seen. This was going to be the best vacation of my life, I could feel it. She asked me my name. I handed her the beer I'd just purchased for her and replied: "I'm Catherine."

5

Barry's hands, thin and spidery, still gripped the supple flesh of Sarah Childs' shoulders.

His lips, still puckered from the last words of the tale, were near the joint of her neck and spine. His lips were close, but they did not encroach. There was no attempt to move them closer, nor would she have stopped such an attempt.

Sarah stared forward, as though in a trance but more accurately in a fugue. Otherwise, were she cognizant of it, she could have felt the swampy heat of his breath against her hair. Her mouth, like his, was agape, not with his hunger but slack from use. She stared at her fellow travellers, moving through the exhibit and wandering towards the next. Her pupils had dilated into small pin-pricks of their former selves, leaving only her haunting blue irises.

She swallowed and swallowed again, but no matter what she did, she could not get enough saliva.

"Was it a good story?" Barry asked, his voice wispy. Gossamer. Ethereal.

She tried to speak, but it was as futile as her attempts at swallowing. Her tongue refused to wrap around the words, so she nodded.

His right hand moved from its proprietary grasp on

her shoulder. It moved up, up, *up* until it grasped gingerly at the swell of her neck. "Your turn, then. Tell us a tale. Tell old Barry a story, why don't you?"

"That's not really how this works," David said, appearing in the doorway.

Barry snapped to him and for a moment, just for a moment, the old man wasn't an old man. It was gone in a flash, and David knew it must have been a trick of the light, but for a second he'd been something else. Something paler, and somehow, smaller.

Sarah turned at David's voice as well, and when she did agency returned to her gaze. She smiled at him, with her eyes as equally as her mouth, her pupils returning to the sea of black they had always been before this day, only rimmed with blue.

She stepped toward David and out of Barry's grasp, his fingers falling from her like leaves from a tree as the autumn air chills them to death.

David stepped towards her as well and into the light from the window, and when she saw how stern he looked, Sarah stopped short and suddenly. She recoiled and his hand was on her arm, lightning quick, snapping her to his side. Then, with him leading the way and she in tow, they walked back to the rest of their party.

"I told you..." he started, his voice hushed and immediate, before turning over his shoulder and seeing Barry lumbering behind them.

The others had stopped their browsing in the time it had taken Sarah to get from her view of them in the mirror to her view of them unobstructed, as though her vision of them had been fake. As though they were one way when viewed through the glass and another way when not.

They all stared at her, shoulders slumped forward.

John Barker, Rowe Saunders, and Bernice Fletcher were chewing something. They chewed without eating, a horrible image that conjured thoughts of cows and chud, or more aptly given their blank expressions, of cattle.

Alphonsus Buck, Charles Henry, Gary Linehan, and Derek Rose all stared at her, each in a different corner of the room, their eyes dark, shaded from tilted brows in a Kubrickian stare.

Each of them gave her *that* look, that look her Nan had first given her when she'd stayed out late with a boy one summer night. It wasn't quite the disappointment she thought it would be, but anger. The look that said, "You got one over on me, and I'm telling you now, I don't like it none."

Sophia Valentine stared at her, but her stare was the only respite from that look. Her look was one of concern. Concern and concerning, her Nan used to say. That was the second time in as many seconds that Sarah had thought of her Nan and suddenly, solemnly, she remembered why she was here, and her shoulders sank.

When hers sank, the others in the room, theirs arose, their slumped postures straightening and becoming alert, like a spell was over. They'd told her what to feel and now that she'd felt it, that in itself was good enough.

"I'm taking over this tour," Erin Valentine said, stepping from her space off to one side into the center of the room. "I think that's best for everyone."

She paused, straightened, then, with more emphasis. "Rare coins are next. We have some of the earliest. Some of the pre-Confederation—"

David stepped forward, and as he did, so did Barry, past David, as though he wasn't there, and past Sarah. "No…" he said, trailing off.

He wasn't looking at Erin when he spoke. He rarely looked at Erin when he spoke, rarely regarded her in the slightest.

Barry instead, looked toward Rowe Saunders. Rowe had his head turned back to one of the glass cases. He didn't notice that Barry's eyes were on him at first, nor that all eyes of the room were on him for a second. He was tall with an unkempt mop of blonde hair and a thin, pointy face that still bore the scars of acne cheeks not long healed. One of his elders from Current Island once referred to him as "the man you couldn't hang," and it had taken some time for Rowe to realize he meant that his height would have required an incredibly large gallows.

Rowe turned only when Barry put a hand on his back. Then, seeing the small man in the too-big bowtie with his hands on him and that everyone's attention was on them, all of the blood left Rowe Saunders' cheeks and suddenly he looked sallow and gaunt.

"No, I think I'll stay," Barry said, clapping Rowe's shoulder blade and finally finishing his thought. "Why, I know those old coins like, well, like the back of my hand," he said, splaying his hand in front of himself as if to demonstrate. It was peppered with liver spots and scars from disuse.

"Come, everyone. Come. Come, come. There is one thing, you simply must see it. It is a single Carolingian coin, dating 812-814 CE. Not remarkable in any way in and of itself… except. *Except* for where it was *claimed* to be found."

He paused, turning to make sure the others were following him and Rowe.

They were.

He smiled. "Come."

NOTES FROM THE
CATHEDRAL EXCAVATION
Andrew Hawthorn

Appendix ii to description of artifact 1893.175

Carolingian coin, silver, denarius, circa 812-814 CE

Excerpt from the diary of August Markham[1], September 1893

St. John's was far from destroyed, as I had been informed, when I arrived in the town along with Mr. Addison[2] and a small work crew from the university. Here and there a stone facade remained like the headstone of the building that once had been. A forest of blackened chimneys was being propped up or demolished. Piles of scorched brick and melted pipe crowded the narrow roads. While desolate, with ash and soot still being shoveled into carts to be drawn away, at least the skeletons of many of the structures had been preserved from the fire and the framing was already well underway with others. Temporary structures had been erected in a nearby park to house those not yet possessing a home, and we availed ourselves of these as well. By this time, many had already found alternative living arrangements or indeed had even

---

[1] August Swancourt Markham, 1845-1932, professor of history at Yale University with an expertise on seafaring cultures and tradition. Discoverer of the Ouranic Inscriptions. Known primarily for his work excavating the Antinaxos shipwreck.

[2] Othniel Henry Addison, 1851-1893, historian and anthropologist, also a professor at the university. Addison did not survive the excavation.

moved back to the site of their former homes as they completed the new buildings around themselves.[3]

After locating our place on the outskirts of the general construction, we made our way to the cathedral site, eager to begin. Our destination lay in the middle of town, just up the hill from the harbourfront. Rising even now from the ruins around it, the great hulk of the Anglican Cathedral of St. John loomed like an English castle, transplanted and out of place in the New World. Vast walls of stone thrust into the air, defiant in their rise from ash. It was a gothic structure in the revivalist style, reminding me instantly of the college library back home.

Yet here the proud walls met only with empty space. The entire roof, and what must have been much of the top half of the church, was gone, obliterated by fire, leaving the interior exposed to the sky. All but one of the stained-glass windows had fallen, their lead having melted in the blaze. In a moment of perhaps unfortunate levity, Addison, himself a Papist, pointed out that the Basilica, some further way up the road, had escaped the fire.

Entering at what once had been the main door of the building, we gingerly picked our way across a network of beams that had been placed for the safety of the workers over an unsteady floor. It was a sorry wreck for a place of worship, charred stone and sodden debris first burnt then soaked with rain.

I was struck by the residual impression of the cathedral's former grandeur and the feeling that it would have been a beautiful place just months before.[4] We were in-

---

[3] The desolation Markham describes is due to the Great Fire of 1892, which destroyed two thirds of St. John's. Keith Allen, author of *1892: The Great Fire and its Consequences* says the fire began with the dropping of a lit pipe in a barn but went on to do $13 million in damage and leave 11,000 people homeless. Much of the city was rebuilt by 1895.

[4] Markham is incorrect about his dates here. More than a year had

troduced to Mr. Slade[5], who took us forward past blackened pillars that he explained had been erected only a few years previous. Teams of men were working to clear rubble from the nave and transepts. Slade told us that at the height of the blaze, neighbors had been invited by the church to store their furniture and belongings inside as the great stone walls were believed to be impermeable to fire. But rather than protection, due perhaps to an errant spark or smoldering wood unknowingly introduced, the pile of possessions became a raging pyre, burning the church from within as well as without.

It was this concentration of heat and flame on the floor of the cathedral that had led to the ground being now so treacherous, the mortar and blocks falling away in several places. It was this particular nature of the fire, its very excavation of the building's foundations, that had allegedly uncovered what we were there to see.

In the center of the nave, the floor had given way entirely, leaving a yawning pit that we were forced to skirt on secure wooden beams tied together into a makeshift scaffold. As we approached the transepts, however, Slade led us to a stairwell off to the right that had been largely untouched by the fire and was now marked only by the ashen bootprints of the workers.

From below now we looked up and out of the ragged mouth of the pit. The lower levels of the cathedral had also been laid bare by flame; the dissolution of the floor above had opened parts of the crypt that had suffered horribly. But even more damage had been done in the area where the fire had burned hottest. Before us, we saw the opening had continued deeper still. Heat from the fire had eroded a century or more of wood and stone, and what the

---

elapsed between the fire on July 8, 1892 and his arrival in the city. The damage he is describing must have been extensive.

[5] George Slade, 1851-1920, one of the chief excavators of the Cathedral of St. John after the fire.

fire hadn't accomplished had been finished by rain and weather, and the weight of the building itself.

Slade took us to another ladder descending into the pit. There was no staircase going down now, he explained. The designers and caretakers of the cathedral had thought the crypt was the deepest floor. No one had been aware of the floor below.

We were now some forty feet below the nave on the main floor. It was dark in the room at the bottom of the ladder, but Slade had brought a lamp. This he now lit, shining rays first across the walls, then pressing forward. It was not so much a room as I had thought, but a hollowed-out cave. The walls around us were living rock, raw and wet in places. It smelled damp, but not foul.

Some work had already been done to clear the debris from above, and a simple pulley system had been set up to raise larger sections of the sunken floor. Slade took us past this into the dim recess of the cavernous room and focused his lantern on what we had come to see. There in the dark, like the ribs of some giant beast, was the burntout hull of a wooden ship.

The two men who had uncovered the scene were to be made available to us, but only one was on site for the time being. The other man had been injured in a fall shortly before our arrival and was now resting. By the finder's account, they had been digging through the debris before the discovery, still surprised as no one had known of the cave's existence. His recollection was that the hull had not been touched by the collapsing floors above, and though it had clearly burned from the heat it was a ways off from the void of the pit, tucked, as it were, into a small hollow at the back of the cave.

We were given leave then to study the find at our leisure. It was perhaps 75 feet in length, only 13 feet wide at the waist. Its sides, which had fallen away, appeared at one point to be made up of overlapped timbers in the clinker fashion. We found it did not at all match records of the canoes of the local tribes of the region. As I later discovered, the Beothuk were recorded in their time by David Buchan[6] as making birch bark vessels with high gunwales and rounded bottoms more suitable for oceanic travel, similar, to the single-gunwale canoes of the Mi'kmaq. This was neither, but a much longer, thinner vessel, with lower sides and a deep, round bottom. It was suited for the rough water of the North Atlantic, though initially we could not imagine a European crew crossing the ocean safely in such a vessel.

The wood had been freshly scorched in the near end, but we soon realized that much of the damage was as old as the ship itself, perhaps done intentionally as a ritual, or burial practice. Indeed, the scorching of the wood had hardened it against further damage and must have been the reason the remains we were inspecting were as well preserved as they were.

What we could see from our first day's investigation was more reminiscent of a small Viking longship if nothing else.[7] There was no mast but space for fifteen or so sets of rowers, two abreast. Whatever the walls of the vessel had been before rotting or falling away we could not say, but timbers running along the length, from stem to stern, protruded out in a proud "beak" or pincer from the prow.[8] It was clear that whoever had constructed the ship

[6] Lieutenant David Buchan who explored the Exploits water system in 1810 and made contact with the Beothuk in an ill-fated expedition that left two men killed.

[7] Speculation of a pre-Columbian Norse presence in North America was eventually confirmed in 1960 with the discovery of structures at L'Anse aux Meadows dating to between 990 and 1050 CE.

[8] The vessel Markham describes here has been compared to several other ship burial sites, most specifically the *Nydam* and *Hjortspring* boats, both recovered from bogs in southern Denmark between 1859 and 1921. The problem of this comparison is that the former vessel dates from around 400 BCE, the latter, 310 CE, or around 1,400-900 years before confirmed Norse presence in the region.

were skilled seafarers, coming from a tradition hitherto unknown to the modern sciences.

The next morning, we began our excavations around the remarkable ship, taking care to record our findings as exactly as possible. For each layer of ash and earth was removed we took particular advantage of the pulley system that I have previously mentioned, and I imagine for the passerby our efforts were indistinguishable from those of the workmen excavating the modern cathedral above us.

Our work was soon to be rewarded, as a rich hoard of artifacts was uncovered before our eyes for the first time in untold millennia. Before we had even removed the first spadeful of earth, one of our men discovered a bent and broken iron blade, which seemed to have been pulled from the dirt quite recently. This was cracked and sharp where it had snapped in two and seemed even to have fresh blood now dried along its edge. Perhaps one of the workers had run afoul of the thing in the dark. Next, we unearthed seven richly carved spearheads of bone and three of iron, along with a half dozen more iron swords, each bent and with a single edge.

The remains of tools and shield bosses were soon found, as well as cups, bowls, and the stubs of what may have once been utensils. Near these, we uncovered two coats of ancient mail, richly decorated and etched with knotwork, but yet not bones or bodies. Traditionally in a burial site such as this, for that is what we now were calling it, such a display of wealth would denote the resting place of a figure of some importance. It was no small thing in ancient times to lay aside riches, or even a fine boat, for no reason. And if this was a site that had been robbed some time after burial, why disturb the bodies but not the wealth beside? Yet we found no body whatsoever. Our ef-

Thorkild Randsborg of the Danish National Museum notes that while it is possible that Iron Age Norse had visited North America, Markham's account of the cathedral excavation does not provide enough reliable information to verify the claim one way or another.

forts revealed grave goods without a grave.

The most curious find was the remains of a wooden casque, filled to the brim with coins of precious metals. These had been partially melted and fused, but not so worn that I could not excitedly discern them as Carolingian in origin due to the clear image of an equal-armed cross on the face and a temple structure on the reverse.[9] None of the other artifacts matched the region or period of this curious find, and as it was well outside my areas of study, I put it aside for future consultation.

These excavations had taken us approximately two and a half days' work. On the afternoon of the third, Mr. Slade came with the unhappy news that the second worker to have discovered the ship, a Mr. Bugden[10], had taken a turn for the worse and had fallen into a deep brain fever which the town's doctors said was unlikely to lift. I asked if we could visit him, at least to pay our respects, and we were directed to the makeshift hospital that had been

---

[9] The coin mentioned here, catalogued at The Roomsas item 1893.175, is the only remaining artifact alleged to have come from the cathedral excavation.

However, despite matching the description provided by Markham, later scholars have been almost unanimous in pointing to the lack of provenance, and only Markham's word that the piece was discovered in Newfoundland at all. Chief among these, Markham's rival John Harte of Oxford who denounced news of the find as "fantasist posturing." Decades later, prominent medievalist scholars Kirk Foster and Jonas Moeller would write extensively poking holes in Markham's published discovery. His own colleague and contemporary Egbert Slanski refused to comment on it. Even Joseph Frahm in his landmark 1982 biography *August Markham: Promise and Prize* glosses over this discovery, agreeing the coin continues to fascinate but suggesting perhaps a simple error in dating.

Setting this aside, were it true that the coin now in possession of the museum had been found beneath the Anglican Cathedral of St. John, it would set the *terminus post quem* dating of the site at approximately 812-814 CE, still two hundred years before the traditional date of Norse contact with the region.

[10] There is no record of the worker mentioned here, but that isn't unusual for the period of reconstruction following the fire.

erected in the area called Bannerman Park, a field close to the country's capital building, now a wreck of tents and shanties, and in which we too had found our lodgings.

Addison and I came upon the hospital, little more than a crude barn hastily constructed behind the capitol building. I couldn't imagine the walls of the thing standing up to a stiff winter breeze and was reminded again of the desperation of the St. John's men rebuilding their small city while left to fend in shacks and tents.

We were shown in by the nurse and discovered a man in a sorry state of being. His face was swollen and purple with thick bruises from his fall, and his right arm was tightly bandaged. His breathing was ragged, and as we approached he seemed to be speaking prayers to himself, or else talking in his sleep.

He was not asleep, however, and after he weakly turned to see visitors, he seemed to brighten up. I introduced myself and Professor Addison and asked after his wellbeing, but in the typical Newfoundland fashion he downplayed his grave injuries, repeating that it was nothing and that he would soon be able to return to St. Anthony, which we were given to understand was another town on the island, somewhere to the north.

The conversation took a turn when we asked about the circumstances of his discovery of the ship. His expression instantly darkened and he simply said, "I fell." Addison suggested this happened after the discovery, and gently asked about what happened before his unfortunate fall. Again, he turned away and began lowly talking to himself, but soon he cradled his bandaged arm and explained that he only fell because he had cut it so badly on a piece of metal in the pit and that he would feel better when he had gotten out of the hospital and made it back to his people in St. Anthony.

When I asked if he or anyone had ever heard of such boats around the island, he became distant for a brief moment, then, looking me straight in the eyes he reached out and in a raspy voice, issued the phrase, "It's a dragger."

I was mystified by what he could mean by this but had little time to consider it when without warning he shouted and slammed his injured arm down on the side table, knocking a pitcher to the floor in a crash. He continued in an incomprehensible stream of words in that strange Newfoundland dialect and slang. The only phrases that were comprehensible were that he wished to "skip" for (or perhaps skip out of) this place and leave St. John's, but yet wished to return to Newfoundland despite clearly being in it. And again, dragger and dragger on and on until the nurse, along with some others roused by his racket, succeeded in soothing him until he fell into a fit of coughs and moans.

I was so shocked by this turn of events that I am afraid I stood dumbstruck for many moments before Addison suggested we take leave of the poor fellow. I fear his sense may have truly left him, an opinion reinforced when, while chatting to the nurse as we left, I expressed my hope that could be returned to his family in St. Anthony, only to be informed that he was a St. John's man, who as far as she could tell had never once in life left the city.[11]

---

[11] Markham's incident with the worker is among the most contentious passages in the manuscript.

Most early scholars writing on the text paid attention to the exchange only in Bugden's rustic identification of a buried longship as a "dragger," or fishing vessel that tows a trawl or weighted fishing net. However, the issue was popularized when the passage was extensively cited, along with select other works by Markham, in new age philosopher Armin Danheim's 1968 book *The Discovery of Valhalla*, which argues amongst other things that there were wide pre-Columbian Norse settlements throughout North America as far back as 1600 BCE, with their leaders and citizens forming the basis of Norse mythology.

Danheim argues that Bugden is actually speaking in a dialect of ancient Norse, and that his desire to return to St. Anthony, a place he had never been, is refering to the L'Anse aux Meadows site, a place he could not have known about before its discovery by Helge and Anne Ingstad in 1960.

The next day, we returned to our work determined to discover the bones of the presumably highborn person that had warranted such a burial. That is to say, if a burial indeed it was, for what other purpose could it have served? We had at this time cleared away much of the earth around the frame of the ship and had begun to hit stone. This gave us ample room to reexamine the craftsmanship that went into creating the strange vessel, and to take more accurate measurements of the frame. In doing so, we soon recognized an odd pattern to the damage.

Thus far we had identified two stages in the destruction of the once-proud vessel, the initial burning and burial, and the rot and ravage of time in the intervening millennia. These were different enough that they were easy enough to identify and catalog. However, we soon began to recognize a third damage that had been visited on the site sometime after its creation.

The waist of the ship was crushed, which is common enough in burials of this type. However, unlike other such sites as found in Norway or Denmark, this ship had not been fully buried but was rather placed in a cave. As such there was no pressure of earth to lead to any breakage.

Still, in a section toward the middle of the frame, the blasted timbers seemed to my eye to have been crushed together and downward, along with the keel of the ship. It was as if they had been secured by some great rope or other device capable of enforcing immense pressure, but if so, such a thing had long ago rotted away. I believe it was Addison or one of his men who began to suggest the theory that the ship was not a burial but an offering or

---

The book uses several pseudoscientific or debunked sources and has been dismissed roundly by scholars, including the Ingstads in 1972. However, Danheim identifies the phrases recorded here by Markham as "skip for," "Newfoundland," and "dragger" as the ancient Norse phrases skipför meaning to voyage on a ship, *Vinland*, the Norse name for the North American settlement, and draugr, meaning ghost or demon.

sacrifice. He said the sight of the ship reminded him of nothing so much as an Iron Age site, where a skeleton of a man had shown signs of being ritualistically bound and broken over a stone.

Regardless, it was shortly following this discovery that we ended our work for the day, and in the name of God I wish we had never taken it up again.

On our last day, we returned to examining the waist of the ship, gently removing the splintered sections of ancient wood, and clearing away the decrepit earth from around the keel. I had mentioned previously that we had struck stone in places, and here again we got but a few inches down below exhausting the soil. But this stone seemed different. It was smooth to the touch with the softened edges of an ancient rock that was different from the craggy walls of the cave around us. Clearing away the earth, we could clearly see delicate carvings etched into the surface, representing plants, trees, and flowers, all seemingly placed at random but in great numbers and concentrated and overlapping more and more at the keel of the ship.[12]

These must have predated the ship burial by hundreds, if not thousands, of years. We briefly spoke of the possibility of this as an ancient ritual site or temple. But the concentration of the carvings around the keel, particularly in the area profuse with pressure cracks and damage seemed to be drawing us on. With renewed zeal, we began as carefully as possible to clear away the shattered timber and earth that remained, first with trowels and brushes, then with our bare hands, possessed as we were in an ec-

---

[12] Frahm was the first to suggest that what Markham is describing here is in fact the Mistaken Point Formation, discovered and identified in 1967, a layer of shale, argillite, and siliceous sandstone running beneath most of the Avalon Peninsula, including St. John's. It is possible what Markham is describing as carvings were fossils, indeed some of the oldest examples of Ediacaran and Cambrian fossils in the world, some dating back as early 570- 485 million years, or at least up to the end-Botomian mass extinction event.

stasy of the passion of discovery.

It was Addison who first identified the corner of the thing. A small point, like a deep carving of a pyramid, emerged from grey earth, lit only by our gas lamps held far away from the delicate frame of the ship. The carvings seemed to wrap their viny tendrils around this new, deeper design. It reminded me of the carved Solomonic columns of Rome, with leaf and vine effects spiraling beneath their doric capitals. We hadn't time to reflect then, as there was more to uncover. Each of us followed a furrow running out from Addison's corner, and with a few more sweeps of the brush, the entirety of the thing was revealed. It was a door.

While I had little enough time to examine our discovery, the scene is now burned into my brain, I fear, forever. Settled into the stone beneath the precise center of the ship was a deep recess holding what first I tried to convince myself was merely a rectangular design or frame for some other carving. It was not plain but not carved either. Instead, it seemed a beautiful, natural formation as though, like a stalagmite, it had grown there centuries ago.

Its surface sparkled with crystalline deposits amidst the stone, which seemed to give it a depth of appearance that made it hard to focus upon, tricking the eye and inviting deeper study. Indeed, though it may have been the poor light, it seemed to somewhat pulse with magmatic energy, and after I wondered if what I had seen was not in fact a solid piece of stone but merely a squared-off opening into some deeper chamber of molten rock. But then I remembered the cool touch of the stone under my hand as we cleared away the earth.

What makes me certain that it was indeed a door was this: At the center of the thing, again appearing a naturally grown formation subject to the laws of all stone, was a twisting handle, or knob. It was set as if waiting for a human hand, and of the proper size for one to turn.

I was not the only one to think so. We only had moments to behold the thing before one of the work crew, Stevens, made to open it himself. He knelt, or fell forward, hand outstretched before any of us could act to hold him back. His hand closed on the handle and turned.

As soon as I registered his intention I moved forward to act, but when his hand touched the door, a deep sound issued forth from somewhere beneath us that shot through my head and lodged somehow behind my eyes. It was a scream, high pitched and sustained that I could see as much as hear in an explosion of colour and pain.

I could not stop him, but Addison had been ahead of me, and even as I saw the aperture crack open, releasing a sickly, burning stink, he had thrown himself against Stevens to slam it shut again. But the closure was worse. A detonation of force, as from standing near a cannon shot, knocked me back and echoed across the walls, causing the loose earth and rock above us to fall in from above. I was buried.

The ground seemed alive, but I could see nothing. However, in moments I felt an iron grip close upon my arm, and I was pulled free of the falling stone. Several of the cathedral workers from the floor above had heard the scream and come running to our aid. I do not recall how we emerged from the blacking pit back into the light of the church, but I recall being carried bodily by two men toward the stairs.

When I came to my senses we were on the floor of the nave, myself and all the men fortunate to have been found. Addison, God rest him, was not among us, nor Stevens. Some of the men went back to look but it was far too dangerous and unstable to dig. The single image I now recall, as feeling returned to my body, was staring unfocused toward the altar of the great cathedral. It was just past the yawning opening of the pit, and I realized it had been placed directly above the waist of the ship below, and that hellish, prehistoric doorway.

Was it by design? Coincidence? Or was it that same elemental, subconscious impulse, that made poor Stevens helplessly open that which should have remained shut and buried?

Almost all our discoveries were lost. We return home tomorrow, and I shall never again set foot on this cursed island that drinks the lives of its sons, burns their cities, and hides such secrets as these.[13]

---

[13] The fantastic nature of this account, and the fact that no evidence of the cathedral excavation's findings remains outside the Carolingian coin Markham later found in his pocket, have led many to dismiss this account as an attempt to embellish his reputation.

It goes without saying that the parish of the Anglican Cathedral of St. John, while acknowledging the cave-in, denies knowledge of any secret cave, or its influence on the construction of the cathedral, begun in 1847 for a congregation that had existed in that area since at least 1699.

Professor Othniel Addison and two other men did die as the result of a collapse in the chamber beneath the cathedral. After the initial rescue the area was deemed unsafe, and no further attempt was made to reach it before it was filled in during the restoration of the cathedral complex.

No other part of Markham's diary for late 1893 has ever been located, either among his papers at the Yale Beinecke Rare Book and Manuscript Library or elsewhere. His son Corinth Markham later claimed that his father had burned all materials relating to the event but this document, which had already been given to the museum along with the artifact.

Fabrication, hallucination, or something more sinister, the excavation was a turning point in Markham's career, which some critics have likened to Arthur Conan Doyle's obsession with the Cottington Fairies. After 1893, his work saw increasing instances of far-fetched accounts such as these, culminating in the disastrous Black Forest expedition of 1932, which claimed his life.

Markham never did return to Newfoundland and Labrador.

6

"That's a hard story," David said, gruffly.

Barry turned and, for a flash, he wasn't the small old man in the bowtie. Just like when David entered the room to find Barry with Sarah, he was briefly something *else*.

His eye sockets sank deeper, his shoulders hunched more, so much so that they could properly be called haunches, and his fingers, already long like spider's legs, now came to points.

Again, it was only a flash and was gone so quickly that it was easier to think that it had not been there at all.

He straightened, composed himself, and wiped his mouth. "There are no hard stories," he said, finally, when he could. "All stories have value. All stories can tell us something."

"Even those that terrify us?" David asked.

"*Especially* those that terrify us. They can tell us so much. You can learn *so much* about a people from what they are afraid of." He paused. "About a *culture*. Society has used scary stories to understand the real things that have scared them since time immemorial. All those slashers in the 80s that punished people who had sex, it tells you what? That society is afraid of the consequences of that act. Is there any wonder they came up as the AIDS epidemic was growing to its peak? The Godzillas and other monsters of the atomic age are exactly that—monsters of an atomic age as a harbinger of the dangers of playing with a science we couldn't fully understand. Even the Wolf Man sees an American across the pond attacked by an Eastern European threat only to become a monstrous version of the beast that attacked him. In this case, he still retains more of his humanity than the wolf that attacks him, becoming a werewolf as opposed to a wolf. Is there anything else in 1942 that this serves as a metaphor for?"

"And here? On this island?" came a voice from the crowd.

Barry smiled, a devilish smile spreading.

His head did not turn, it lolled to the side, as though not attached at the neck. His gaze moved with it until it found Gary Linehan, the unemployed young man from Oderin Island. Barry was short and plump. He looked all of twenty-three but was less than that, in fact, he was almost as young as Sarah Childs. In any other circumstance, you'd consider him too young to be called Gary, but despite his youthful appearance, he carried the middle-aged wariness expected by the name.

Gary squirmed under Barry's gaze and from how the others parted to allow that gaze to be unobstructed. Like a red sea, John Barker, Alphonsus Buck, and Derek Rose all cleared the space between the two men. Bernice Fletcher hesitated, but she stepped aside like the others.

Sarah Childs also stepped aside, and she was the only one that Gary thought might have a valid reason to clear the path. Maybe she felt the growing bruise that Barry's fingers had left on her shoulder, knew just how narrow an escape hers had been, and stepped aside to allow the gaze to fall on Gary. Better him than me, he thought she thought, not knowing if it were the case.

"Here, my good man, here you fear the loss of our children," Barry hissed. "You fear we lose them to wars for a King that cares for us not. You fear that the sea will take them before their time, the rock of a boat so similar to the rock of a cradle. One hard push and it ends as it began. We fear the priests that come to guide them into faith but instead guide them to their graves or worse."

David stiffened. They all did. Barry stepped through them and the path they had cleared, the stiffness of his words making them soldiers snap to attention as he walked past. He reached Gary, put his hand on the young man's back and guided him away from the rest of them towards the next exhibit.

"That's why they tell stories of the fae here. They make up stories about tiny creatures that will take their children if they don't obey the rules. Walk with your pockets turned out, don't follow a voice into the woods, all that. They tell stories about creatures that take their children that are easily beaten by trinkets and superstitions when the real things that take their children don't follow the rules of God or man and succeed by their own chaos."

Barry guided Gary, his hand at the base of his spine, into the next room of artifacts. The rest of them followed close behind. The impulse that had made them part was shaken off when Barry's gaze was not on them, and they fell back into a tight-knit cluster for protection. They watched

Gary, protecting him with their eyes, trying to manifest a shield around him with their attention as though nothing could happen to him while they watched.

"Now, *this*," Barry said, letting Gary go and splaying fingers towards a line of items marked as "donated, graciously, by survivors of the Fire."

There were brass buttons, the singed remains of a straw hat, and a monogrammed handkerchief with the initials F.S. on it.

"This is quite special."

SOME SAY IN FIRE
Ainsley Hawthorn

"Don't go."

Arthur adjusted the tilt of his side cap with one hand. He was striking in his service uniform, jaw and brow and khaki collar all decisive angles. Handsome as he was, the tan drab hazed out his features, and the wool had the effect of absorbing both his identity and his youth. He was now as much her father rigged out in his Great War kit for the yearly veterans' smokers, as much her elder brother Francis looking down at them from his oval frame with fading grey eyes.

"And what kind of man would I be if I shirked my duty?" He kept his eyes forward, but his grin canted to one side.

"Haven't you been doing your duty here with the militia, defending the home front?"

What kind of man was he, indeed. She had loved him as a boy—adventurous, yes, but constrained to the small adventures of youth. The friendly boxing matches, the streetcar jumping, the harbour dare swims. Uncomplicated and unworrisome, limited in space by how far he could walk and in danger by how high he could climb. In this uniform, on this night, he had grown into a man, and his reach and risks had grown with him, or outgrown him. In this uniform, he was old enough to ship out. Old enough to fight. Old enough to die. Only later would she appreciate how very young he was.

The stepped houses of Murray Street huddled over them in the cold, windows blackout-shuttered. The absence of shared light made way for the moon and the frost to steel the street over with their slick glow, and Florrie clutched Arthur's arm to keep from slipping, in stride or in composure.

"They're bringing the war home to Jerry, Flo. Britain's taken a walloping, and they need fresh men on the guns. We can help them finish the job." There was an energy in his voice, a too-noble zeal. Florrie wasn't so easily led.

"And in the meantime, you'll get to see Europe, I suppose. Have yourself a little excitement," she rejoined. "Nice change from patrolling the coast on Bell Island."

"It's the least I can do." Arthur's tone was affronted, but his eyes glimmered in the winter light. "And God knows I need a break from getting shat on by gulls."

"Art! Hey, Artie!"

They were near the main entrance of the hostel by then. A clutch of militiamen and froth-haired young ladies nattered on the steps, their laughter fogging the night air. From among them waved Clarence Hayward. Dropping a cigarette, he scuffed its ember to ash beneath his shoe.

"Artie, Flo, there's someone I'd like you to meet. This is Myrtle."

He swaddled her forward under his arm, petite and airy-boned as a fledgling but brimming with good humour. She extended a feather-fine, leather-gloved hand.

"Myrtle Penney. How do you do?"

"Pleased to meet you," said Florrie, pressing her palm to Myrtle's. The girl looked in her late teens, Clar robbing the cradle again.

"Pleasure," said Arthur. "So, are you both up for a hoe-down tonight?" He cast a glance over at Clar and winked.

Smirking, Clarence tapped the brass NFLD pin on his breast. "Never Found Lying Down—I take it as a personal motto, if you get my meaning."

"You two are incorrigible!" Florrie shook her head but was suppressing a laugh. "Don't you listen to them, Myrtle. I'll be your chaperone this evening, and Arthur will keep Clar on his best behaviour, won't you, Arthur?"

Arthur belted "Yes, ma'am" with military briskness and clicked his polished heels together. Taking Myrtle by the arm, Florrie led the way through the double doors and into the lobby, where they checked their greatcoats and their trenches. In the rec room, couples were jitterbugging to the jukebox and the click-clack of ping-pong balls while on the other side of the reception hall fountain drinks, sandwiches, and desserts skipped back and forth over the canteen counter. Though they were hardly more than fifty feet from the auditorium, they couldn't hear the sound of the concert over the chiming of conversation and cutlery.

Tables had been sardined into the space between the canteen and the reading room in anticipation of a festive weekend crowd. Less than two weeks away, the upcoming holidays filled the downtown streets with middle-aged shoppers by day and young revellers by night, in spite of—or perhaps because of—the strain of the war. Though violence hadn't yet sunk its teeth into their communities, it was lapping at their shores. One hundred and thirty-six drowned in the sinking of the Caribou on its crossing from Cape Breton. Torpedoed piers and seventy mariners dead this fall before even setting sail for Europe. Then, from overseas, the telegrams and the letters in their hundreds: "deeply regret to inform you…", "it is my painful duty to confirm…", "offer you our sincere sympathy,"

The anxiety, the grief, and the suspense wanted balancing, and so the season of comfort, joy, and peace was more welcome than ever. For service personnel far from their ancestral coves and bays—or, further still, from the flatland farms and smoky cities of Canada or the United States—the hostel was a home away from home, where friends and fellows stood in for kith and kin. The hall simmered like a kettle as Newfoundland militiamen, Canadian pilots, merchant sailors, and American soldiers flirted with their local girlfriends, chitchat bubbling over and rubber soles squeaking on the waxed floors like the squeal of steam.

Florrie and Myrtle made their way to a table while Clarence and Arthur went for sodas. Above their heads, crimson and green streamers looped from the ceiling in bright swaths.

"So, tell me," said Florrie as she smoothed her skirt to sit, "how did you and Clarence meet?"

"Oh, at Ayre's! I'm an assistant in hosiery." Florrie could imagine that innocent eagerness behind a shop counter, beaming up at customers and fanning out silk chiffon with delicate fingers. "Funny place to work. Showing ladies the latest fashions, and us more often than not painting seam lines on our own legs."

"Hosiery?" asked Florrie. "Don't tell me Clar was peeping through the ladies' garters."

"No, no. Not as bad as all that," Myrtle laughed. "I was sent up to help in menswear one day when another girl was out sick, and Clar was in to buy trousers. Teased me about taking his inseam. He was right fresh, but," and here her plum lips bowed slightly, "I didn't mind it.

"And you and Arthur," she went on, "how wonderful to finally meet you! Clar's told me all about you both."

"He has, has he?" asked Florrie. Clar would talk the tongue right out of his mouth if he thought it would impress a girl.

"Oh, yes!" said Myrtle. "All good things, of course. You two were real childhood sweethearts, from what I hear. So romantic!"

Florrie flushed. She'd rarely known Clar to be earnest.

"Do you plan to marry when Arthur gets back from the war?"

"If he gets back," said Florrie gravely.

"Now, you can't go thinking like that. He's not the only Newfoundlander going over with the artillery, and they'll stick together. Watch out for each other. The war can't go on forever, and, before you know it, he'll be back home giving you some sweet, bouncing babies."

She and Arthur had never spoken of either marriage or children. She had always thought them still children themselves. In the past three years time had grown wings.

"Myrtle, every boy expects to come home, and not every one does. No amount of watchfulness or fellow-feeling will change that." Florrie inhaled into the void in her belly.

"My brother Francis signed up for the navy with his best friend Dermot," she continued. "They had their service numbers one right after the other and were so proud of it, too. I suppose they imagined sailing the high seas together, serving the king oar to oar.

"They were posted to the same ship, Francis in engineering and Derm on the guns. When they were sunk by a U-boat off Crete, Derm was pulled from the water. Francis wasn't.

"The letter didn't say much, but when Derm was home on leave he told us he hadn't even laid eyes on Francis. The torpedoes struck the engine rooms, and Francis might have been killed in the instant or drowned when the bulkhead caved in."

The backs of the uniformed men who surrounded them on all sides fused into a wall of grey, tan, and blue, as though Florrie and Myrtle were themselves below-decks, hemmed by water and metal and dank, sultry air. The tang of gunpowder in their noses was the after-scent of sweat and cigarettes.

"Derm was asleep in his bunk but made it to a life raft. Four thousand miles across the water together and no help to each other in the end at all. Francis died alone in the middle of a million-man army, and what's to stop Arthur from doing the same?"

Myrtle had been watching Florrie with a gaze that was both unmoving and strangely unmoved.

"What's to stop the same from happening here?" she

asked forcefully. "I don't mean to be glib, I feel for your loss. I've lost an older brother myself. He was a longshoreman down at the pier. One day, the fellow on the crane must have winked, and a crate hit George square on the head. Felt fine, he said. There wasn't any blood or anything. George wanted to keep working, but his super sent him home to sleep it off. He ate his dinner, went to bed, and never woke up.

"Jerry might have a stranglehold on Europe, but he doesn't have one on death. Death's free to find you anywhere."

"Two soft drinks for two hard tickets!" Dropping into the empty seats at the table, Clar and Arthur snapped the tight thread of attention between them, warm bodies bringing them back above water. Myrtle, giggling, swatted Clar's forearm.

"I'll show you a hard ticket!"

There was talk and teasing, but, when they had finished their drinks and were tiptoeing between the tables on the way to the auditorium, Florrie felt like a clockwork ballerina. Was she to be wrapped in a box and stored away until Arthur returned from the Land of Sweets? How long could her magic keep in darkness? At the door, she pulled a handkerchief from her handbag to dab her eyes while the others came up behind her.

"All well, Florrie?" Arthur spoke too softly for the others to hear, screening her from their eyes by the broadness of his back. The concern that furrowed his brow made her throat ache and her stomach clench.

"Yes, all well," she said after a moment. "Just a little smoke in my eyes."

"Flo, look, whatever happens after tonight, just know that my true love *is* true," he said and pushed open the auditorium door.

At the threshold, Florrie hit a curtain of hot, humid air, like walking into a kitchen. The auditorium was, if it were possible, more packed than the hall, with merrymakers ranked elbow-to-elbow in row upon row of folding metal chairs. Along the left-hand wall, the three tall windows that might have let a breath of fresh air into this sweatbox were nailed over with plywood to keep the slightest spark of light from escaping, and the two side doors leading to the outside were barred and manned by guards.

Arthur, having sighted some unoccupied seats near the centre, ushered them through the audience with "excuse me"s and "mind your toes." Emcee Barry Hope, costumed in a ten-gallon hat, white button-down shirt, denim overalls, and incongruous necktie, was warming up the crowd in a put-on Appalachian drawl.

"Howdy, folks, and welcome to Uncle Tim's Barn Dance! We have a swell show planned for y'all this evening, with old Irish favourites, country ballads for you Western fans, and jim-dandy honky tonk tunes that'll make you wanna get up and dance. Speaking of dancing, we have some top-notch hoofers with us tonight who'll be cutting a rug for your viewing pleasure—"

"Why don't you cut your spiel for our viewing pleasure and get on with the show?" hollered a sailor near the stage, starting a group of teenaged boys behind him hooting.

"A sailor, eh?" said Hope. "No grass grows under your feet, I guess, but only because you're at sea. I've heard you've shot down a lot of planes, and most of them were enemies. I've met a sailor who's killed hundreds of men—he's a ship's cook."

The hecklers booed, but the audience howled. Hope was their regular host with good reason.

"And now, please put your hands together for our own rosy-cheeked colleen, the belle of Dublin city, the Irish lark, Biddy O'Toole!"

His introduction seemed to have more of flattery than of fact about it. Though rouge had been amply applied, O'Toole's cheeks were fallen with age, and she had tied a scarf under her chin to girdle her loosening neck. Her voice, though, more than justified the moniker "lark," and, as she crooned "I Met Her in the Garden Where the Praties Grow," Florrie's mood began to lighten. Could anything be more Irish than a potato-field romance? When the dancers came out to "Cowboy Swing," she joined the others in cheering them on.

Next, Eddy Adams, a lanky Canadian, sauntered up to the microphone, his leather chaps flapping over scarecrow legs. He had just warbled out the opening strains of "The Moonlight Trail" when he was cut off by a ruckus at the back of the room. More sailors, like as not, drunk on their own high spirits though the canteen served nothing stiffer than cola. Hope leaned his head out of the wing as though to intervene, but it was a woman's voice that first rang out over the murmur and rustle of the distracted crowd.

"Fire!" it croaked.

The muttering rose to a clamour, but few spectators rose from their seats. Florrie and Arthur exchanged glances, and, at Florrie's left, Myrtle shrugged. Hope now took to the stage, sweeping Adams aside with a calm, expansive gesture.

"Please, folks, no panic," he said into the microphone, then beckoned to the band. "Keep playing, boys!"

Again, from behind them, "She's all afire!" The voice's serrated edge was worn off now, and it pierced the air like a straight blade.

Florrie turned in time to see yellow spines of flame thrashing through the slots in the projection booth. Her hand was already in Arthur's—he'd taken it without her noticing, or she'd taken his—and they leapt to their feet. A crackling noise spun forward across the ceiling to the peak of the proscenium arch, and scorching gas blasted down onto the stage, setting Hope ablaze. The band's instruments clanged to the floor.

All were scrambling then, over metal chairs that collapsed and skidded out under them. Pressed into Myrtle's back, Florrie grabbed the belt of Myrtle's shirtdress with her free hand to anchor her in the stream of bodies that spilled out the auditorium doors. In the reception room, the Christmas bunting, now scarlet with flame, was falling from the ceiling, and people were beating their palms against their own heads to put out their hair as it caught fire. White ash was falling upward like they were in a snow globe, everything turned upside-down.

Between Clar, Myrtle, Florrie, Arthur, and the hostel entrance was a throng of humanity as impassable as any rampart. In the gaps over the shoulders, Florrie saw that only one double door was open, and the crowd as jammed as a flock of sheep passing through a gate. The

heat of fire and the press of flesh seemed to force the oxygen from their lungs. They were hardly moving. Then
there was a rasping draw and sudden discharge, like the
firing of a gun, and a torrent of blue flame coursed down
the stairwell beside the entrance. People on the threshold
were blown out and those further back in the lobby were
mown down.

The mob reared back like a living thing, and Clar,
ahead of the others, wheeled around to shield them from
the surge. Locking eyes with him Florrie could make out
only black and white, his pupils so wide they swallowed
the iris.

"Back. Back," he said hoarsely before smoke dimmed
his features.

Now they followed Arthur, the women shepherded
along between the men. They were four among hundreds
who were crushed onto the auditorium floor, chased by
the flames. Myrtle began to cough, and Florrie yanked out
her handkerchief and pressed it to Myrtle's mouth and
nose. Myrtle took it with a wildly fluttering hand. Though
she stumbled, Florrie didn't look down, wanting to tell
herself that the tender uneven surface beneath the heels
of her shoes was shucked jackets and castoff purses, the
occasional crunch of stiff resistance the strut of a folding
chair.

On either side of them, men were ramming their shoulders and kicking their feet into the bolted exit doors. Some
had climbed up onto the radiators and were clawing at
the plywood shutters that covered the windows, finger-
nails splintering in their frenzy. Flames licked around the
lip of the auditorium doors and someone heaved them to.

It was impossible to tell over the sounds of banging all around them whether anyone pounded on those doors from the other side.

Then the lights went out.

A hush fell with the darkness, and for a moment Florrie could discern the fainter sounds that had been smothered by frantic action. Dozens of people were blessing themselves and praying aloud so that the babel of Our Fathers, Hail Marys, and Glory Bes made of the room a rosary. There was cursing, too, abandoned and obscene. Gobs of molten gypsum were hailing on them from above, and, as the hammering picked up again, the spaces between strikes were filled by clipped shrieks.

"Myrtle? Clar?" Florrie called, but there was no answer, and, when Arthur's hand tugged at hers, she followed that lifeline forward through the abyss, her ribs pummelled by elbows and her thighs by knees. Wavering beams of flashlights began to flicker across the gloom, and she could see the stage ahead of her, a firm horizon in a sea of writhing shadows.

"This way, Flo," Arthur said, and, grabbing her waist in both hands, he boosted her onto the platform and swung himself up behind her.

"Stay low," he said. "There are windows backstage."

They crawled into the wings, keeping their heads below the smoke that smelled of spoiled eggs and leather. As they neared the outer wall, diffuse moonlight lit the haze overhead, giving it the cool glow of mist, and she felt the mildest touch of chill air on her feverish brow. There was a window. Six feet off the floor, its screen had been pried off and its pane glass smashed by the band.

The singer Biddy O'Toole had a hold of the sill and was trying to clamber up the wall, though her feet slid on the softening plaster. Arthur got under her and, her feet on his back, hoisted her up until she tipped over the ledge and out of sight.

"Florrie! You—" he began but was interrupted by a roar as the ceiling above them burst open into a roiling inferno. Flames whited out the window, drawn to the open air. Florrie and Arthur shuffled backward onto the stage, when with a jangling crash the piano plummeted through the stage floor, cutting off their retreat.

In the auditorium beyond, the uproar was quieting. Shrieks of fear and the drone of prayers had given way to groans, perhaps only of straining wood, as the room filled up with fire. Arthur put his arm around Florrie's waist, and they sat together on an island of clear floor as it was gradually sucked under by the blaze.

"I'm sorry, Florrie," said Arthur, and his eyes glowed. He no longer seemed old to her or impersonal. His face was smooth and bright and full, healthy enough to last all the years he wouldn't live.

"I made a mistake," he said.

She didn't know, then, whether he meant the war, the show, or the window. But she edged her body into his, and they breathed and breathed and breathed.

7

"We have to put a stop to this," Erin hissed at Sophia.

The pair were in the far corner of a small exhibit on tree bark, with examples from throughout Newfoundland history from the same sort of trees, showing their change. They were as far away from the tourists and their guide as they could be and still be in the same room.

There was a long pause before Sophia finally said: "...I know."

The words came out like a sigh, like admittance long held back. With breath came acceptance, and both came with a gush. "But I don't know what to do."

"I mean, Jesus," Erin continued, as though Sophia had not spoken, "there are only five of them left."

It was only after the words were out that Erin realized that, for once, Sophia had not disagreed with her.

Before they could intervene, Barry rolled into his next story.

KILLPOP
Paul Carberry

An early snow flitted across the dying sky, dancing on the wind as it swept across the cabin's facade. Hues of orange and amber faded as the threatening twilight pressed it beneath the horizon. The crisp snow crunched beneath Nicole's boots. Her dog, Jack, chased at her heels, nails clattering off the frozen surface. Behind her, the suitcases thudded off the stony driveway without care as Theo and Daniel unloaded the car trunk. Emily and Wilma remained in the backseat, whispering amongst themselves, no doubt forming plans for the moment they got back to the city. They had been against this trip until the last minute. But this counted as Theo's birthday gift and Nicole's boyfriend paid for the cabin, so they begrudgingly came along; the bag of weed Daniel packed helped convince Emily to stop complaining about the long car ride to the middle of nowhere.

Nestled into the woods, the cabin's roof integrated into the canopy of tree branches hanging overhead. Moss grew rampant over the shingles; a thorn bush spread out and snaked around the chimney at the side of the house. Swathed in coils of dead ivory branches, the front corner of the house vanished into nature. Dwarfed by the colossal pine trees, the cabin appeared insignificant against the backdrop of thick, braided trees. The two-story log cabin, squat and sturdy, didn't impress Nicole. Drawn curtains covered the large bay window, giving the house a desolate appearance as the shadows crept over the front lawn, eclipsing everything. On the second floor, two round windows offered a clear view of the valley below; a pale yellow light flickered somewhere in the background, illuminating the bare pine walls upstairs.

When Nicole opened the door, a welcoming wave of heat embraced her. A cluster of mismatched couches filled the spacious living room. Beside the stone fireplace, a stack of wood overflowed from a pine box tucked into the corner, bark and wood chips littering the stone mat. Johnny stood back on to her, using a black iron poker to stoke the fire. A volley of flankers leaped out of the fire and skittered over the stone. Some flankers reached the hardwood, forcing him to turn around and snuff them out with a stomp. He never noticed Nicole standing off to the side of the living room and went back to the fire.

"Hi, dear," she said, her voice hard to hear over the crackling of the wood.

"Hey babe," Johnny said, poking his head up from the hearth. "I didn't hear you guys pull up." He brushed his hands together and rubbed his palms against his faded blue jeans. A red flannel coat worn over a white shirt completed his woodsman ensemble; somehow, Johnny could wear anything and make it work.

The doorknob thumped off the wall as Daniel barged into the cabin, dragging a suitcase in each hand and a duffel bag draped over his neck. Theo trudged in behind, carrying two cases of beer pinned against his chest. With no free hands, they left the front door wide open as they searched for a place to put down their stuff. A rushing whistle of cold air from outside flowed into the cabin, battling the trembling flames in the fireplace.

Nicole rushed across the floor without taking her boots off and jumped into Johnny's arms. "I missed you," she whispered into his ear, afraid their friends would overhear; she hated showing emotion, and she never had a problem hiding them from people until she met Johnny.

Before he put her down, he gave her a squeeze; Johnny's breath warmed the crook of her neck. "It's only been a week," he said, laughing.

"It's so small," Emily complained as she stomped her feet on the mat stepping through the door. "And it's so cold in here," she continued.

Wilma closed the door behind her, hugging herself as she shivered. Theo laid the cases of Busch on the counter and rushed over to her. She pushed him away as he tried to wrap her in a hug. "Don't even," Wilma said, her face scrunched in disgust.

Flushed red, Theo couldn't contain his embarrassment. "But I thought you said you weren't mad at me anymore?"

"Well," Wilma snapped, "I guess I changed my fucking mind."

The veins on Theo's forehead and neck popped out as his blood pressure soared. "Next time Sarah asks me out for drinks, I won't say no."

Wilma crossed her arms across her chest and huffed.

She turned to Emily and said, "Come on," as she grabbed her friend by the elbow and vanished into a bedroom at the end of the hall.

"Smooth," Daniel said, patting his friend on the back. "Are you going to help me get the rest of the bags out of the car?"

A protracted silence passed between them.

"Sure," Theo said, nodding his head. He followed his friend back outside, slamming the door behind him on the way out; the cabin shuddered, and the foundation creaked.

"Please tell me that Wilma and Emily didn't just lock themselves in our room," Nicole said.

Johnny planted a kiss on Nicole's cheek then rested his chin on the top of her head. "Our room is upstairs. My study is just outside that room. Actually, that's where I've spent most of my time."

"I'm not surprised," Nicole said, rolling her eyes. She leaned back, Johnny's arms straining to hold her close. It never failed. Johnny came up here to take a break from his work and he spent most of his time working. "Please tell me you don't plan to spend all of your time in your study while we are here."

Johnny sighed, his massive chest heaving beneath his jacket. "Listen…" He hesitated, trying to gauge Nicole's anger; his eyes studied her, taking in every detail.

Before he spoke another word, Nicole placed her hand on Johnny's chest and shoved herself out of his grip. A frown creased the lines around her mouth, her lips pressed flat against her teeth; a single tear tracked down her cheek. "I've been looking forward to spending this weekend together..." She hesitated, searching for the right phrase to use. She reached out and took his hand. "...without distractions that keep us apart."

"So, you brought all your friends with you?" Johnny said, rolling his tongue over the back of his teeth.

She staggered backward, reeling from his hurtful comment. Nicole let his hand go and shook her head in disbelief, taking a hesitant step backward.

"Wait," Johnny said, reaching out and grabbing Nicole by the shoulder before she could get any further away. "I didn't mean that."

The front door opened, and Theo and Daniel's rambling conversation cut off Johnny. A heavy thud accented their racket as Wilma's suitcase toppled over and banged off the hardwood. Theo cursed under his breath as he struggled to right the suitcase, leaning it against the wall. Oblivious to the argument taking place ten feet away, Daniel pulled out a pack of cigarettes and waved them at Nicole.

"Want to join us?" he offered.

"Later," Nicole snapped.

Lost in his own troubles, Theo grabbed a cancer stick and stuck it in the corner of his mouth as he headed back outside. Daniel stood on the porch for a moment, his hand resting on the doorknob, before opening the door to join Theo outside. He gave Nicole one last worried glance. And he only left once Nicole reciprocated with an *everything's fine* gesture.

Johnny cleared his throat in the silence.

"Listen," Johnny hesitated, waiting for Nicole to turn her attention back his way. When she did, he continued, his tone softening. "I did all that work before you got here, so I could spend more time with you."

"Yeah, right," Nicole spat. "You hate my friends."

"Honestly," Johnny said, placing his hand over his heart. "This weekend is all about me and you. And if that includes getting acquainted with your friends, then that's what you're going to get."

Nicole stared at her boots. Melted snow and slush puddled outwards over the floorboards in the fireplace's warmth. "I'm sorry," she mumbled breathlessly. "Sometimes I can't help myself, I just get so crazy. I guess I hate having to share you with your work."

Johnny tucked a lock of Nicole's curly black hair behind her ear, caressing her cheek with his thumb. "It's fine," he said, "let me show you the upstairs."

Led upstairs by a tender hand, Nicole sauntered up the spiral staircase as Johnny led the way. The top of the stairs opened into a beautiful bedroom filled with elegant, dark-stained teak wood furniture. A pair of matching beaver pelt rugs bordered both sides of the bed. Mounted on the far wall, a deer bust kept a watchful eye over the top of the staircase.

Noticing that Nicole's attention was drawn towards the light spilling from the study, Johnny ducked inside for a moment. The light flickered then puffed out as he turned off the propane. When he stepped back into the bedroom, he gently closed the door behind himself.

"Trying to hide something in there?" Nicole asked. "You always get invested in your work."

"I'm writing a screenplay about a murder," Johnny said, laughing.

"I know," Nicole said, leaning to the side to glimpse the door behind Johnny. "Please tell me it's my supervisor from work, Sandra." A sly smile curled her lips into the corner of her mouth.

"And if it is," Johnny said with a sly grin, "do I get some kind of prize?"

"Maybe," Nicole said, winking at him.

Johnny placed his hand on her hip and guided her backward towards the bed, his fingers unfastening her belt as he did. Nicole moaned softly as Johnny slid her jeans to the floor, the belt buckle clinking off the hardwood. Nicole kicked her pants off, the belt buckle clinking off the hardwood as it skidded across the floor beneath the dresser. Before Nicole could say anything, Johnny eased her onto the bed and knelt down on the beaver pelt. As Nicole glanced down, Johnny's face melted between her thighs; her gaze shifted towards the ceiling as a wave of euphoria washed over her.

"Jesus Christ," Wilma lamented, gawking at the ceiling. "Don't they realize we're down here?"

Upstairs, the bedsprings squeaked, and the headboard knocked off the wall with an expeditious rhythm. The four friends stared up as the noises intensified; Emily's jaw hung open in admiration. Theo took a swig of beer and fumbled as he blindly tried to place the glass on the coffee table, unable to pull his eyes away. Suddenly, Johnny grunted a conquering moan and then one final thud as he crashed into the bed.

The sound of the dog clawing at the back door drew

Emily's attention away. "The dog wants to go out," she said to no one in particular.

"It's too cold and dark outside," Daniel answered.

"And it's Nicole's dog," Theo added. "She should be the one to watch over it. I didn't show up here to babysit."

"Grow up," Wilma said with a snort. "They're nice enough to let you come up here without asking for a single dime. It's literally the least you could do."

"I don't recall you pitching in to help pay for any of this," Theo growled, his arm fanning across the room. "Now why don't you go tell Nicole her dog needs to be let out?"

"Why don't you go up there?" Wilma pointed her index finger towards the staircase. "Or are you worried about stumbling in on a real man in action?"

"Maybe if you were as hot as Nicole, I wouldn't have to force myself to go through the motions with you.

"Fuck you," Wilma snapped, her face flushed bright red. "Just let the dog out."

Emily and Daniel exchanged a quick glance, neither one able to maintain eye contact without bursting out laughing.

Wilma sat across from Theo, glaring at her boyfriend. Without saying a word, Theo brought beer to his lips and started chugging; his Adam's apple bobbed up and down as he tilted his head back and the glass up. When he finished, he slammed his empty glass on the table, wisps of white foam sloshed into the air. Theo used the back of his sleeve to wipe the foam from his chin, leaving only his mocking smile on his face.

Ignoring their bickering, the dog continued to claw at

the door, her nails scraping the screen as she stood on her hind legs. Outside, the wind howled, pelting the windows with snow and sleet, a reminder of the raging storm outside. The first real snowfall of the year had left them all unprepared. Neither car had its winter tires yet.

"Don't worry about it, you guys," Emily said, forcing herself up from the wooden rocking chair.

She staggered drunkenly towards the back door, using her hand to brace herself against the wall as she leaned down to pat the dog on the head. The dog's nail clanged on the floor, eager to go outside to do her business. Emily cracked the door and put the leash hanging on the hook in between the doors onto the dog's collar. As Emily pulled the door open, the wind ripped it from her hands and the screen door smashed into the side of her head, knocking her back into the wall. The dog darted into the swirling snow and out of sight, the momentum ripping the hook holding the leash from the wall. Emily reached her hand out to grasp the leash, but it swerved out of reach. From the darkness, the dog let out a choked yapping bark and then fell silent.

"Are you ok, Emily?" Daniel asked, rushing over to his girlfriend. His hands combed through tangled locks of strawberry blond hair, already wet from the snow blowing inside. He examined his hands, "At least you're not bleeding. But you're going to have a headache later."

"The dog," Emily said, pointing towards the darkness with an agonized expression plastered on her face. She held her hand to her forehead, grimacing in pain.

Daniel called out to the dog, the wind stealing his voice. A hint of silver shone at the edge of darkness, the porch light reaching the hook as the snow buried it. The wind howled across the yard, piling snow up against the side of the cabin. Two-foot drifts had formed along the stone wall that formed the basement of the cabin. At the edge of the cabin, two wooden doors rattled in the frame that covered the basement steps, the metal latch struggling to hold them together.

Heavy footsteps thundered through the cabin as Theo tramped towards them. "Close that damn door," he yelled. When he reached the screen door, he slammed it shut, the frame rattling with a metallic screech.

As he was about to close the door, Emily stuck her arm in the frame, forcing Daniel to yank the door out of Theo's grip before he could slam it closed on her arm. Emily dragged herself to her feet and pressed her head against the glass. "Do you see that?"

"What?" Daniel stood beside Emily, turning his attention to the outside.

Emily tapped the glass with her finger, pointing towards the unknown. "Over there," she said with a hint of hysteria, distorting her tone. "Over there, towards the shed."

Melting snow obscured the view, forcing Daniel to open the screen door again and poke his head outside. Theo grumbled about letting all the heat out and Wilma told him to shut up. Daniel ignored them both and tried to focus his vision through the blustering snow. At the edge of darkness, two flaring orange circles burned bright, then deteriorated into a festering glow.

"Hey," Daniel called out into the darkness, using his hand to shield his face from the ice pellets stinging the subtle flesh of his cheeks. "Is anyone out there?"

A blistering gust of wind tossed a sheet of snow across the yard. When it cleared, the slight orange radiance vanished with it. Daniel stuffed his feet into a pair of rubber boots that were two sizes too big and grabbed a red, green, and blue flannel coat off the hook and darted outside. He leaned into the wind, trudging through the snow towards the dog's leash. Faintly, he heard his name called; Emily's voice was no match for the blustering wind.

When he reached the leash, he bent down to pick it up and pulled, expecting no resistance, but the leash stiffened as he pulled. The red nylon cut a straight line into the darkness. Daniel gave a sharp yank, trying to dislodge the leash from whatever it had gotten snagged on—it didn't budge. He leaned back with all of his weight. The line went slack and Daniel flopped into the snow, the fresh snow finding its way down the back of his pants.

"Fuck!" he shouted as he got to his feet.

He wrenched the leash out of the darkness, the collar scampering through the snow in sharp surges. When he picked it up, a tuft of gore-matted fur clung to the collar. Daniel took out his phone and turned on the flashlight, following a trail of crimson blotches towards the forest. He pursued it deep into the forest, winding between trees and fallen stumps, the snow thinning out the deeper he plunged into the woods. He glanced over his shoulder no longer able to see the light of the cabin behind him. A shiver raced down his spine—and not from the glacial air. He called out to the dog. The only response was a faint, whimpering bark.

Daniel cupped his hands together and hollered, "Jack!"

He brandished the glaring white light back and forth, the tree trunks casting threatening shadows that meandered across the snowcapped forest floor. The flashlight on his phone lost the battle against the darkness as it encircled him, growing tighter around him with every passing moment.

"*Daniel*," a throaty voice materialized out of thin air.

"Theo?"

"*Come get your doggy, Daniel.*"

The sound came from everywhere and nowhere all at once. Unable to pinpoint the source, he spun around, shining the light in a desperate arc around him. Jack's whimpering cries caught Daniel's attention, centring him on the sound. He faced the sound, nudging the flashlight forward, trying to glimpse the dog.

"Come here, boy," Daniel pleaded. "Jack, I have a treat for you." He ruffled his hand around in his jacket pocket, hoping to fool the dog.

The dog barked a warning then scampered off into the darkness. A shrill blast of frigid wind pushed Daniel back towards the cabin, the wind driving pellets of ice into his face. Despite the growing fear in his stomach, he wandered deeper towards the sound.

"*That's a good boy,*" a deep voice grumbled.

"Who's out there?" Daniel yelled, the wind stealing his voice away. In the distance, a fallen tree branch snapped. The wind howled, pelting Daniel with snow, forcing him to cover his face with his arm as he stumbled forward. He thought he could hear the dog's haggard breathing, wisps of steam swirling in the air.

"*Just a little further,*" the voice urged.

The dog yelped, urging Daniel into a frantic run. Tree branches clawed at his face, the roots threatening to trip him with every footfall. A bright orange light flared in front of him. Frightened, he jumped backward and stumbled over an exposed root. His head smashed off a thick tree stump, the rough bark gouging at his scalp. A warm trickle ran down his neck and cooled at the pool of his back. Daniel patted the back of his head with both hands, feeling the dampness against his palms, his hair matted with gore.

The snow in front of Daniel crunched, drawing his attention. A pair of polished black army boots reflected the glare of his flashlight, casting the figure in front of him into shadows. As he moved the camera up, the form remained veiled in a swirling blackness; a fetid, sulphurous odour poured from the enormous figure in front of him.

Daniel pressed his back against the tree trunk, trying to steady himself before making a run for it. Stoic, the figure lurked over Daniel, staring down at him with glaring orange eyes. He tilted his head at a strained angle, pulling the skin tight over his neck's bony vertebrae. Dark, red slashes crisscrossed his stubbly face as if someone had tried to edit the undesired features by scratching them out but then gave up on the project, leaving it a terrifying mess.

"What do you want?" Daniel asked, tears stinging the corner of his eyes.

The men bent down to one knee, the joints cracking boisterously, and, without a word, reached out with a gloved hand, the leather warm as he caressed the wound on the back of Daniel's head. With a sinister smile cut across his face, he stuck a finger into his mouth and sucked the blood off. The slurping and sucking sounds made Daniel nauseous.

"Who are you?"

"They call me mean names," the figure rasped, his voice hoarse and gurgled as if speaking through blood.

A red bubble formed in the corner of the stranger's mouth and burst, sending a spray of blood into the wind. Plumes of steam trailed off the man's body. Daniel felt the warmth radiating from him. A glob of blood splattered over Daniel's chin, and the bitter taste of pennies filled his mouth. He lurched forward, driving his shoulder into the man's face. The man stumbled backward a single step. Daniel tried to get to his feet, but the man grasped Daniel by the shoulders and pinned him to the tree.

"Why are you here?"

"Your friend invited me in," the stranger cackled.

Confused, Daniel asked, "Which friend?"

"The one who calls me Mr. Scratch."

Mr. Scratch's mouth opened wide. Tendrils of noxious black smog erupted from his throat, cascading over Daniel, oblivious to the blustering snow. His jaw unhinged, opening wide, the rancid stench of burnt and rotting flesh oozing out. The encompassing blackness swallowed Daniel's anguished screams.

Gasping on a cigarette, Emily waited in a lawn chair by the back door, staring out into the darkness through the fogged-over window. The forbidding cold from outside stung her face through the window. Her lips were a muted shade of blue and her teeth chattered as she hugged her arms around herself for warmth, but she refused to take her eyes off the edge of the forest. After being gone for over forty minutes, Emily wanted to head into the storm in search of him, but she was afraid of getting lost, so she decided to wait here for him. She tried to convince Theo to search for his best friend, but her feeble words landed on deaf ears.

"Here," Wilma said, startling Emily. "Drink this. It will keep you warm and settle your nerves."

Wilma held the cup out in front of Emily, appreciating that she wouldn't take her eyes away from the window for even a second. Steam whirled from the mug, rising over Emily's face, turning her cheeks and nose a vibrant shade of rose.

"Don't worry." Wilma paused and placed her hand on Emily's shoulder, giving it a delicate squeeze. "He's going to stomp his way into this house at any moment now."

Tense, Emily leaned forward and blew into the mug; whorls of vapour fanned out and vanished. She took a tentative sip then drained the mug in four giant gulps. "Thanks," she murmured, holding the mug against the small of her neck, absorbing the dying remnants of warmth.

Outside, the wind flung the snow sideways across the backyard, the thinner trees bowing to its will. Branches rustled against each other, sending clumps of snow falling to the ground, leaving dark imprints in the drifting snow piles until the falling snowflakes filled the hole, which didn't take long. Hidden beneath a cluster of clouds, a faint glow of silver offered the only indication that the sky hadn't vanished into a black hole.

Behind Emily, Wilma paced the hallway. "He's been out there a long time now," she said, her voice trailing.

"No one asked him to go out there," Theo said.

The sound of Theo's voice made Emily sick to her stomach.

"Coward."

"What did you just say?" Theo asked, his voice wavering between astonishment and anger.

"Don't," Wilma said.

The sound of her shoes scuffling down the hallway drew Emily's attention. Trembling, she got up from the lawn chair, both hands balled into tight fists. Neither Wilma nor Theo noticed her, entangled in their argument. Emily yanked her coat off the hook on the wall and flung it on. The sound of her zipper gained Wilma's attention.

"I'm going out there," Emily snapped.

"Wait," Wilma pleaded, holding her hand out to Emily. "I'll come with you. You're in no condition to be out there by yourself in this kind of weather."

"If you two think I'm going out there with you, you better think again."

"Who gives a shit?" Wilma said, pulling on her jacket.

"Thank you," Emily said as she leaned in to hug Wilma.

Before they left, Wilma turned to confront Theo. "You should be ashamed of yourself," she yelled, thrusting her finger at him. "Too cowardly to brave the storm for your best friend."

Behind them, a blustering gust of snow barged into the cabin as the door burst open, snatching Emily's breath away. She turned, and a silent gasp escaped the pit of her stomach. Her face twisted in horror at the figure stumbling through the door. She stumbled backward, her shoulder knocking a picture off the wall; it landed with a shattering crash, glass cascading across the floor.

"Daniel?" Emily sputtered, unable to recognize her boyfriend through the blackened blood splattered over his face, the wounds on his face festering a greenish-yellow puss.

Daniel collapsed into a heap, the screen door banging back and forth. Loud, metallic screeches erupted with every gust of wind. Theo hurried past Emily, scooping Daniel up into his arms with a strained grunt. "What the fucked happened to you?" he asked Daniel.

Driven to action by Theo's response, Emily guided them both towards the living room where they eased him onto the couch. Wilma slid a pillow beneath his back to keep him propped upright.

"Something must have attacked him," Wilma said. Her eyes widened with terror at the realization that whatever attacked Daniel still roamed the woods. And that the back door flapped in the wind, still wide open, the light from the cabin inviting. Without hesitating, she rushed down the hallway and hauled the door shut; a metallic thud echoed as she slid the lock into place.

Unconscious, Daniel shivered and convulsed on the couch. When he opened his mouth, Emily noticed a crystalline black grease that covered his teeth. His swollen tongue lolled around the inside of his mouth, sloshing the liquid against his cheeks. Emily placed a hand on his jaw, pressing it against his trachea, her fingers braced against his collarbone. When she leaned in to check for an obstruction in his throat, a vile stench wafted from his mouth, but she ignored it and used her fingers to probe around his mouth; she felt his breath, warm and sticky, against the back of her hand.

"He's breathing," Emily said out loud, more to console herself rather than to anyone else in the room. "We need to get him warm. His body is frigid."

Theo helped Emily push the couch closer to the fireplace. The flames danced in Daniel's vacant expression, reflecting in his glazed-over eyes. A racket of banging pots and pans from the kitchen drew Theo's attention. Emily remained concentrated on Daniel. The propane stove ignited with a whoosh and the tap spurt water into the kettle as Wilma raced to get some water boiled. Emily struggled to unbutton his jacket, the fabric frozen stiff, and the holes clogged with snow and ice.

"You're going to be okay," Emily reassured Daniel, trying to keep her voice steady.

"I'm so cold," Daniel mumbled, his lips trembling and his voice weakened by fatigue.

"Theo," Emily called out, "get that fire roaring."

Theo grabbed an armful of logs from beside the fireplace and haphazardly tossed them into the fireplace. He grabbed the iron poker from the floor and stoked the fire. The hungry fire caressed the fresh fuel, the withered bark sizzling as the flames gorged on the timber.

"Don't let Mr. Scratch in," Daniel urged then passed out again.

Nicole jerked to a seated position, startled awake by a loud thump. Beside her, Johnny lay motionless except for the delicate rise and fall of his ribcage; the deep, satisfied snoring of a restful sleep taunted her. A suppressed pandemonium downstairs lured Nicole into a semi-wakeful state. She swung her feet over the side of the bed, rubbing her eyes with both ends to push the sleep out. Downstairs, a door slammed shut and raucous voices spoke hurriedly.

"Drunken fools playing outside in this kind of weather," Nicole mumbled to herself.

A constrained sigh departed her lips as she stood up, the fur beneath her feet comforting. Vivid memories of Johnny's passion flashed through her mind. She peered over her shoulder at him, considering waking him up for another round, but she didn't want to interrupt his pleasant slumber.

A slit of flickering yellow light seized Nicole's attention. It took her a moment to realize that the light was coming from the other side of the door to Johnny's studio. At some point, he must have gotten up to work on his screenplay and forgot to turn off the light before slipping back into bed. Angered, Nicole decided she would go into that room and take the laptop to hide someplace where he wouldn't be able to find it. That would teach him a lesson and force him to take a break from his work.

She edged the door open, the waning light spilling into the bedroom. As she entered, she pulled the door closed to not wake Johnny. Beneath the two windows that peered out over the snow-covered hills, Johnny's white frame desk clashed with the pine-board walls and the rest of the rustic furniture that filled the room. She couldn't believe he went through the effort to lug that desk from his apartment all the way here, but she knew he loved being able to stand up or sit down while he worked, so it didn't surprise her.

Covered in pictures and hastily scrawled words, Johnny's whiteboard sat in the room's corner. There were pictures of the cabin, surrounding woods, and a few pictures of Nicole with her friends. Each picture aligned beneath the three acts of Johnny's screenplay, painting a picture of the story to tell, inspiring him and keeping him on track. By the third scene, only her picture remained, her friends only showing up in acts one and two.

She sat at the desk and opened the laptop, the white screen blinding compared to the pale propane light. The screenplay was left open on the final scene, the screen blank except for two terrifying sentences.

Mr. Scratch stood in front of the hearth, the roaring fire searing the flesh of Nicole's back as she struggled to get away from the monster. No, not a demon, the devil himself.

Her stomach churned at the thought of Johnny using her in a screenplay about horrific events that took place in the cabin where they were staying now. The legs of the chair scraped over the rough hardwood as she pushed herself up from the desk. When she turned around, she jumped back, started by the shadowy figure standing in the doorway.

"Sorry," Johnny said from the shadow of the bedroom. "I didn't mean to startle you."

"What is this?" Nicole asked, her finger thrust at the open computer screen.

Before Johnny could answer, a thunderous hammering rattled the windows.

"Go away!" an indistinguishable voice from downstairs screamed.

"Who could that be?" Nicole wondered out loud. "We're in the middle of nowhere."

Another thundering blow jolted the frame of the cabin; more panicked screams followed. Nicole rushed past Johnny as he stepped into the room. She reached out and grabbed his wrist before he vanished into his study.

"Where are you going?" Nicole screamed.

"The owner left a shotgun in this room," Johnny answered. "But I moved the bullets into a shoe box in the closet downstairs. Grab them while I get the gun. It will save us time."

"Johnny, what the hell is happening?"

"Just go!" he roared. "There's no time to argue."

Nicole nodded her head and raced across the bedroom. As she reached the top of the stairs, the door to Johnny's room slammed shut, punctuated by a bolt sliding into place. She rushed back to the door, pounding on it and screaming his name. But the door wouldn't budge, and Johnny didn't answer. Her friends' blood-curdling screams drew her attention downstairs; fear of getting trapped upstairs forced her to head down to join them. She ran towards the stairs on unsteady legs, her feet blindly carrying her safely down the spiralling staircase.

Chaos erupted at the bottom of the stairs. Squat against a cabinet, Theo strained as he pushed the heavy furniture into place against the front door. The door convulsed in its frame as the unknown hammered it with ruthless blows. Emily screamed from the back hallway, begging for help to move the dresser. Frozen in the center of the kitchen, Wilma held a butcher's knife.

Burning logs tumbled out of the roaring fireplace and

rolled precariously close to the couch where a dishevelled Daniel lay unconscious. Nicole tried to grab the poker to shove the logs back into the hearth, but the iron handle seared her palm. With his back against the cabinet, Theo struggled to hold it in place as the door rattled in its frame, his feet sliding all over the floor with every vigorous blow.

Nicole raced into the back hallway and got beside Emily, using her shoulder to drive the dresser against the back door. Emily's eyes were wide with unfathomable fear, her chest heaving as she struggled to catch her breath. In the kitchen, the kettle whistled as the water inside boiled. Nicole headed into the kitchen, flicked the dial off, and lifted the kettle off the red-hot burner and placed it down on the stove.

"Get out of here," Theo bellowed, his plea falling on deaf ears. The only response was a sickening, curdled laughter.

A sizzling hiss filled the room, followed by the putrid stench of burning flesh that soured the air.

"Daniel?" Emily gasped, shuffling towards him. She ignored the manic grin that warped his features. His pupils expanded, two glossy oil drops staring blankly at Emily as she rushed to embrace him. She never noticed the iron poker in his grasp, a trail of black smoke rising from his scorched hand.

"Emily!" Nicole called out too late. Her hand covered her mouth as she watched the horrible event unfold before her.

Daniel jabbed the spear straight towards the ceiling as Emily opened her arms to embrace her, the pointed tip searing through flesh and lodging in her skull. A clout of bubbling blood splattered over the floor at their feet, making a wet sloshing sound. The burning hot tip burned the inside of Emily's skull, and a piping hot stream of blood spouted from her ears as her eyes erupted in a sickening pop. A dark blotch formed on Emily's crotch as her muscles let go. The sour stench of piss fused with the burnt flesh made Nicole gag.

Wilma shrieked and ran towards Daniel. When he turned to face her, she threw the knife at him and ran towards the back door. Daniel didn't flinch as the blade tasted the flesh of his neck before clanking off the stone hearth and falling to the floor at the base of the steps.

Outside, the stranger continued to pound on the door, the wood splintering and cracking with each crushing blow. Theo strained to hold the cabinet against the door, beads of sweat rolling down his forehead as he watched the horrific scene unfolding right in front of him. His boots scuffled over the floor as the door burst inward, sending a rush of frigid air into the cabin. The flames in the fireplace swelled and lashed out, greedy for the fresh air.

With a cruel thrust, Daniel discarded Emily's body unceremoniously into the back wall, her neck cracking from the impact. Daniel raised the iron tip to his face, studying the burnt-on flesh with a sadistic smile on his face. He licked the gore-spattered iron with a disturbing moan, his eyes rolling into the back of his head as he savoured the taste of flesh.

Run, Theo thought. And it was obvious on his face that he thought it.

"There's nowhere to run," Daniel snickered, his words

booming and throaty. The voice belonged to someone else—something else. He staggered forward, his movements jerky and forced. "Nowhere to hide."

A crashing boom echoed through the house as Wilma tipped over the dresser, her feet scrambling to climb on top. Nicole ran towards the back hallway, but Daniel lunged forward, blocking her path. His scowling grin pressed thin, revealing blood-stained teeth beneath. The screen door clattered open as Wilma slammed it against the dresser until there was enough room to squeeze through.

"Wait here," Daniel snickered, swinging the poker in a wide arc, forcing Nicole backward.

Daniel's boot thudded manically off the floor as he stomped down the hallway, driving the iron poke into the wall in wild arcs, delivering a spray of splinters and drywall flying through the hallway as he went. Stuck between the door and the frame, Wilma screamed as Daniel grabbed a fistful of hair. He wrenched the coil of hair around his fist and jerked his arm back. With a sickening rip, Daniel yanked a clump of hair out of Wilma's head, tearing a bloodied piece of scalp with it. He tossed it down the hall, and it landed with a wet thunk as Wilma screeched a horrible howl of agony.

"Wilma!" Theo cried out.

Daniel wrapped his arm around Wilma's neck and hauled her back into the cabin. Her nails dug into the wooden frame and bent back then ripped out at the quick. She tried to scream, but no sound came out. Theo raced to her rescue, leaving the cabinet as it skidded across the floor. Nicole rushed over and slammed into the cabinet to keep the intruder out. She watched in horror as Theo crashed into Daniel, the three bodies embroiled in a dance of death. Fists flew and legs kicked in a blistering fury; bones cracked and flesh bruised.

Theo gained the upper hand, wrapping his fingers around Daniel's throat and pressing down with all of his weight. Black spittle frothed in the corner of Daniel's mouth, his eyes bulging out of the socket, his skin a brilliant shade of purple from the lack of oxygen. When the bones in Daniel's neck splintered, Theo relinquished his grasp, deep, hitching sobs rocking his body.

"Daniel," he groaned, "I'm sorry."

"Don't be," Daniel replied with a smirk.

Reaching out with both hands, Daniel grasped Theo's shirt and hauled himself up so that he could bite his friend's neck. Blood poured down Daniel's chest as he gnawed on the soft flesh beneath Theo's chin. He jerked his head back violently, tearing out a chunk; the grotesque flesh quivered, dangling from his crooked smile.

Nicole abandoned the front door, grabbed the kettle off the stove, and rushed down the hallway. She swung the kettle in a violent arc, slamming it over Daniel's head. The glass shattered, sending a spray of boiling water cascading over Daniel and Theo. In an instant, bright red blisters formed on their exposed skin. Theo tried to scream, but the sound vanished into the bloody mess of his throat.

Shards of glass protruded from Daniel's scalp. A torrent of black blood oozed from the savage wounds, splattering over the floor and against the wall as he spun around, driving the back of his hand into Nicole's face. Her nose erupted in a gout of blood and she staggered backward. Dazed, she stumbled into the living room and tripped over the leg of the coffee table. She fell face-first onto the floor, her wrist bending back painfully as she landed.

Dragging Wilma by a fistful of hair, Daniel sauntered towards the front door. He threw Wilma against the wall, driving the wind from her body as she slammed against the pine board. With one hand, he sent the cabinet toppling over on top of her. A horrified scream was cut short as the cabinet crushed the life from Wilma. A pool of blood seeped out from beneath the wreckage.

Nicole crawled towards the front steps, using the furniture to drag herself along as the room spun around her. Nicole's knees and hands slipped out from beneath her on the pools of slick blood coating the floor. She came face to face with two gory black holes that stared at her—Emily's jaw frozen in a permanent scream. To get to the steps, she dragged herself off Emily's corpse.

She could hear Daniel's haggard breath growing louder, but she couldn't hear his footsteps on the floor. Forced to turn to face the living room, she eased back against the first step and felt something dig into the small of her back. Nicole put her hands behind her back, her fingers probing for the handle of the butcher knife Wilma had thrown at Daniel.

Daniel stood on the couch, the poker gripped lightly in his hand, digging the iron head into the flames once more. "This has been fun," he said, cackling. "But I should finish up here before Mr. Scratch comes and steals all my thunder."

He jumped from the couch, landing on the floor with

a heavy thud, the pointed tip of the iron poker glowing a smouldering orange. When Daniel stood in front of Nicole, he raised the poker and pressed it against her cheek, the tip searing into her flesh with a sizzling hiss. As Nicole screamed, Daniel raised the poker above his head. The iron tip vanished behind his head as his body tensed, gathering all of his remaining strength for the blow.

With her remaining strength, Nicole drove the blade into Daniel's stomach. The steel vanished to the hilt, buried in his abdomen. Daniel stared down at her, his eyes wide with shock. She screamed and twisted the handle with both hands, the contents of his stomach falling out and sloshing at his feet. The iron poker fell from his hand with a heavy thud; Daniel collapsed on top of it, his arm falling into the flames. The flames engulfed his flesh with a sickening crackle.

Heavy footsteps thundered through the front door, the entire cabin shuddering in fear as the mysterious figure lumbered through the madness. Nicole used her elbows to drag herself up the first stairs, her face contorted with agony as she fought to escape. A quick glance towards the top of the stairs offered nothing except a dark place to die. Nicole gave up, slumping against the stairs as the monster lurched into view.

"You're here…" Nicole gasped for breath as blood flooded into the back of her throat, "…to kill me."

"I don't kill people," the man said, a hint of smug righteousness in his tone. "People do that on my behalf."

A fit of laughter strangled and sputtered in Nicole's throat. "I killed your servant," she said. She couldn't help herself, a wide, defiant smile plastered on her face.

The man stood in front of the hearth, his shadowed form veiled in her blurred vision.

"Now, what are you going to do?" Nicole spoke rapidly, the approaching march of death hastening her words.

"Me?" the man asked, laying a red metal container at her feet. "I don't need to do anything. My work here is done." He turned and methodically lumbered through the living room, admiring the fruits of his labour. "But I believe you still need to get your vengeance."

And without another word, Mr. Scratch left the cabin. Nicole peeked over her shoulder and then back at the red can. She gave it a kick, the gasoline inside sloshing around.

Johnny sat in front of his laptop, finishing the last act, using the dying song below to guide him; he pictured it as clear as day in his mind's eye. His fingers raced back and forth on the keyboard, words appearing on the screen at breakneck speed. All it cost him was Nicole and her friends. But it would be worth it. With his new fame, he'd have no shortage of girls who'd beg to take her place.

An overpowering stench wafted into the room, marring his concentration. He shook his head, refusing to tear his eyes away from the screen. Nauseating vapours made him lightheaded, tickling the hairs in his nose. Light footsteps thudded on the other side of the door, trailing across the bedroom and down the stairs. The words kept appearing without having to think about it. But the tone changed drastically.

Nicole poured gasoline over the bed and furniture, creating a trail down the stairs. She hugged the red gas can, a present from Mr. Scratch. Then, with a smile on her face, she threw the metal can into the flames and embraced the euphoria of revenge as the gates of hell opened up to devour them both for their atrocious deeds.

"What the hell?" Johnny yelled at the computer. "I'm not supposed to die!"

A deafening *whumpf* rocked the cabin as the windows downstairs exploded, sending a shower of glass outwards into the snow.

Thick plumes of black smoke billowed in through the crack in the door. The intensity of the heat was immediately unbearable. Johnny rushed to the door, the handle searing his hand as he tried to open it. Greedy yellow flames licked at him from the walls as the fire raced through the upstairs. Before Johnny could escape through the window, the floor collapsed beneath him, plunging him into the inferno below.

8

Sophia hadn't disagreed with Erin because she was right. There were, in fact, only five tourists now on the tour surrounding Barry as he spoke at length about the effects of the Grand Falls fire on the surrounding forest: David Hunter from the Northern Coast, and Derek Rose, Bernice Fletcher, Charles Henry, and Sarah Childs of Tickles.

They followed Barry in a tight little circle, walking almost as one, none of them ever acknowledging how small their sphere had gotten.

"How do they not notice?" Sophia whispered, her voice breaking. "How do they not see what he's doing?"

"It's what he does," Erin chided. "I told you, *it's the thirteenth*. It's the height of him, today. He's at the height of what he is today."

Sophia's hands started to shake.

Barry finished what he was saying about the fire, then gestured the group of only five forward into the next room, devoted to the various traditional vocations of Newfoundland.

Erin stepped forward, quickly, and grabbed David by the arm, spinning him and separating him from the group as the rest stepped through the door.

"Unhand me!" he cursed. The melodrama of the grandiose act, pulling his arm away with a jolt while barking such a stilted command would have been comical had the situation not been so dire.

"You have to stop this! Don't you see what's happening?" She grabbed him again as she spoke, one hand taking either of his arms. "It's near the end, don't you see? There's only five of you left!"

David stared at her, and after a moment, leaned in to speak to her in hushed tones as Barry's voice echoed through the room as he began his next story.

CRESCENT LAKE
Brad Dunne

"I hope you boys aren't planning on going out on the Crescent," the gas station clerk said, eyeing the grooms-men in their shorts and tank tops.

Jamie laid his beer on the counter and was about to ask why before Bryan interrupted him.

"No, ma'am," Bryan assured her. "We just got a cabin rented for our buddy's bachelor party. You should drop by."

The grey-haired woman gave Bryan a wary smile like she knew he had the devil in him, but it was charming, nonetheless. Jamie wondered how often women gave Bryan that smile. Mark, Devon, and Sean all gave each other knowing smirks. The groomsmen bought their beer, Gatorade, and snacks then piled into Bryan's SUV to drive to Crescent Lake.

"Why did she say we shouldn't go out on Crescent Lake?" Jamie asked.

"I can't believe you were flirting with missus," Mark said to Bryan.

"You'd stick your dick in a bowl of soup if it was still warm," Sean said.

"If I had to choose between her and a snake's mouth, I'd take the snake," Devon added.

Jamie didn't share in their laughter because he didn't feel like he'd been included in the jokes.

"Why did she say we shouldn't go out on Crescent Lake?" he repeated.

"Don't worry about it," Mark said. "Can we do a Timmy's run before we hit the lake?" he asked Bryan. "I'm not fit here this morning."

"The groom has spoken!" Bryan announced.

Jamie groaned to himself. He was cramped in the back between Devon, and Sean. "We should've brought another car for this."

"Yeah, you should've brought yours," Bryan said.

Everyone laughed at this.

"Do you even have your license?" Sean asked.

"Yes," Jamie lied. "I just don't have insurance."

"How old are you?" Devon asked.

"I'm twenty-seven," Jamie replied. "Same age as Mark."

"We met in Kindergarten," Mark said.

Devon seemed surprised by this. Everyone thought Jamie was younger than he was.

Jamie looked out the window and caught glimpses of Crescent Lake between the trees. A green wall of Balsom concealed the blue mass from the main road, which curved along the lake's convex shape then twisted and turned like so many of Newfoundland's rural roads. The small outport community was a one-road town, but it was one of the few big enough between Gander and Corner Brook to support a Tim Hortons. A few old-timers in rusty pickups stood outside Tim's, nursing coffees with cigarettes dangling between their yellowed fingers. The groomsmen pulled into the drive-thru, and Bryan handled the orders. Everyone got extra large double-doubles. Jamie asked for a blueberry muffin as well, but before Bryan passed it back to him, he bit off the top half, which made everyone laugh again. Mark glared at Bryan, who shrugged in response. Jamie caught this exchange in the rearview mirror. He imagined that they must've talked about this. Mark had asked Bryan to go easy on Jamie, not to give him too hard of a time. Because Jamie can't pick up for himself. But he'd show them that he could. He'd punch Bryan in the face with the bottom half of the muffin. Smear it all over that pompous smirk. That would put him in his place. He didn't, of course. Instead, he swallowed his anger with sludgy coffee and what was left of his muffin.

They pulled out of Tim's and back onto the main road. Once they were about twenty minutes out of town, Bryan took a dirt road into a cloistered area near the lake. The boys tumbled out of the SUV and stretched their stiff, dehydrated limbs under the sun. Sean passed around a bag of magic mushrooms. Jamie was grateful for the coffee's cream and sugar to help wash down the bitter fungus. Once the mushrooms were all consumed, the guys got busy unloading their floats. Bryan laid his keys in the driver's side wheel well.

Jamie noticed a sign by the water's edge that forbade swimming, boating, fishing, and just about any other potential water-related activity. "Should we be worried about that?"

"Don't be such a pussy," Bryan replied.

"I imagine the local municipality introduced some by-laws to avoid liability," Sean reasoned.

Jamie rolled his eyes privately at Sean's lawyerly tone.

"That's just baymen," Bryan said. "Couple b'ys probably got drunk one night out on the lake and went tits up. You know hardly any of them can even swim. Sure look at the water. Even Jamie would be fine if he fell in."

Crescent Lake reclined in the mid-day warmth, dappled with sunshine. A speckled trout leapt from the water to catch a fly buzzing too near the surface. The ensuing ripple was the only blemish on the mirror-like tableau the brilliant sky had cast on the lake.

"Bob Ross couldn't have done better himself," Mark declared as he walked out onto an old wooden dock that extended from the shore. The rotted boards bowed so severely with each of his steps that Jamie was afraid Mark might fall through. He pissed off the dock, and the splashing droplets were about the only thing the boys could hear for miles.

"Here." Bryan passed Jamie an electric pump that was connected to his SUV. "You got little bitch lungs."

Devon and Bryan used bicycle pumps to fill up their floats. Devon managed to keep up with them using just his prodigious lungs. As the groom, Mark sipped his coffee in the sun, and Jamie filled his float. Once the floats were sea-worthy, the guys disembarked and began paddling toward the centre of the lake. Mark carried a Ziploc bag of joints and attached a little shower radio to his float. After paddling for about half a mile, they cracked some beers while bobbing in the lake's centre. Crescent Lake was encircled by gently rolling hills, which made Jamie feel like he was bobbing inside a giant bowl. In the distance, heavy clouds lumbered toward them, but they would take hours to reach the lake. The groomsmen still had the better part of the afternoon to enjoy before heading back to the cabin for another evening of BBQ and more beers.

Devon and Sean tossed a Nerf football back and forth; Mark and Bryan were having a semi-serious conversation, likely work-related; and Jamie just floated. They passed around soggy joints, tossed empty cans of beer into the river, and listened to the staticky radio. The combined effect of caffeine, psilocybin, THC, and alcohol helped ward off the groomsmen's collective hangover. The guys complained about their wives, girlfriends, kids, bosses, co-workers, and some other topics that Jamie had no opinions of. He couldn't help feeling like they danced around certain topics like government, social justice issues, and, in particular, the pandemic. Had there been a conversation between the other groomsmen to avoid an argument with Jamie? Maybe. That was OK by him; he was fine with keeping the peace this weekend. Besides—and maybe it was the magic mushrooms—Jamie felt connected to everyone and everything. That was until Bryan spoke.

"Did Sam RRSP after?" he asked Mark.

"No," Mark answered.

"Too busy with the new baby," Bryan continued. "Is that her second?"

"I think so," Mark replied.

"How did you fumble that," Bryan asked Jamie. "She's up there making loot. You could've been a stay-at-home dad, playing video games all day."

"Didn't want to move to Labrador," Jamie said.

"Didn't want to leave mommy," Bryan said.

Jamie saw Mark shoot Bryan another one of those glares. Jamie had heard it all before. It didn't matter how many times he explained that he didn't want to move to Labrador, the guys all still gave him grief for letting Samantha go.

"Did you find us any strippers for tonight?" Devon asked Bryan.

"I didn't want to insult your sister and embarrass your future brother-in-law," Bryan replied.

"What Jocelyn doesn't know won't hurt her," Devon said.

"Bryan can smell strippers from a hundred miles away," Mark said. "He's like a shark."

"I'm merely a fan of the choreography," Bryan protested.

"Do you still have to wear a mask for a lap dance, I wonder," Sean asked. Mark shot him a reproachful look, but it was too late.

"Probably need proof of all five boosters," Jamie said, but his tone lacked the same joking mode of the other guys.

"That's what was wrong with those freedom convoy truckers," Devon suggested, trying to steer the conversation back to the same light-hearted mood as before. "Not enough lap dances."

"Nah, they were just fed up with the bullshit lockdowns," Jamie said.

"Are you like a conspiracy theorist?" Devon asked.

"Jamie is unvaccinated," Bryan said.

Jamie saw Mark shoot Bryan another meaningful glare. We talked about this, it said. I said not to bring it bring it up.

"Honestly," Devon said. "I don't agree with all either. I only got the vaccine because my job said I had to. I never said any of that to Jocelyn, though."

"Here we go," Mark said before Jamie could start. "We're here to have a good time, not argue about the vaccine."

Jamie had enough social grace to leave it there. He leaned back into his float and surveyed the sky. The clouds seemed to be approaching at a faster pace than they'd expected. No matter how much beer he drank, his mouth was full of the metallic flavour of ozone. Like burnt wires by an overly chlorinated swimming pool. Or maybe that was just the mushrooms. Whatever the case, he suddenly got an overwhelming feeling of being watched. Was there a boat out there on the lake's horizon? He looked around and noticed a peculiar ridgeline running along the water. They were jagged like mountains, not the slopping hills of Newfoundland. And now that he looked, they also seemed to be undulating in the water like a string of buoys. That's when the ridgeline peeled off the horizon and snaked toward the group. Jamie rubbed his eyes and tried to focus, but before he could get a good look at them, they slipped under the water, causing a placid wave that lifted the group as a dark shape glided underneath them. No one else seemed to notice except Jamie. He told himself it was probably just the mushrooms. The vaccine talk had gotten him a little worked up and was tanking his buzz.

"I gotta piss," Sean said, struggling to balance his knees so he could fire into the water without splashing himself.

"Here." Bryan tossed Sean an empty Gatorade bottle. "Piss jug."

"Piss jug!" Devon and Mark cheered along. Now they all suddenly had the urge to piss, and the anointed jug was passed around.

"How about you, Jamie?" Mark asked.

"Nah, I'm good," Jamie responded.

"C'mon!" Bryan cajoled. "Everyone's got to Christen the piss jug!" He tossed the bottle over to Jamie, who recoiled.

"That's disgusting!" Jamie protested.

"Oh, don't be a sook," Bryan responded. "I rinsed it out! I promise you won't get COVID."

"Fuck this," Jamie said and started paddling toward shore. The guys tried to convince him to come back, but Jamie was fed up.

Sean slid into the water and swam toward Jamie. "Wait!" he called out. Jamie ignored him. Sean swam out in front of him and blocked his way. "Hey, dude, sorry about all that. Don't take it personally."

"He's always giving me a hard time. All day yesterday too. I'm sick of it."

"I'll talk to Bryan. Tell him to ease up. He's having trouble at home. I think he's just trying to blow off steam."

"I don't care. I can't stand that guy. He's always giving me shit about my job, Samantha, my mom."

"I hear you, but you got to stick around for Mark. You're his best friend. He'd be devastated if you bailed."

Best friend? Jamie wanted to ask. So why aren't I his best man? Not Bryan, a guy Mark had only met in university. Mark and Jamie had been friends since kindergarten.

At the very least it should be Mark over here trying to talk him into staying. Jamie was the one who had introduced Mark to Jocelyn in the first place. She was friends with Samantha in nursing school. That was before Jamie dropped out of the engineering program and they all left him in the dust, which wasn't his fault. But they didn't get that. They just saw him as a loser who played video games all day and lived with his mom. Guys like Sean—who breezed through life, who got into their first choice of law school, who got all the girls—they didn't get it.

"What did you just say?" Sean asked.

Jamie hadn't realized he'd said anything. He closed his eyes and rubbed his face, massaging the bridge of his nose. There was a gnawing feeling in his guts that was more than just the mushrooms. Lately, his mind had been going to some dark places he didn't like. He realized he was probably being unnecessarily hostile to Sean, who he actually liked. And he was right; Jamie didn't want to ruin Mark's bachelor party. He opened his eyes and was about to agree to rejoin the group, but Sean had disappeared.

"Sean?" Jamie asked in a near whisper. The water was too dark to see any sign of him.

"What's going on?" Mark called out.

"I don't know," Jamie replied. "Sean went underwater. He hasn't come up."

The rest of the guys paddled their way over. Devon dove into the water. After about thirty seconds, he came up for air, then went back down. He repeated this half a dozen times.

"There's no sign of him," he said between big gulps of air. "This lake is crazy deep."

"How did it even happen?" Bryan asked Jamie like it was his fault.

"I don't know," Jamie replied defensively. "He seemed fine."

"Does Sean have seizures or anything like that?" Devon asked.

"Not that I know of," Mark said.

"Maybe there's something wrong with the mushrooms," Jamie suggested. "Like he had an allergic reaction."

"Shit," Devon said. "What if they're poison?"

"Alright," Bryan insisted. "Let's just stay calm."

Jaime groaned at Bryan's I'm-the-boss-now tone.

"Huh?" Bryan asked.

"Nothing," Jaime said.

"Let's make our way to the shore," Bryan continued. "We'll call 911. Devon, you hang back in case Sean pops up."

Devon climbed back atop his float and began scanning the water for any sign of Sean. Bryan, Mark, and Jamie started paddling back toward the shore. Just as the old dock came into view, they felt a wake pass underneath them, scattering the floats. Jamie nearly tipped over into the water.

"What the hell was that?" Mark asked.

"An undertow? Like a riptide?" Bryan suggested. "Maybe that's what took Sean?"

"That doesn't make any sense," Jamie said. "Riptides are along the shore."

"And how would you know?" Bryan asked.

"Hold up," Mark said. "I don't think we should leave

Devon behind."

"Why?" Bryan asked.

"If the mushrooms are poisoned then he might go under too. And I don't like this riptide shit. Or whatever it is. Jocelyn would kill me if something happened to her brother."

Yes, Jamie thought, we mustn't do anything that might upset precious Jocelyn. He remembered that Jocelyn was one of the first people to unfriend him on Facebook after he started sharing dissenting views on the vaccine and the mandates. Then it was Samantha. Had Jocelyn turned her against him? Not that it mattered. She'd married some douchebag doctor up in Lab City, and now she was popping out little crotch goblins that looked just like him. They were living their little normie lives, driving luxury Sierras, taking trips to the Dominican Republic in the winter. It all made Jamie want to puke.

"Devon!" Mark called out and waved his hand, gesturing for him to come join them.

Just as Devon began paddling toward them, he was catapulted dozens of feet into the air. A gigantic tail bigger than Bryan's SUV emerged from a cascade of foamy water. They heard Devon's screams as he was thrown across the lake for what seemed like minutes. When he finally crashed into the water, he didn't emerge.

"Jesus Christ!" Mark yelled. "What the hell was that?"

"Maybe a killer whale?" Bryan said.

"That tail looked way bigger than a killer whale," Jamie said.

"How could a killer whale even get in here?" Mark

asked.

"This lake is connected to the Atlantic," Bryan explained. "It could've swam in here."

"That's probably what those signs were about," Mark said. "What missus was talking about."

"I really don't think it's a killer whale," Jamie said.

"I saw on a documentary that when sharks attack people it's because they think they're seals," Bryan continued. "Maybe that's what's happening now."

"Yeah, I saw something similar," Mark agreed. "There was a video on YouTube of an orca launching a seal into the air just like that. Like it's playing with its food."

Jamie remembered those jagged hills that were floating in the lake before Sean disappeared. In his drug- and anxiety-addled memory, those things loomed larger than Godzilla's spiked back. "Whatever it is," he said, "it's way bigger than a killer whale."

"I think you're just freaking out because of the mushrooms," Bryan said.

"So we all hallucinated the same thing?" Jamie asked. "That doesn't make sense."

"Sure it does," Bryan countered. "We all saw something traumatic, which our brains exaggerated. I don't think that's so implausible."

"You just don't want to admit that I'm right," Jamie said.

"Guys," Mark interjected. "C'mon."

"Here we go," Bryan said. "Maybe it's an experimental giant squid Joe Biden created to fight the Russians."

"This isn't helping," Mark said.

"Do you think an orca could throw a grown man

across the lake like an Aaron Rodgers Hail Mary?" Jaime asked.

"Maybe Jamie has a point," Mark suggested.

"I'm not surprised the only football player you know is Aaron Rodgers," Bryan shot back.

"What makes you so sure I'm wrong?" Jamie asked. "Because you're an engineer and I'm just a GameStop employee?"

"Ex-GameStop employee," Bryan said. "You gave that up because you wouldn't get the vaccine, right? You say I'm a know-it-all because I'm an engineer, but you're the smug little cunt who thinks he's better than everyone. I see all your posts on social media calling us the 'jabbed' and how we're just a bunch of 'sheeple' because we consume mainstream media and don't believe the insane conspiracy bullshit you read on the internet. But let me tell you something, it's all a big front, and I think you know it. You think you're persecuted because of lockdowns and vaccine mandates, but that was the perfect excuse to sink further into your hole. You look down on me, Mark, and Sean because we're 'normies' or whatever because we have middle-class jobs, families, houses, but you're just too scared to go after any of it. You'd rather rot away playing video games and jerking off to porn down in mommy's basement."

Jamie's mind was blank with rage. Bryan leaned back in his float satisfied with his diatribe. Jamie was about to let him have it when Bryan disappeared within a black column that burst from the water with the propulsion of a rocket. The impact scattered Jamie and Mark from their floats. Jamie was able to get to the surface just as the pillar crashed back down into the water, accented by that massive tail slipping under with a sickening grace. Jamie never saw its head, but the thing must've been thirty feet long. The splash rocked Jamie again, driving him under the waves. He struggled to figure out which way was up as he fought the water's momentum.

Stay still, a voice told him. Sink to the bottom and let that thing take you. Just be over with it, over with everything.

It was a comforting thought.

As the beast's wake settled, Jamie allowed himself to float in the water, numb from the cold. But when there was no longer any air left in his lungs, his eyes flashed open. He looked up and saw pale sunlight breaking through the water. His limbs flailed of their own accord toward the surface. He broke through and saw Mark struggling to get back atop a float. Jamie saw one nearby and swam toward it. The shower radio attached to it crackled "Everybody's working for the weekend!" They both used their hands to gently paddle toward each other. Neither spoke while the water was still agitated, afraid they might agitate the creature again. The steely clouds were above them now, blocking the sun. Crescent Lake lay motionless like a monolith.

"Are you OK?" Mark asked after a few minutes.

Jamie nodded. "Do you believe me now?"

"Are you seriously going to pull that 'I told you so' shit now?"

Jamie shrugged. "Do you think Bryan was right?"

"What? About the orca?" Mark laughed. "No, I don't think so."

"I meant the other stuff."

Mark sighed. "I don't know, man, I'm more concerned about getting the hell out of here alive."

"I figured you'd agree."

"Hey, you're my best friend."

"But not your best man?"

"You're my best friend," Mark repeated. "But you don't make it easy. And the last couple of years, it's gotten worse. I invite you out with friends and you either bail at the last minute or don't show up at all. And if you do show up, you act like a sook. All you want to talk about is video games or politics, and then you throw a tantrum whenever someone disagrees with you. Do you have any idea how miserable that is?"

"I guess I trigger your friends because I'm politically incorrect."

"Oh c'mon, you know that's not the reason. Devon is pro-Trump, and he gets along with everyone just fine. Bryan is right that you're just using all this culture war shit to isolate yourself. But you've always been that way. Ever since we were kids. I love hanging out and playing video games and all that, but you've got to leave the cave eventually. You're almost thirty and you've got no real job skills, you've never lived alone—"

"You know why."

"You say it's because you've got to help your mom, but your dad left a long time ago."

The two friends floated in silence for a while. Up above, the grey clouds turned black.

"I've never told you this," Mark continued, "but your mom has been calling me lately. She's really worried about you. She says you stay in bed all day sometimes. And you won't apply for jobs. Most days you're either gaming or rotting your brain on Twitter. I thought that if you came out for the bachelor party you'd finally start coming out of your shell, start getting your life together or something."

Jamie's knee-jerk reaction was outrage. He was about to rip into Mark for talking to his mom about him without his knowledge when a thought occurred to him, a thought he'd been avoiding for a long time: What if they were right? What if he was just using this all as an excuse to hide? But to hide from what? Life? The truth was that his anxiety had been metastasizing long before the pandemic. It had gotten so bad that he had to reduce his hours at GameStop to part-time because nights before a shift he'd get so anxious he couldn't sleep. All he wanted to do was lose himself in virtual reality—Hyrule, the Mushroom Kingdom, Tamriel, or San Andreas. Twitter, YouTube, podcasts. Anything that distracted him from the unsatisfying and unpredictable real world.

"Are you kidding me?" Mark exclaimed.

Jamie hadn't noticed it was raining. The lake reverberated with the rain's constant drumming. He started to zone out with the pitter-patter of droplets hitting his head, which is probably why he didn't notice Bryan bump into his float until Mark started screaming. The rest of the groomsmen bobbed in the water, semi-digested and stinking of bile. Jamie considered their chewed-up bodies with the detached curiosity of a mortuary assistant.

"Shit shit shit shit shit," Mark repeated to himself in a loop.

Listening to his childhood best friend muttering to

himself on the precipice of a nervous breakdown, Jamie decided he was going to get them out of this mess. He would be the one to save him and deliver him safely to his beloved Jocelyn. Then everyone would see his worth. Then he'd be the best man. He'd prove Bryan wrong. Prove his dad wrong for walking out on him and his mom.

"We need to make a break for it," Jamie said.

"That thing will just hunt us down," Mark said.

"Maybe, but it'll just do that anyway if we stay out here."

"Yeah, I think you're right about that. Any ideas?"

"I was thinking it can't make out our shapes so well now that it's raining. Maybe that's why it spat up the others. It was hoping that we'd freak out and give ourselves away." Mark didn't seem fully convinced. "I'll chuck this too," Jaime added. He unclipped the shower radio that was attached to the float. "All together, it might give us enough time to get to the dock."

Mark thought it over. "That's probably our best chance."

Jamie started the countdown. "Three…two…one!" He surprised himself by how far he threw the radio. Aaron Rodgers would be proud. Or maybe that was just the mushrooms. When the radio plopped into the water, Jamie turned and saw that Mark was already swimming furiously toward the dock. Jamie dove in and swam after him. He kept his head up and drove his arms while flailing his legs with all the technique he'd learned in Tadpole swimming lessons. Between his splashing, the rain, and his frantic breathing, he had no idea if that thing was behind them. There was no sense looking back, so he put his head down and kept swimming.

Once his arms and legs felt like they were so full of lac-tic acid that he couldn't bear another stroke, he looked up and saw the dock was near. Mark had made it. He clam-oured up the steps and looked back on the lake. The thing must have been closing in because Mark started running toward land. Jamie couldn't believe it. His childhood best friend was abandoning him there to be eaten alive. The outrage gave him that last boost of adrenaline to swim harder. He made it to the dock and climbed up. Again, he didn't bother to look back. Up ahead, Mark fell through the rotted boards. He screamed and tried to extricate him-self, but one leg was awkwardly trapped between the boards, and his hands kept slipping on the greasy dock. Jamie was on his way to help when he heard a splash be-hind him. He turned to see rows of jagged spikes emerge from the water, cutting through the water like a snake. A diamond-shaped head with two great yellow eyes broke the surface. The beast rolled ashore and rose atop his belly, casting a long shadow over the dock. Jamie looked up but could barely make out the top of the creature towering above them. It bent over them and split its mouth open to reveal a mess of serrated teeth, and a black abyss full of ancient hunger. Jamie froze in terror, unable to move.

"Help!" Mark cried.

That startled Jamie from his inertia. He looked at his friend, then looked back up at the monster, and then took off running. Behind him, he heard the thing crash into the dock. Mark's cries were lost amid the splintering wood and splashing water. Jamie didn't want to discover if that thing was amphibious, so he grabbed Bryan's keys in the wheel well and started the SUV. The wheels kicked out clusters of rocks as he peeled out of the dirt road and onto the highway. His driving skills were about the same as his swimming. The rain splashed across the windshield like he was in a carwash, but he never thought or knew how to turn on the wipers. He was still dripping wet. Water poured down his face. Or were those tears? He didn't know. The SUV was stifling with humidity, so he lowered the windows.

"There wasn't time," he told himself out loud.

No, there wasn't time. That thing would've gotten them both. Besides, good riddance, right? Mark was going to leave him there to die, so it was only fair. Abandoned again. Mark, Samantha, his dad. They were all the same. In the end, they all bailed. Friends, girlfriends, family. None of it meant shit. All he wanted to do now was go home, lay on the couch, and game.

But was he headed in the right direction? Where was he? He'd been driving for what felt like ages, but he hadn't seen any cars or houses. He squinted to see the road ahead of him, which lifted and curved along the shape of Crescent Lake. The rain intensified as he struggled to see the road ahead of him. He finally managed to pick out the yellow traffic line, but it kept twisting erratically. Then the dotted passing lines became spikes like an alligator's scute. He was driving on top of the beast's back; he was sure of it. The road flexed with the lazy motion of a snake waking from sleep. A head crowned by asphalt turned its attention to the SUV. Jamie screamed and swerved the SUV out of the way before it could strike him. The wheels careened toward the cliff. He'd been going too fast and the

SUV punched through the guardrails. It tumbled down the cliff and splashed into Crescent Lake.

Water rushed through the open windows. Jamie fought to get out, but he couldn't fit through the gap. The heavy SUV sank quickly. No matter how hard he kicked at the doors, the water pressure had them sealed shut. The last his mind processed before it snapped were the two yellow eyes approaching through the dark.

9

Barry finished explaining the sealing equipment and moved on to another display.

In it was a small lobster pot, too small to have ever actually caught a lobster, filled with small beach stones. Next to it was a wooden anchor and a knife carved from obsidian to a sharp, jagged edge set within a whalebone and held with sinew.

"These were toys," Barry said, laying his hands down on the case. "The pot was too small to catch anything but was otherwise exact, the anchor too small to hold anything substantial. But they are not plastic; the pot is functional, just a smaller version of what they would use. And the blade is real, as real as they get. Obsidian can cut so sharp that the blade is not felt."

Carefully, gingerly, Barry took the lid off of the case, removed the obsidian blade, and examined it in the light. "It can cut between atoms, we know now. Can you imagine? But these were children's toys. In the same way we used to give young girls baby dolls to prepare them for their roles as mothers, we gave little boys the implements of hauling the fish, or helping with the fishing, the jigging." He paused then turned the blade to point at those in attendance. "The gutting."

It was only then that Barry noticed that David was not with the group.

He took stock of the rest of them, Derek Rose, Charles Henry, and even Bernice Fletcher. They parted, without even knowing they were doing so, and it seemed again as though only Bernice resisted the urge, though she did follow after a brief hesitation.

"Come here," Barry said, gesturing with the knife, one last threatening action with it before he put it back into its case. He replaced it, closed its lid, ran his fingers along the edge of the glass, then spread them out over the display.

Sarah was close to him again, with only the glass of the case between them, and at this distance, that looked like nothing at all. Like only air.

"Let me tell you a tale of these things, yes? Let me tell you a story of what it's like knowing, even at this young age, the stench of fish."

BOG LEGS
C.H. Newell

The entirety of Colleen Cull's life can be summed up in a single phrase: the stench of fish. Even before she was legal working age and got a job at the fish plant in Comfort Cove, she helped her father Kevin with his skiff, fishing, hauling, jigging, or gutting. Colleen's existence is the stink of fish. She doesn't much notice it anymore, but others do, aside from her coworkers at the plant, and all the rest of them who work on the water. People turn up their noses when Colleen's around town after work before she gets home to have a wash. Sometimes even a wash doesn't remedy the years of built-up stench—fish was only the half of it, too, then there were the crab, squid, mussels, lobsters, and on and on and on; it all reeks.

One big reason Colleen actually *doesn't* mind the stink is that, for the most part, it repels the men from wanting to have sex with her, even the lads on the boats who stink to high heavens as much as her. That's just fine by Colleen. She's never been interested in them. She hates how they treat her, anyway—a woman in a supposedly man's world—like she needs male muscles to help her female limbs accomplish work she's been doing mostly on her own since before she ever knew what a period was, let alone had one. Colleen's thankful that at least the men at the plant have given up trying to hit on her. At work, she's just one of the guys, like most of the other women who work there.

Many nights after work, everyone from the plant goes to the bar for a few drinks and a chat, usually bitching about the amount of work, or when the season was slow, the lack of work, or the latest union news. Lately, they've all been talking about the three men who went missing, each disappearing from different spots along the shore around the edges of town. At first, people assumed it was foolish men who strolled drunk by the water and wound up slipping and hitting their heads before getting pulled out in the current. Not out of the realm of possibility, the town has its fair share of drunks, not to mention its fair share of choppy water right at peoples' doorsteps. One of the only places to get a drink in town isn't far from the Atlantic's edge. So the idea that a few men fell into the water drunk in the span of only a few months wasn't far-fetched. And most folks around Comfort Cove who knew the men would've believed it for the rest of their lives. If it weren't for all the stories over the past several decades about a strange creature that, so the tales go, watches people in the evenings along the shoreline, sometimes hiding in the woods, other times wading in the dark waters when the moon was obscured behind stuffy clouds. An old lady in the '70s claimed that the creature tried to pull her into the trees while she was on a late summer walk; she still swears that if a couple of young men hadn't saved her it would've gobbled her up. These past six months with men disappearing is the first anybody's ever accused the creature of murder.

Bog Legs, they call it. At least that's what some of the people around Comfort Cove were calling it; others didn't even dare to talk of it, worried that the more they spoke about it the more they might call it out of the murky depths it surely calls home. But all the stories about Bog Legs are similar: it supposedly has giant fish eyes on either side of its fat head; gangly legs like those of a crustacean but far longer; a neck full of gills in several rows; and while it's in the water it uses its body to swim like a fish, then on land it scuttles like a hulking, awkward crab.

The first time Colleen heard the tale of Bog Legs she found it sort of funny, considering how odd most of the things she's pulled out of the Atlantic over the years look already. She actually believes the rumours floating around town, just not in the same way as everyone else. She's always assumed it was just an undiscovered animal, not a monstrous cryptid. She's said from the beginning that those men died of their own drunken foolishness. She, like all women in Comfort Cove, knows that men who have little to do except drink and fight at the local bar on the weekends do all manners of stupid things hazardous to their health. Colleen insists whenever others bring up Bog Legs that it's all a matter of bad timing between oceanic evolution and male idiocy.

When Friday comes and work's done, Colleen goes for beers and darts with a group of coworkers. The conversation naturally turns to the latest disappearance—a forty-five-year-old man called Gerald Trelegan, a local welder known more for hitting his wife than his welding skill—and how Bog Legs is, without doubt, the culprit behind it. The whole thing's become a bit boring to Colleen, especially when a sack of shit like Gerald's involved, yet she still engages a little, mostly to toss a wet load of skepticism on her friends' gossip-fueled fire. Not that they were really her friends. They never did anything together except for work and go for beers. Colleen's real friends have gone away. A few were just, gone; not dead, just not part of her life anymore.

Colleen gets up to claim one of the free dartboards. She doesn't even want to play with anybody. She'd rather toss darts herself and not keep score. She starts to play aimlessly while drinking her beer. The creature conversation is all Colleen can hear, even over the blaring country music coming from the world's oldest jukebox. She decides to step out for a piss.

Despite nearly being summer, Comfort Cove is still chilly on a night when a constant breeze rolls in off the Atlantic. Colleen steps out and feels the chill, but it's not enough to make her go back inside to use the bar's bathroom. She heads to the treeline across from the bar, not far from a couple of the wharfs off the town's main drag. She ducks behind trees then slips off her pants to squat in the darkness. All Colleen hears is the sound of urine softly splashing between her boots. It's quickly replaced by a sloshing in the water. Colleen recognizes a lot of ocean sounds instinctively; all those years of working on her father's boat. This splash isn't a random wave, or a fish flopping up out of the break. It was somebody making their way out of the surf—legs pulling beneath the surface like a mini undertow, the clap of thighs trying to get free of water. Colleen finishes peeing and stands up, forgetting to pull up her jeans. She looks out towards the shore but sees nothing, even outside the bar nearby. Then, the sloshing. Colleen darts her eyes up the shore through the inlet and spies an oddly shaped figure moving out of the water onto land. The figure's body is huge and its legs are tiny, as if it were the shadow of a big, fat ant. The figure disappears into the trees. Colleen frantically scans the tree-line farther out for any sign of movement. She sees trees and alders bend then sway before settling still. After that, nothing, only a light howl on the breeze. Colleen laughs. *Yes, b'y. Bog Legs out for a stroll.* Colleen finally pulls up her jeans, zips up, and heads back for the bar, feeling the call of more Dominion Ale.

Some state this morning, Kevin says.

Colleen smiles at him while he laughs, and she goes on pulling up a trap. Despite all the alcohol consumed the night prior and a lack of sleep, Colleen's out with her father in his boat. They're hauling in lobster traps that Kevin sets around the same few places every season.

I'm only teasing, girl. I used to be at the same stuff. If it weren't for the diabetes, I'd still be at it.

Oh, I heard all the stories.

Colleen grins at her father. He returns a similar smile. Their faces look alike, as if Colleen was looking into an old, wrinkling, greying mirror. She keeps on grinning while she drags the trap she pulled aboard over to the end of the boat, settling it against several others already stowed away.

How's everyone down to the plant getting on? Kevin asks.

Ah, they're fine. Same old stuff.

I s'pose they're all talking about Gerry, hey.

Lots of talk.

Ol' stuff about Bog Legs, is it?

Colleen nods, thinking about the figure in the dark last night. She'd laughed about it when she went back into the bar. She didn't tell anybody, but she laughed and laughed to herself quietly. Now, standing out on the water, the boat rocking on the waves, Colleen can't help wonder what her father might've seen over the years.

Colleen says, All the time you've spent out in boats… ever see anything weird?

Kevin stops what he's doing. He looks at his daughter with a curious eye.

I mean, like, something you couldn't explain.

Kevin pushes another lobster trap over against the rest then sits down and pulls a battered pack of cigarettes from his flannel shirt pocket. He lights a smoke.

When I was nineteen, Kevin says, I was working for Uncle Mart on his boat. He used to be some hard on me— my lord! There were days I'd be out in boat so long that when we got back on land, I'd lie in bed, close my eyes, and feel like I was drifting out to sea in the pitch dark.

Uncle Mart was always tough as nails.

You got that right, my dear. One time, it was just me and Mart. We were out around the bay up towards Lewisporte. Far, too. Couldn't have been past five in the morning. Sun was about to rise up. Mart was over on one end of the boat, and I was up at the bow for a smoke. And I saw this flash out on the water. It was like someone had a mirror out there and caught a beam of sun. I let me eyes settle out there, and after a minute or so I noticed this strange, scaly tail whip up out of the dark blue. Then I seen the skin: it was a *person's* body. There was still a tail, scales, all that. The whole thing came out of the water, curved like a dolphin's body when it jumped, then dipped back in—but I seen it! I yelled for Mart to come look, but by the time he came 'round, the thing was gone. I was sure I seen a mermaid. 'Course he laughed at me. Made fun of me until the day he died—called me Mermaid Boy every single time we were out in boat after that. Arsehole.

Kevin never mentioned anything like his story before this, so it's a surprise to Colleen. His story breathes truth into the idea that she may have, indeed, seen the creature everybody calls Bog Legs.

How come you asked something like that? Kevin asks.

Just all the Bog Legs stuff. And last night, I maybe saw…*something*.

Kevin looks at his daughter with eyes full of wonder and a tiny drop of fear.

Colleen says, Probably nothing. But I was curious if you'd ever seen something.

I can tell you this, darling: the world is full of very real, very odd things. I just try to remember that not everything we don't understand is bad. You try and remember that, too.

As the weekend rolls around and May Two-Four celebrations are about to begin, Colleen prepares for a few days off, starting with another round of drinks and a few flicks of darts down to the bar. Comfort Cove is a bit busier than usual since some people are back in town from university and college. This also means familiar faces returning after time away—time away from the town and also its many memories. One familiar face that Colleen notices in the bar is Allison Crocker, an old friend from childhood. Things got awkward between them after a sleepover for a friend's birthday when they were only twelve and shared a secret kiss. Neither of them even knew the word *lesbian* but knew what they did wasn't small-town-approved. Though they remained friends until high school was over, they remained so at a distance.

Colleen's refreshed seeing Allison after so long. When the two eventually lock eyes across the small yet crowded bar, Colleen's relieved to see happiness glowing from Allison's eyes. They come together in a hug then chat in between lulls of music and drunken banter, catching up on each other's lives in brief anecdotes.

Lord, I almost forgot, Allison says. I heard about Gerry Trelegan.

Yeah, he's missing.

No, they found his body over on the shore just near Culls Lookout.

Colleen can't believe what she's hearing. News typically travels fast around town. Nobody said anything to her about Gerry turning up dead.

Allison asks, You never heard?

I was at work all day.

I heard it on VOCM on the way into town.

Christ, Colleen says. That's the fourth man in six months.

What's everybody saying around town?

Colleen laughs and swigs her beer. She says, A lot of talk about the creature. You remember.

Oh my god. Bog Legs. You're joking.

Not for a second.

I can't believe people are still telling those stories.

Yes, maid. This place loves to talk.

Allison chuckles and leans over, butting her head playfully against Colleen's shoulder. Colleen smiles nervously.

So, you got any plans to get out of this place? Allison asks.

Honestly, I've been so caught up in the routine of working at the plant and on Dad's boat that I haven't thought much about it.

We used to talk about getting out all the time.

Allison looks Colleen in the eyes, smiling warmly. She sips her beer, holding eye contact. Colleen can't stop smiling, full of nervous energy. Allison scoots over in the booth closer to Colleen and throws an arm around her, squeezing their bodies together tightly for what Colleen imagined was minutes but, in reality, was only a handful of seconds.

I missed you, Colleen. I'm sorry we didn't keep hanging out in high school.

Sometimes people grow apart.

I guess when you get out of this place for a bit, you get a bit of perspective. You remember that time we were at that sleepover, and it was just the two of us up late and—

Colleen leans in further towards Allison to kiss her lips. Just as their lips nearly touch, Allison recoils with a disgust typically only reserved for the unexpected scent of death and decay. She looks around to see if there are any witnesses.

Colleen says, I'm sorry. I thought—

I know what you thought. What's wrong with you?

There's nothing wrong with me, Colleen says. She stands up from their table defiantly, though without any thought as to what she was going to do next.

We're not kids anymore, Colleen. Grown women don't do this kind of shit.

Colleen's stunned; not by the rejection, but by how she's being rejected.

And you *reek*, Colleen. Even if I was a lesbo, I wouldn't wanna make out with someone who stinks like the caplin's rolling in.

Listen, you don't have to be a bitch, Colleen says. Her voice cracks. She feels tears welling. Her throat goes thick; she worries she may choke on a mix of anger and embarrassment.

Allison gets up from the table. She puts on her jean jacket, all the while looking down at Colleen, lording above her with the same look on her face as a human looking down upon a bug they've just crushed.

Call me a bitch again and I'll tell everybody around here about you, Allison says.

The words are a knife blade running up Colleen's spine—their danger tingles along the surface, their sharpness threatening to push deeper and leave awful wounds. Allison says nothing and walks out through a crowd of people to leave the bar. Colleen's left cold and alone and scared. She looks around in disbelief that nobody even saw what happened. Everyone's too involved in their own Friday night to have noticed two women talking closely in a corner of a crowded little bar. Colleen finishes her beer and the beer Allison left behind then pops a cigarette in her mouth, lights it, and shuffles her way out into the humid May night in a series of drunk stumbles.

Early rays of sunlight break through Colleen's eyelids. She gradually slips out of her drunken dreams. She doesn't know where she is immediately, then sees a canopy of trees above her that almost block out the sun entirely except for a scattered ray. For a second, she thinks the canopy is her eyelids. Everything else drains away when Colleen sits up to look around more and sees what can't be anything other than the creature everybody calls Bog Legs. There the thing is, standing atop its spindly crustacean legs, its torso hunched and slimy, lurking quietly in the shadows cast beneath the canopy. Colleen's startled but doesn't make any noise. She pulls herself up off the ground, though right away feels the lingering effects of her previous night's bender and nearly throws up. The creature doesn't move, it just keeps watching.

What do you want? Colleen says.

The creature stares out of the shadows, its head slightly tilted to one side so that one big, wet fishlike eye can have a look over Colleen. It makes no noise, except for the inhale-exhale of its gilled neck puffing in and out.

Are you going to hurt me?

This question appears to hurt the creature, whose large, fishy eyes beam with an undeniable sadness. It steps forward a bit out of the shadows. Some thin sunlight peeking through the canopy reveals the rest of its body to Colleen, who's stunned to see that all the stories were, more or less, true.

The creature says, I would never hurt *you*.

Colleen's speechless, in spite of all the things she's dying to say.

Don't be scared of me.

I'm actually just surprised at your voice—that you speak English, says Colleen.

Many years I've listened to the people in their boats, how they talk to each other. It took me a long time. But I learned.

Colleen's brain is moving too fast for her to keep any of her thoughts straight.

The creature says, Are you okay?

Yeah, I'm just hungover.

The creature tilts its head silently.

Oh, Colleen says. Hungover. Um, it's like...do you know what beer is?

Bear?

No, not the animal. It's a drink. Buh-ee-rrr.

Colleen makes a drinking motion and a slurp sound.

Ah, yes, drink, the creature says.

Anyway, beer's not that good for you. At least not the morning after.

You looked sick last night.

I probably was, I can't remember much.

The creature says, I pulled you off the rocks. You were falling. And there were, men.

Men?

Watching you. Talking about where to take you.

This makes Colleen's bones feel as heavy as concrete.

I threw rocks and the men thought there was something in the woods, the creature says. Gave me time to pull you here. Safe.

Colleen fills with a warmth she's never known. The creature's strange voice saying *safe* echoes in her body, from her ears to her heart.

Thank you so much, Colleen says.

Nobody ever talks to me.

This makes Colleen sad. She says, I think people are afraid of you.

You don't look afraid anymore.

Well, you've been very sweet to me. Who knows what could've happened last night if you weren't there.

Men are bad, says the creature. Always hurting—on land, in ocean.

Oh, I know *all* about men.

Used to try to talk to people when I first came here, long years ago. But men attacked.

The creature shows Colleen a long scar on its back—a thick, white line.

My god, Colleen says. I'm so sorry.

No family left. All gone. Killed by men.

Men kill a lot of things.

Colleen suddenly realizes she's forgotten the time. She checks her watch: 6 am.

Oh, for the love of—I'm late, I have to go help my dad.

The creature says, Please be safe. Don't drink the beer.

Colleen smiles and giggles as she brushes her clothes off. She says, Maybe we could see each other again.

Something inside the creature lights up. Its big, gelatinous eyes are wide and bright.

Will you be around later when I get off work this evening?

Yes, the creature says. I am here. Maybe swimming.

Colleen instinctively goes to the creature and puts her arms around it for a hug. The creature puts its clawed arms around her, too. They share a brief squeeze then Colleen runs out towards a break in the trees leading to the shore. She turns back to the creature.

Colleen says, I forgot to ask your name.

Name?

Mine's Colleen.

No name. I'm just me.

Colleen finds the creature's response adorable. She says, I like that. I'll be back to see you later.

Colleen steps through the treeline. The creature waves a claw as its new friend disappears into the blinding daylight beyond the forest.

Colleen turns up late at the plant in a mix of hangover and dreams. She can't quite believe she met the creature. She wonders if she might've conjured up a vision of ole Bog Legs from the churning pains in her gut from all the booze last night. She can't deny there was a strange connection between them. Even the way she resists calling it Bog Legs, feeling that the name insults the creature—*feelings* for the creature. She tries not to think so much about it, nor the way her own warm flesh felt pressed against its slick, firm exterior. She finds herself curious if the creature's outer bits are a shell, or perhaps a very thick skin. She stops working altogether, her head swimming in new ideas she could've never imagined before this morning. One of her coworkers, Patsy Brinson, notices Colleen standing still and silent.

You okay, Col? says Patsy.

Oh, lord. Sorry.

Colleen jumps back into her work.

No worries, love. Thought you was looking rough.

Don't be talking, Pats. I barely made it in.

I saw you storm out the bar last night.

Ugh. What a state.

Colleen's face brightens.

Can you keep a secret? Colleen says.

Patsy looks around and nods.

Colleen says, I seen the thing this morning—the creature.

Go on, b'y.

I'm serious. And it sp—

Hey, b'ys. Colleen caught a look of Bog Legs this morning.

Everyone comes flocking like gulls descending upon a greasy bag of stadium fries, all chirping and asking their own questions in a symphony of cackling.

For God's sake, Colleen says.

You chase it away or what? says one of the men.

No, I never.

Another man says, I would've smashed it to bits.

A couple of the women laugh.

I'd kill that if I ever seen it, the first man says. Take me .22 and put it right to that fishy ole head, then *BANG!*

Colleen's horrified. She can't get a word in amongst the chatter of violence and death, each of the men proposing a new, terrible way they'd murder the creature. She lets them carry on and slinks into the background of the conversation. She goes back to work, as the conversation of cruelty continues in the background.

As the sun's light becomes slippery and leaks into darkness, Colleen leaves the fish plant and walks over past the bar to the woods where she left the creature early that morning. She has a flashlight with her from the plant and uses it to guide herself through the trees. She looks around a while, beginning to think maybe the creature was too suspicious of her—a human—to meet again. No sooner does the thought enter her mind when the creature comes barging through an opening in the trees and surprises Colleen, whose smile rips through the dark suddenly.

Really glad to see you, Colleen says.

I see *you*.

Colleen laughs. The creature makes a strange noise that Colleen assumes is a laugh since it also shuffles around in a half circle, which can only be described as a happy motion. It doesn't last long. Colleen remembers the people at the plant and all the awful things they talked about doing to the poor creature.

I'm worried for you, Colleen says. The people I work with want to hurt you.

Hurt me?

They think you're bad.

Those men I killed were bad.

Colleen says, So, you *did* kill them.

They were doing… bad things.

Colleen doesn't doubt the creature. Something about its demeanour says only calmness and honesty.

I don't want you to get hurt, Colleen says. Maybe you should find somewhere else to go.

This wounds the creature visibly, and Colleen sees it. The creature's eyes become less like those of a fish and more like those of a dog: big, wet, sad.

The creature says, You want me to leave.

I didn't mean that.

You hate, like the men.

I do not hate you. I thought about you all day.

The creature's eyes change—they become tender with a longing glow. It says, What did you think about me?

Well, I thought about your body.

Colleen points at the creature's body. The creature lifts its arms up, almost like it's showing off, modelling its figure. Colleen turns off her flashlight and reaches out, putting her soft, warm palm against the creature's stomach. She looks into the creature's eye facing her as she touches, making sure it's fine. The creature's eye blinks slowly and lovingly. Its mouth forms what must be a smile; that's how it looks to Colleen. And then, Colleen feels the creature's stomach shift. She looks down to see the stomach open like a wide mouth, running up and behind the creature's legs. She looks back to the creature's eye, her own eyes surprised.

You can touch, says the creature.

Colleen slowly moves her hand inside the creature's stomach opening. The creature lets out a deep, beautiful sigh, as Colleen feels its stomach muscles contract. The creature pulls Colleen in tightly, and Colleen continues to touch the creature gently, now with both hands. In the quiet dark of that little patch of forest, they become one.

The Atlantic is choppy the next morning, so after hauling in a decent bit of fish Colleen and her father head back to the wharfs. The sky is dark grey. The clouds are bloated and ready to piss everywhere. Earlier in the morning, still floating from her time in the woods last night, Colleen was only thinking of being with the creature, recalling the beautiful scene of their bodies wrapped up in each other under sparse moonlight dribbling through the forest's canopy. Now, as the waves clap and spray, and thunder starts to roll far off in the distance, everything feels bleak to Colleen. To make matters worse, Colleen can barely work on gutting fish for her father. Each cut, every pull of guts, all the splashes and splats of gore that come along with ripping out a fish's insides revolt Colleen. She remembers being close with the creature, her hand within its stomach opening. She remembers feeling the vibrant and erotic life inside the creature. And it pains her to tear everything out of those fish. She's never once questioned the work she does, but everything changed last night. And it won't ever be the same again.

Later that day, Colleen can't stop thinking all the same things while she works on the line at the plant. All the cracking of carcasses, the gutting of fish, the slight crunchy pop of different sea life's eyes that you can't hear above the machinery but feel even through the gloves everyone has to wear; it becomes a grisly orchestra that rattles in the depths of Colleen's soul. It's all too much to take, so Colleen tells her supervisor she needs to leave, then she nearly runs out of the plant so that all those cruel sounds of fish and crustacean murder don't deafen her.

Colleen wears away the day at the bar and soon it's nighttime. Others start to crowd the bar like usual. Colleen decides to leave and hopefully avoid any coworkers, or even her supervisor, questioning why she left work early just to hang off the end of the bar sucking on bottle after bottle of Dominion Ale. She slips out of the bar and into the humid air outside. She strolls along the shore with a meagre buzz from her day drinking. The cool night air feels good. But feeling good doesn't last long for Colleen. She can only think of all the violence she and everyone else inflict upon the sea and all its inhabitants. She hasn't stopped thinking of the creature for the past couple of days, ever since they first met. She wants so badly to protect the creature. The thoughts start to pull at Colleen like a puppeteer with its puppet's strings, and before Colleen's brain recognizes the body moving, she's sprinting up past the wharfs and across to the forest to that special place she and the creature share once more.

Once Colleen makes it into the forest canopy, she starts to call out.

Where are you?

Colleen doesn't even know what to call the creature.

Please, Colleen says. I want us both to get out of here. We can't stay here anymore.

Colleen hears splashing and sloshing, that familiar sound alerting her to the creature's presence. She rushes out of the trees towards the noise, and she watches the creature emerge from the waves. Her eyes are full of love. She feels lucky to witness and know this creature. Colleen thinks about how the existential lottery of birth and the long historical reach of time, along with evolution, collided to allow her and the creature to live at the same time, to come together in the same place, to fall into each other's arms and claws.

When the creature makes it up over the rocks, it hugs Colleen close, and then Colleen pulls them both back in through the trees so they're safe from view. They hug. Colleen kisses the creature's face and its wide, strange lips.

We have to leave this town, Colleen says.

Go where?

Anywhere. Me and you.

You would leave your family?

Colleen says, Dad will understand. He knows I don't belong here. Never did.

I can go anywhere. But you need a home.

We could make a home. Somewhere.

The creature's eyes are big and bright and full of love, just like Colleen's smaller yet no less shining eyes.

I will go, the creature says. When?

Maybe tonight. I just need to say goodbye to my dad.

I know many words already, but I don't know how to say what's inside me right now.

Does it make you feel, warm?

Yes. My blood is cold, but my heart is warm.

The creature and Colleen hug again. They kiss. And a branch snaps under a foot, startling the pair of unexpected lovers. The creature and Colleen turn, noticing a man standing near the edge of the trees. Colleen recognizes him from the plant.

You freak, the man says.

Con—what are you doing here? Colleen's voice shakes out of her throat.

Watching you and this goddamn monster. Colleen and Bog Legs making out in the woods. God almighty.

The creature says, You go away. Now.

It speaks, says Con. What else are ye two doing out here now?

Don't say a word to anyone, Con. Don't. They'll kill her.

Her? Oh, my. Figures you'd be after anything with a gash.

What did you just say to me?

You heard me, Con says. We all knows about you.

The revelation nearly knocks Colleen over.

The creature says, Stay away from her.

I heard enough from you.

As Con speaks, he reaches behind his back and pulls his rifle around into his hands. He cocks the rifle, then points it right towards the creature, who recognizes it as a weapon and moves behind a tree, though its body is too big to stay hidden.

Don't do this, Colleen says. You don't have to.

This goddamn thing you took as a lover *killed* people,

Colleen. You're both freaks.

While Con turns his head to Colleen, he doesn't notice the creature creep closer. He goes on yelling at Colleen. In the middle of a sentence, as Con opens his mouth to scream a bit more, his voice goes silent. It takes even Con several moments before his brain understands his body's predicament. Con drops his rifle and his eyes look around in panic. The creature stands back alongside Colleen and they watch a dribble of blood leak from a thin, jagged line stretching across Con's neck flesh. Con's body eventually topples over as blood squirts from his wound. Colleen and the creature both stand over the corpse, neither of them making a sound.

The creature and Colleen manage to get the corpse into the water after some effort, but it does nothing to settle Colleen down. She's more nervous by the second. And the creature can tell just from Colleen's body language that things aren't going well.

Colleen, talk to me.

My life has changed so much in just a few days. Now, this.

That man wanted to hurt. He hurt me with his gun.

I'm part of this, though. I could go to jail.

The creature doesn't understand. Then it dawns on Colleen that her life has become a strange fairy tale of some kind, a twisted folk story that people will tell for years. She's overwhelmed to the point she feels she might burst out of her flesh. So, she starts to run. It startles the creature, but it doesn't chase after Colleen, letting her go.

It gets up after a moment and tries to give chase, except it never evolved to run on land, and soon it loses complete sight of Colleen. But the creature keeps going.

Off in the woods somewhere ahead of the creature, Colleen picks up speed. She still feels all those feelings that first rushed into her when she and the creature met, when they held each other in that quiet place amongst the trees. It's a fear of all the consequences—not just for what happened to Con, but for being outed as someone whose love and lust go beyond the boundaries of what others can understand in a small town. Colleen doesn't want to abandon the creature, yet she can't keep herself from running.

The air rushes hard and fast into Colleen's face as she feels her body lift from the ground into the air, only seconds before her body twists in midair and her weight pulls back down where she crashes into the rocks on the beach. If there were anybody around to witness Colleen's fall, they probably would've assumed that she died on impact, as her face landed first, then her body crumpled over top of itself and sank down with a rattling wheeze like a flesh-and-bone accordion.

By the time Colleen comes back to consciousness and manages to make it back home, it's nearly eleven o'clock, and the worst has happened: Con's body was discovered. Cops already made rounds to several people who work at the plant, according to Colleen's father. Briefly, Colleen's stuck in silence, even her body incapable of movement. Kevin stares at his daughter. He sees how bad she's banged up.

Honey, what happened to your face?

Colleen fades away a moment, concussed from her fall, except some thoughts cut through the fog. *What are the cops going to do? Sure, you saw Con die, but even if you confessed what you actually saw, they're not about to believe that the creature, or any other so-called mythical creature, killed Con.* Colleen settles her nerves for the first time since she walked through the door.

I'm gonna take you up to the cop shop in Lewisporte shortly, Kevin says. First, we'll get a few Band-Aids to glue you back together.

Kevin heads to the bathroom. Colleen stands alone with only her thoughts about the creature and getting away. She loves her father so much. She doesn't want to leave him, but she needs to leave this place and so many of the people in it. She tries not to think about telling Kevin she's leaving, at least for a while. Soon, Colleen's relatively fixed up and they're heading to the truck. Inside, Kevin turns on the radio and music bursts out of the truck's damaged speakers. For at least what Colleen assumes is the next short while, she doesn't have to break her dad's heart. Neither of them realize that the creature caught up to Colleen, right before they were ready to leave, and it's lying in the truck's pan, covered in a tarp, along for the ride.

What you're saying is that you have no alibi, a mustached cop says.

No, I forgot to bring that.

Goddamn it, Colleen, Kevin says.

Sir, if you interrupt our conversation again, I'll ask you to leave.

Kevin nods reluctantly and sits back down in his chair against the wall.

People from the plant say you left work early, Ms. Cull. They also said they saw you at the bar after their shift was over. One of your coworkers claims you left as soon as they showed up. Where'd you go?

For a walk. On the shore. In the woods. Like I told you before.

The cop says, And you slipped, you fell, blah, blah.

The cop's attitude surprises Colleen, even if she's long known that police are cruel and silly people. She zones and thinks of the creature then of Con's corpse. *Don't feel bad for a man like that. He wouldn't feel bad if it was you they found with your mangled, open throat and your head beating off the rocks in the cove.*

The cop says, You expect me to believe that a woman with no alibi for where she was last night when Conrad Wells is estimated to have been murdered coincidentally turns up hours later with a bunch of wounds all over her hands and face from a fall?

Officer, I know you said I'm to be quiet, but you're going awful hard at her.

Mr. Cull, your daughter's our only suspect at the moment.

Kevin says, That don't mean she's guilty. Don't even mean she's the *best* suspect. So, if I was you, I'd let me and Colleen go, and we'll be back again when we gets a lawyer.

A knock on the door comes, which takes the cop up

from his seat and outside. While Colleen stares into the door, as if she'll somehow start to hear what's being said on the other side, Kevin looks at his daughter remembering the day she was born. Kevin doesn't care even if Colleen did what the cop's accusing her of, even if she did it a hundred times. He feels a panic set into his gut. He scans the room like he's going to become an action hero and break his daughter free. But he can't do anything. Seconds later, the cop and his tobacco-stained moustache return. He has a smug look smeared across his face.

Kevin says, We're going. You'll talk to us through a lawyer.

Your daughter will go nowhere, the cop says.

The cop turns to Colleen and looks down at her, eyes filled with disgust. He doesn't say another word. He opens the door, and in comes Allison with fear and hate in her eyes. Colleen knows what's coming before Allison ever parts her lips to speak.

The cop says, Tell Ms. Cull and her father what happened at the bar the other night.

Colleen tried to kiss me, Allison says. When I refused, she flipped out and tried to hit me. Other people saw it.

Colleen jumps from her chair and Kevin has to grab hold of her so she doesn't start swinging on Allison.

See, she's a crazy dyke.

Colleen thrashes in her father's arms, but Kevin keeps hold of her tight.

The cop says, We have enough circumstantial evidence to put you under arrest, Colleen.

While the cop officially arrests an angry, wild Colleen, Kevin sits back in his chair devastated. Allison slips out of the room, a wretched thing crawling back under its rock. Colleen soon stops fighting and lets the cop handcuff her. In the truck outside, the creature sits up and sheds the tarp after Allison comes out of the station's front door. It gets down out of the pan with its long, weird legs, and then makes its way up to the front of the police station. The place is relatively empty inside; outside is a ghost town. The creature stares in through the window where a cop stands at the front desk with his face down in papers. It opens the door and heads inside, though the front desk cop doesn't budge or look up.

How can I help you today? says the cop.

Colleen.

The cop looks up and jumps with fright. He tries to unbutton his holster. He fumbles at it but gets the gun out. He cocks the gun's hammer, then shoots a bullet at the creature. The bullet goes through the creature cleanly, near where its shoulder might be if it had human shoulders. The creature angrily raises a claw and chops the cop's head off right above the Adam's apple. Several spurts of blood shoot out of the cop's chopped trunk of a neck. His carcass collapses in a widening pool of blood so dark it looks like ancient red wine.

Colleen, Kevin, and the cop hear the commotion from the interrogation room.

Stay *right* here, the moustached cop says.

The cop pulls his gun and moves out of the interrogation room, leaving Kevin and a cuffed Colleen behind. He slowly moves out through the hallway, checking around corners, then comes all but face-to-face with the creature, who's now covered in blood.

Bog Legs!

The creature looks at the cop, tilting its head and leaning in to stare with one of its huge eyes. It scans the cop up and down, noticing the gun in his hand. It doesn't hesitate and raises its claw to chop off the cop's hand—the hand, still gripping the gun, hits the floor with a sickly thud. The cop screams and tries to run but he's in shock, as blood pours from the meaty stump at his wrist and splashes loudly against the tiled floor. He slips in a miniature creek of his own blood and slams against the floor with a crunch of bone. His skull splits. While the cop bellows a haunting moan and his legs start twitching, the creature steps over him and looks him in the eye with one of its own. It sees the fear—the same fear it has felt every time it comes across a human man, particularly one with a gun. After basking in the fear, the creature raises one of its lobster-like legs as high as it can, and it brings down its foot so that it strikes the cop at the temple. A squishy burst sends brain matter squirting up out of the cop's temple, now a fleshy cave through which the creature's slender leg stands. The creature pulls its leg from the hole in the cop's head like a syringe so the carcass flops against the floor with dead weight. Just as it does, the remaining two cops at the station come around the corner with their guns drawn.

The first cop says, Get your hands u—wait.

Neither of the cops can comprehend the large aquatic beast standing barely fifty feet away in front of their eyes. Quickly, the creature charges at them both. One cop puts a bullet into the creature's claw. But the creature barrels forward and tramples over the cop then in a single motion smashes his head with one of its claws. The other cop shoots several bullets and misses. He panics, dropping the gun. The creature turns and pins him against a wall, trapping him at the neck with its open claw.

I will grow back, the creature says. But you are gone.

The creature effortlessly snips the last cop's head like a dandelion being popped from the stem. It stands there in silence amongst the blood and gore. Its chest heaves, letting a sigh that's part pain and part relief from the strenuous exercise. It only takes a moment to itself before going to look for Colleen.

I can't believe you're real, Kevin says.

The creature snips the cuffs off Colleen, who hugs it in return. Kevin's amazed at the whole scene.

You're real and you killed them fellas.

Dad, those men were bad. They weren't like you.

Kevin looks at the creature with angry eyes, but he sees the way Colleen stands next to it, how his daughter's eyes look at the creature, how his daughter's voice sounds defending it.

I am allowed to live, says the creature. I only protect myself, this place.

The sound of the creature's voice makes Kevin feel something he's never felt before, a soft and warm feeling from the bottom of his heart.

Kevin says, Of course you are.

Dad, I wanted to tell you this before, but…I'm leaving. *We're* leaving.

Kevin doesn't need any further explanation. His face starts to quiver and tears unleash down his face.

It's nothing to do with you. I just have to get away.

I have to go and be who I want to be and go wherever I need to go to be the woman I've always been inside.

Kevin's body shakes as he cries. Colleen goes to him and hugs him close. She and her father stand quietly crying together. The creature soon goes to them, wrapping its clawed arms around them to embrace them together, comforting the father and daughter while they say goodbye.

Many in Comfort Cove looked at what Colleen did as the fire that lit the kindling of a terrible tragedy involving the loss of precious lives and still do. Just as many, if not more, eventually saw what Colleen did as the necessary steps she had to take to free herself from the shackles that the town, and even other parts of the big, wide world out there, placed upon her. No matter what people think, wherever Colleen goes, at the side of the creature they call Bog Legs, she's now forever free.

10

"Is that story true?" Sarah asked, voice quavering slightly.

"Oh, they're all true," Barry whispered. His hand was on her shoulder again, but the sensation of it wasn't the feeling from pressure on a tender bruise she expected, it burned. Yet, she could do nothing about it. Her body wouldn't let her flinch against the pain.

They walked together, away from the exhibit.

And, some dim part of her realized, away from the group. "Why are we—"

"All stories are true, in their own way, you know," he interrupted. "All of them. There's some truth to all of them, and that truth—why, that truth can *feed* one. One cannot subsist on bread alone as Matthew said in the Good Book, my child. But I have found that one *can* subsist on *stories*."

They were in a new room now with new artifacts. None of these were real, she recognized. They, more than anything else throughout the place, were props.

These were displays, tributes to Newfoundland authors.

One was a picture of Percy Janes and the typewriter

he used, but it could not have been the actual one he used. It was a facsimile; there was an indefinable lack of verisimilitude that created a weird sort of uncanny valley for the inanimate object.

"How…" she started but did not finish.

"I tell you, all stories, my dear, they feed the soul. All of them."

He gripped both of her shoulders. She felt his breath on the back of her neck again. When had he gotten behind her?

"Even the stories of those with less to tell. Even the stories of the *young*." He smacked his lips. They were so that she felt the impact from the air on her flesh sending the hair on her neck straight up as the skin broke into gooseflesh.

She was trying to get her breath, to say something, but he barreled on.

Before she could find the words to address one point, he had moved on to another.

"Sometimes, I think, when you devour the stories of the young, what you're actually taking are all the stories they have *yet* to tell. The young, they are so *ripe* with the experience they have not had yet. You say these things without saying them, the words lost between words, and you feast on those as well. You can engorge yourself on those stories. Stories within stories. Stories all the way down."

He paused.

"Do *you* have a story, Sarah?"

Sarah swallowed. Her lower lip quivered, then she raised her arm and pointed to the display of the typewriter. "What story does *that* tell?"

WRITER'S BLOCK
Nicole Little

The small, embossed nameplate is adhered to the wall at eye level next to the door.

"She was a famous writer; did you know that?" The porter nods at the placard, grinning at me, his many back molar fillings shining silver in his wide mouth. "She died here too …" He trails off and waggles his brows, trying to gage if I'm into the story or not.

I am already well aware of what happened in this room. I smile politely, wanting the exchange to be over.

"I've asked not to be disturbed," I remind the kid. I slip him a crisp fifty.

His eyes bulge. "You got it, my buddy." And then he's gone.

I close the door behind me and take a look at my accommodations for the next month. It's not much, but it's about what I expected for a cheap downtown hotel. It's clean at least.

I toss my suitcase on the bed and slide my laptop onto the small desk that's crammed beneath the window.

It's time to get to work.

I'm on a deadline. I've got a publisher and an editor so far up my ass…

This first draft is due at the end of the month. So far, I have nothing. That's fine though. It's better when I'm under pressure. It feeds the beast.

I order room service at seven: a salad and sparkling water. I chew methodically, not really tasting anything, just dutifully gnashing and swallowing. I put the dishes back on the tray and place it outside my door for collection.

The gold nameplate catches my eye as I turn to go back inside. I consider who might have placed it here. Family? Friends? The hotel owner hoping to make a quick buck, charging extra for the room where a local writer had written her most prolific work? A book that had turned out to be her last.

I open my laptop. From my carry-on, I remove a small velvet bag. From within it I take a stub of a black candle, matches, a velvet cloth, and a bundle of herbs.

From my luggage, I remove a chipped pottery bowl. I open a packet that holds a sterile lancet and prick my finger, wincing at the brief stab of pain. This is never my favourite part. I place the bundle of herbs in the bowl and liberally drip blood over the top. I hastily wrap a piece of gauze around the finger and then light the candle and turn the flame to the herbs. A sickly sweet aroma permeates the air. I inhale deeply and blink rapidly as my eyes water.

I chant the ancient words by rote. The laminated cheat

sheet in my wallet is something I no longer need—not my first rodeo.

The room grows hot. Sweat prickles my hairline and gathers in the short stubble on my upper lip. I keep up a constant low murmur.

A pressure builds in the room now, and my ears feel stuffed with cotton. Then, a shift in the atmosphere, an audible pop, and I feel a physical release, a fission down my spine—I gasp at the pleasure and open my eyes.

"Welcome." The single word is a husky, low rasp. The best I can manage at the moment.

The look of bewilderment is almost comical.

"What…am I doing…" she croaks, voice rusty from disuse.

I grin at the ghost in front of me. "You're going to help me write a book."

"So, this is how it's going to work," I explain conversationally. "I will let you in, I will relinquish just enough control to allow you to write, and then you'll be on your way, back to where you came from."

She tries to move but cannot. It's the binding spell.

"Let me go," she demands.

"No," I reply, "You must agree to my terms."

She stares at me. "What's in it for me?"

This is new.

"You get to write again, to have people read your work. You'll live on in your words."

"What if I don't want to?" She struggles against the corporeal bindings once again.

"Then I'll send you straight to hell."

"What makes you think I wasn't already there?" she asks. "But if you do...where will that leave you?"

She has me there, but I won't let on. "I'll just write it myself."

"Hmm. I don't think you will, or else why would I be here? Let me have a little bit of fun on this side of the sod again and I'll do as you ask. A few hours behind the steering wheel. I think that's a fair exchange."

I sigh but I nod. What harm could it do? She'll go for a walk, pick some flowers, have some wine.

The ghost smiles.

I take a step close and mutter a few more words to release the binding. I feel her slither inside my brain. Heat suffuses me; it's almost sensual. I hear her voice in my head.

"Oh my. You have some very dark thoughts up in here. Let's have a little fun, shall we?"

Then the lights go out.

A laugh awakens me. My head throbs. The sour taste of Irish whiskey coats my tongue. My nose burns and I know in an instant that liquor has not been my only indulgence this night.

I am in my hotel bed. The poor excuse for a curtain at the window does little to dispel the bright morning light that streams through it. I squint against it. Something heavy lies across my legs and I struggle out from beneath it.

It's a body.

A dead body.

I crawl back against the headboard in shock and revulsion, rubbing my eyes, hoping it's just a dream. But the bedsheets are soaked in blood. I am covered in dried red and crusted gore. I urge.

"What the fu..." It's all I can get out.

"Yeah, sorry about that," says the voice in my head. "I got a little carried away."

"A little..." I stare at the body. I think I might be in shock. "What the hell did you do?"

"I was having fun," she pouts. "I've been dead a long time, and I deserve to let loose."

"Deserve to...murder someone?" I ask.

"Well, maybe not that part," she admits. "I'm just not used to it in here yet, that's all."

"Yet?" I shout. "Get out."

I begin to chant the expelling charm.

Nothing happens.

"Oh yeah, about that." The voice has the decency to sound chagrined. "I snooped around the old noggin. Had to make a few changes, I'm afraid. I'm what you would call a free agent now."

My breath comes in gasps. I might pass out.

"Now," she says, "Shall we order food before or after we get rid of this?"

It's certainly not how I expected this day to go. A corpse, wrapped in a heavily stained bedsheet, is in the hotel bathtub, and I have yet to type a word.

The most bizarre form of writer's block I have ever

experienced.

"We need a really big suitcase," she suggests. "Soon. Before rigour sets in. Then, tonight, into the harbour with it."

She is suspiciously knowledgeable about what I have to do next. The size of the suitcase, how to contort the body. I throw up twice, but I do it. Funnily enough, no one bats an eye at a grown man talking to himself while dragging a suitcase down Water St.

Afterwards, I stand under the hottest water I can stand and use an entire bar of hotel soap plus the tiny bottle of shampoo. I beg her to shut herself away for a bit, to give me a modicum of privacy as I clean myself.

"I'm afraid that ship has already sailed, darling," she replies. She hums while I scrub.

I know I have messed up this time. It's always been so easy. The others I'd summoned had been confused at first of course, but they were more than happy to have one more published work. I always wrote a heartfelt dedication, thanking them for being my inspiration, my muse.

But this one. This one is different.

I dry myself and don comfortable clothes.

"Your turn!" Despite it all, I feel a little thrill at these words. "Let's get to work."

I sit at the desk; I feel her take control and suddenly my hands are not my own, but I am still aware. I see the words appear on the screen. Chapter after chapter, she is unstoppable. This is the best stuff I have ever written. My misgivings begin to melt away.

A car horn blares, and I startle back to reality. There is cold, wet asphalt beneath my feet. I'm not wearing shoes and there is a reusable bag crumpled in my hand—Dollarama. I toss it aside. Though I am drenched with rain, my throat is dry. I am somewhere along Duckworth, a short distance from the hotel. I pick up the pace.

The voice in my head is strangely silent.

I stumble past the front desk; the porter from when I checked in raises a hand in greeting, but I pretend not to see him. I step gratefully inside my room and close and lock the door behind me. I hit the wall switch. The room floods with light and it is then that I notice the dried brown crust embedded beneath and around my nails.

"Yeah, you might want to give those a good scrub."

She's back.

In fact, I don't think she ever left.

I decide I don't want to know what we've been up to tonight. Ignorance is bliss. I scour my body in the shower, taking care to get all the nooks and crannies. If I had bleach, I think I'd use it.

Clean (I hope), I sit in front of the laptop and wait.

"I'm not even sorry this time," she purrs.

I shiver in revulsion.

"Don't worry," she says in response to the movement. "You enjoyed it."

My fingers are already tapping away at the keyboard. I just let it happen.

The pattern repeats itself again and again. I sleep... at least I think I do. There are big chunks of time missing, times when I know she has taken over completely. I've lost weight. My hygiene is questionable at best. My facial hair is as long as it's ever been.

She makes sure to let me through when it's time to write though. I suppose she wants me to know she's holding up her end of the bargain.

In my lucid moments, I am wracked with anxiety. I think about the body in the suitcase, sunk to the bottom of St. John's Harbour. I think about the others (because I am sure there have been others). I think about what will happen when this book is done.

And we are getting close.

Another week goes by in a blur—the bits I can recall anyway.

Finally, it's done. My hands type "The End" with a flourish.

It's fantastic. I know it, she knows it. So, what happens next?

I must have spoken it out loud.

"I kinda like it in here," she says. "Might stick around."

"No."

"Oh, come on. This is better than any relationship I ever had when I was alive."

I don't know what to say to that. It's oddly relatable.

"We're good together," she insists. "I get you, you get me."

I think about the 80,000 words she's churned out for me since this whole thing started.

Maybe I can make this work.

I pick up the phone and dial the front desk. "Hello, this is room 140 and I would like to extend my stay."

11

"Oh, look at that, we lost our way," David said, speaking with a faux joviality that sounded actually quite hostile. He stepped into the room with Sarah and Barry in it, with Bernice in tow, his back turned to her. "We're so clumsy, you and me. We got lost from the group."

Barry stared at them for a long moment with narrowed, darkened eyes. Then he relented. "Yes," he said, finally. "Yes, you really must keep up."

Sarah pulled forward, released from his grasp. Her hands went to her shoulders, feeling the uneven landscape where he'd dented her flesh expecting blood but coming back dry. She shook, convulsed, like someone who has discovered they have been covered with spiders and continues to feel them even after they're gone.

Barry squinted. The staff, Erin and Sophia, entered behind David and Bernice. They formed a wall between the exhibits, and Barry went from one to the other. "Where are the others?" he asked, finally.

David narrowed his eyes at him. "I'm sure they'll be along," he said, making no attempt to hide his contempt. "You know how we are, the lot of us. We get to gabbing, lord knows where we get off to." He turned to Bernice. "Sure, even we got separated from the group, didn't we? We got to talking."

"Got to talking," Bernice nodded and inhaled as she spoke. "Tell me, David Hunter, if the whole group is made of only four and two of them leave, did you leave the group or did the group leave you?"

David clapped his hands. "That sounds like one of those mighty philosophical quandaries, doesn't it? Did you leave the group or did the group leave you? Is this glass half empty or half full? What is the sound of one hand clapping? All that stuff, we'll leave to the philosophers, don't you think?"

"I suppose we shall, David Hunter, I suppose we shall." Bernice turned her gaze, then, fully to Barry. "What say you then? Have you got a tale for me? A story for this old librarian, or are you only interested in the pups? I've read a lot in my time; I'd love to see what you might have for me."

Barry splayed his arms, suddenly a game-show presenter, and spoke.

JIMMY'S LITTLE HELPER
Kelley Power

Management told the newspapers they shut down Hotel Newfoundland that week in the summer of '66 because of flooding—not rats. Not big Norwegian browns with plump rumps and thick tails. Everyone knew the grandest hotel in St. John's did have more holes than a cheese grater, and those dockyard rodents did make their way up there from the harbour, and they did shimmy in for the food and heat the hotel offered. But to admit it and close the hotel because of it? Never.

Look, it wouldn't have been the truth anyway. Not like they could tell the real story; who'd believe it? Sure, I was there and, 60 years on, I have to look at the two finger stumps on my left hand to prove I didn't imagine the whole thing on a drug trip.

Nineteen sixty-six was a big year for me. I graduated high school. All my summers of Boy Scouts were behind me. Jenny Dwyer let me feel her up under her shirt on our first date. Father said I was ready to become "A Man," so he got me a job as junior custodian at Hotel Newfoundland. He was a concierge there and proud of it.

On my first day, I walked to work with him from our

place on Signal Hill. The whole time, he was breathing fire and brimstone telling me to keep my mouth shut, my chin up, and myself out of trouble with Mr. Jimmy Lush, head custodian.

"If Mr. Lush tells you to fish a turd out of a toilet like bobbing an apple out of a barrel, you do it," he said as we crossed the parking lot behind the hotel and took a turn around the corner toward a handleless steel door. My father rapped on it. A crack and rattle later and the door swung slowly open. It revealed a bear, somehow transported to the heart of the city and trapped inside this hotel. After a brief grinding click, a flame licked up from a lighter to reveal grey eyes set in a sunbaked face of creases and cracks and an outthrust jaw covered in black whisker stubble, lips holding tight to the cigarette he was lighting.

I must've made a sound—and I tell you straight, it was something between appreciation and apprehension, since I'd never seen a man this big in my life—because he and my father glanced at me with matching frowns.

"Bob," the man said, nodding to my father. "You're early."

My father took a step back and dragged me with him as the bear-man nudged the door wider and stepped outside, sucking a drag off his cigarette that burned half the stick.

"Big day today, Jimmy, with the CN people coming through," my father said, checking his watch. Canadian National Railway owned the hotel back then. Their hotel services people came every year to inspect the place and look for reasons to sell it. Or shut it down. Like Father said, it was a big day.

The bear, revealed to be Mr. Jimmy Lush, tilted his head as if confused, letting small curls of smoke leave his nostrils.

"Jimmy?" my father said, an edge of worry creeping into his voice. "CN? The inspection?"

Mr. Lush breathed out a giant cloud of smoke and the air around him vibrated when he unleashed a cackle. He stubbed out the half-smoke cigarette on the sole of his heavy brown work boot and clapped my father on the shoulder.

"Don't worry, Bobby. I got it under control." Nobody called my father Bobby, not even my mother. But my father didn't seem to mind. In fact, he sagged under the weight of that meaty paw and sighed in relief. "Probably even get to patch that pipe behind the coat room before they get here." He laughed again. I half expected him to ruffle my father's hair with his giant hand.

The steel door closed behind me and Mr. Lush, cutting off the sunlight. It took my eyes a minute to adjust to the dimness inside and spot the stairs leading down to the basement. Upstairs where my father was headed might have been a grand spectacle of mezzanines and barbers and travel agents and dining rooms, but the service floor was stark. Cinderblock walls, unpainted. Concrete floor, painted grey. Water dripped from the ceiling of pipes lining the central corridor. A couple of secondary hallways shot off the main hall, each lined with doors. Everywhere I looked, people in service uniforms or overalls were walking with a sense of urgency. An ant colony, buried beneath the ground, supporting the luxuriousness above.

Mr. Lush pointed out different areas and their uses as we passed open and closed doors. Too many for me to remember. Behind one door, I heard a scratching scurrying as we passed by. A mouse emerged halfway from under the door before it disappeared again, looking more like it was yanked in than crawled back. I jumped. Mr. Lush didn't seem to notice or hear the squeal or scratching that followed as he continued my tour of the hotel's underbelly.

"Laundry's in there," Mr. Lush said, pointing to a room filled with shelves of folded towels and sheets. A woman stood with her head down at a long table covered with linens in mixed stages of tidiness. She folded one towel after another like they were coming at her on an assembly line, not heaped in an untidy pile next to her. White canvas duffle-style bags were stacked in one corner. A second lady stood at the foot of that pile stuffing a long sheet or tablecloth into the top of another canvas bag before pulling the drawcord tight and tossing it on top of the pile. The tumble-thump of a commercial-sized washing machine and dryer underscored the sweaty industry in the room.

We took a turn after the laundry room down another hallway, and Mr. Lush stopped outside a wooden door with "Custodian" painted on it in curving blue letters. He led me into a small office and sat at a desk lit by a single lamp. A floor-to-ceiling cage was at the back of his office, securing a shadowy storage room with scant shapes of shelves, what could be buckets on the floor, and something larger in the middle, too dark to make it out.

"Your father says you aren't afraid to get your hands dirty. But you look like a hippy. Are you a hippy, kid?" Mr. Lush sized me up as he said it. His frown made clear he wasn't a fan of how my hair came down into my eyes, or my untucked shirt, or the flared bottom of my jeans. He turned his chair without waiting for my answer and riffled through a cupboard.

"No, sir," I said, crushing the urge to salute him. Jimmy's not to be taken lightly, my father had told me. Tough, but fair.

He produced a pair of blue overalls. His frown turned full scowl as I struggled to pull the legs on over my work boots (I know, a rookie mistake), no doubt garnering from my thin frame that I wasn't much of a worker. But I was fit. I worked two paper routes on my bike and played hockey on the ponds all winter. I had stamina. And I was wiry.

"I'll plunge a toilet, empty the rat traps, whatever you need me to do," I said, working my arms into the sleeves of the overalls.

Mr. Lush leaned toward me. "Rats are the one thing you won't have to worry about here, my boy." He slapped his knees, then thumbed over his shoulder toward the supply cage. "Jimmy's little liquid helper took care of that."

I looked in the cage again, this time able to make out that the large dark shape was a green metal barrel. 40 gallons for sure. "In the barrel?" I asked.

He nodded. "The magic mix! Sprayed it around two weeks ago, haven't seen a rat since. You want something done right, leave it to the army."

"You're in the army?"

"For God's sake! Your father said you were smart. I *bought* it from the army. Well, from a guy who bought it from the army. Worked just like he said it would. Poof! Rats-be-gone."

I was going to tell him about the mouse and the scratching I'd heard earlier but pressed my lips shut. He seemed really pleased with himself and it was a bad idea to piss off your boss with unwanted news on your first day of work.

"Well," he slapped his knees again. "I've got all my guys working on the last bits of tidying up upstairs before the CN crowd come this afternoon. I'm short down here today. That'll be your place. In the basement." He turned back to his desk and flipped up a few papers clamped to a clipboard. "Here you go. Clogged floor drain in the laundry room. Good job for your tiny little fingers." He wiggled his corndog-sized digits at me as he said it.

"Got a pair of gloves? Or a plunger?"

He smiled. "Plunger broke. All the gloves went to the kitchen crowd this morning." He turned back to his paperwork. "Come back when you're done. I'll have something else for you."

Clearly dismissed, I retraced my steps up the hallway, buttoning up my overalls, and followed the thickening scent of detergent until I was back at the hazy entrance to the laundry. I don't know how the women worked in here. I'd barely crossed the threshold and sweat was already gathering in my hairline.

The towel-folder glanced up.

"You Bob's youngster?" She waved me over. "Don't be shy, won't help you down here. I'm Marge. Iris! Bob's fella." Iris was still stuffing canvas bags at the back of the room but glanced up with a wave before getting back to it. "You don't have much of your father in you. More like your mother. You here for the floor drain? Over there, near the sink."

She kept stacking neat squares of towels while she talked. All business, Marge. It was easier for me to nod than try to break into her string of words.

"Drain cover's been gone for two weeks. I told Jimmy this would happen. Face cloth probably jammed right in it. Broke off the plunger trying to get it out."

The puddle had pooled in a slight depression in the floor and was covered in brown foamy film. I dragged the toe of my boot across the surface to break the film and find the drain, but the water was dense grey beneath. I rolled up my sleeves and squat down, wishing my father had gotten me a job as a bellboy instead.

My fingers felt slippery the second I touched the water. The drain opening, when I found it, was slick and gummy. I reached in, felt a tangle of something, and pulled. A clump of hair and thread came out of the pool, dripping and slimy. It smelled like mouldy wool.

"Whoo! Biggest one yet!" Marge chuckled.

The clump hit the tile floor with a wet smack as I flicked it off my fingers. The drain burped a large air bubble to the surface of the puddle, but the water level stayed the same.

I got four fingers into the drain on my second try and couldn't feel anything. I shifted my weight and curled my thumb under so I could wedge my whole hand down. If this didn't work, I'd have to ask Jimmy for a pole, or a hook. The scummy sides of the drainpipe worked in my favour, allowing me to slide my hand past my wrist with little effort. I felt another obstruction with the very tip of my middle finger. I strained and shifted again so I was hovering over the puddle, my weight balanced on the balls of my feet and my free hand, palm flat on the tile. I got another inch or so down and got enough room to make a small claw with my bunched fingers and felt them sink into a jelly-like mass. A dry heave rose from my throat without warning.

"Stop—" Iris started but was cut off by her own barking yak.

Marge cackled like a teasing crow.

I heaved again. Iris replied with another. Call and response gone horribly wrong. Oh God. My gag reflex was strong; if she kept going, I'd puke. Had to finish.

My fingers gripped the soft mass in the drain and met something firm enough to pull on. I swallowed another dry heave and yanked hard. My hand came out of the hole and I sat back on my heels. The dour water bubbled and belched, and the drain gave a feeble gurgle. Finally, a whirlpool formed as the puddle started its journey down the unplugged drain.

So busy was I congratulating myself as I stared into the spinning water, I forgot I had a handful of muck until Marge said, "Haven't seen *that* before."

Her tone was enough to make me snap open my fingers and let "that" drop to the floor. Marge came over for a closer look. The pink gooey mass was spiked with white prickles and trailed a tangled end of scraggly rope.

"Wouldn't have guessed that," Marge said. "Arse-end

of a rat by the looks of it. Tail's thick as my thumb! And...
what's that on it? Blisters or..."

I blinked hard and looked closely. What I'd thought
were white prickles were in fact the ends of bones—a
spine for sure, maybe a few ribs. And Marge was right:
the rope was indeed a rat tail, but with spots of raw red
bubbled flesh. One bubble was the size of a marble, and
I'd swear a black rat eye, complete with eyelashes, was
growing on it.

When I heaved this time, there was no keeping it
down. It went straight into the dwindling puddle of grey
water, where the tiny chunks of my bacon-and-eggs break
fast swirled down the unclogged drain just as Iris started
yacking up on the other side of the room.

"Don't exactly have an iron gut, do you?"

Marge had taken Iris off to get a cup of tea; it was
just me left to explain to Mr. Lush. He was poking the
goopy rat arse with the tip of a pencil he'd pulled from the
breast pocket of his overalls, no sign he was bothered by
the smell of rancid rodent. An empty salt beef bucket and
shovel were on the floor at his feet.

"When I was younger than you, I found my dead cat
in the woods behind the house, crawling with maggots.
Picked her up like that with my bare hands and buried
her, then went home for turkey soup. With rice."

"Gold star for Jimmy," I said under my breath. I stood
a yard away, out of smell range. I had washed my hands in
the harshest detergent Marge could provide. It might've
even been bleach because my skin was on fire. It wasn't

enough—I could still feel the slick corpse on my finger-tips.

"Well," he said, stabbing a couple of the tail bubbles with the tip of the pencil. They were soft but didn't burst. He moved the pencil tip to the one with the eye and I looked away. "Hmph." When I thought it was safe to look again, I saw him wipe the tip of the pencil off in the leg of his overalls, leaving a glistening slug trail behind. "It's a rat. But can't say I've seen a tail like that before."

"Maybe your new rat poison burned it?" I asked.

Mr. Lush rubbed his stubbled chin. "Maybe."

Marge came back into the room at that moment. "Rat poison?" she said, squaring up to her folding table again. "Weed killer, you mean. I told you that stuff was use-less."

"Mind your own business," Mr. Lush replied. "Have you seen a rat down here since I put it out?"

Marge raised her eyebrows and tipped her chin at the gooey mass on the floor.

Mr. Lush huffed and shook his head. "Yeah, before that. Because I haven't heard a peep out of you about it in two weeks. Because they're gone. Because I won."

As the back and forth continued, it was clear I'd be-come part of a long-standing struggle over the rat popu-lation in the hotel. It was weird to know that just above, while the fancy people were having tiny cucumber sand-wiches, wearing their silk dresses and tailored suits, a rat war was going on in the basement.

"Do they ever get upstairs?"

Mr. Lush and Marge stopped mid-argument to look at me.

"What?" he said.

"The rats. Do they ever get upstairs? Like in the kitchen or the lobby." Or in a bed.

Marge blessed herself and Mr. Lush pointed a finger in my direction. "Don't even think such a thing. And you with your father up there today trying to make everything perfect for the inspection today. You trying to jinx it?"

I put my hands up to ward off the onslaught. "Ok, ok. Jeez. It's just, this one's dead, right? But…" I took a breath. "Earlier, I heard some scratching and squeaking behind one of the doors. There was a mouse, but seemed like something bigger—"

"Goddammit!" he thundered. "Why didn't you say something? Scoop up that thing and come with me." He clomped out. I picked up the shovel and scraped the metal spade across the tile to collect the rat-thing. When it hit the bottom of the beef bucket, it jiggled like the fruit-in-Jello Mom gave us after Sunday dinner. I ignored the revolt in my stomach and hustled out, catching the last of Mr. Lush's tirade: "…said it could take up to a month to get them all. Always a straggler, right?"

I shuffled quietly behind him, certain the question wasn't meant for me.

He flung open his office door and fumbled with a set of keys hung at his waist.

"Leave that there." He nodded at the bucket of decay I was holding. I dropped it outside the door and leaned the shovel on the wall next to it.

"Shouldn't I dump it in the garbage or something?" I said to the uninterested oxygen in the room.

Mr. Lush stomped toward the supply cage, unlocked

it and threw open the door. He pulled the cord on a single naked bulb in the middle of the room. The matte green barrel I'd seen earlier stood apart from the other supplies, like nothing else in the room wanted to be near it. The thick orange stripe around the middle of the drum showed starkly against the green. Mr. Lush grabbed two sides of the barrel's lid and tilted the whole thing side to side, a move I'd seen my uncle do a million times with oil drums at his garage to see how full they were.

"Plenty left," Mr. Lush said. "We'll go round two. And three. Ten. Whatever it takes." He removed the plug from the large hole in the lid and fumbled around on a shelf behind him. A faint astringent smell reached my nose.

"What is it?"

"I told you: rat killer."

The tilting barrel gave me a view of words on the lid in yellow paint. Most of it was either rubbed off or a collection of letters and numbers that meant nothing to me. I could make out one word. "It says herbicide on the top."

"Yeah, the guy I bought it from said they used it to kill off trees and shrubs around the roads and powerlines at that army base up on Red Cliff. Made the leaves fall right off. But he said it wiped out the rats and mice and birds, too. Can't get this over the counter locally, if you know what I mean. Soaked every room down here in it. No stone left unturned. Best part, they seem to crawl away and die. Never did find a dead rat here. Just gone."

Turning back from the shelf, he laid a metal pump sprayer on the floor and unscrewed its top. Down went a tube through the barrel's hole. He sucked the other end of the tube to get the flow going. I'd done the same many times to siphon gas out of my father's car for my Honda minibike. He gurgled and spat to the side as he transferred that end of the hose into the empty pump sprayer. Clear liquid flowed into the bottle.

"You, ah, don't mind getting that into your mouth?" I had growing doubts about Mr. Lush's approach to rat warfare.

"Well, you know, the Yanks were probably going to throw it all into the ocean anyway when they closed the base, like they did with the trucks and pots and pans and anything else they didn't want to cart away, so how bad can it be? Just bad enough to kill a few critters and limb out a few trees. You hippies today, all afraid of the chemical boogieman. Sure, when I was your age, I delivered coal all around the city. Was covered in coal dust at the end of the day. In ears, my eyes. Breathed it in, ate it. Don't see anything wrong with me, do you?"

His rant continued in this vein until he was interrupted by a hollow thud and sharp crack of metal on concrete in the hall outside the office. Mr. Lush started and jerked the hose out of the pump sprayer. The acrid chemical spilled over the floor, his boots and his pant legs.

I backpedalled from the spreading poison toward the doorway and poked my head out. I had a second to notice the beef bucket I'd left there had tipped over and the shovel was on the floor next to it. But only a second. Because my eye was drawn right after that to the sight of the gory, ass-end of the rat I'd pulled out of the drain being dragged up the hallway by a convulsing mass of pink flesh peppered with tufts of brown hair.

Have you ever seen a naked mole rat? That's the best

real-world animal I could compare this thing to. I'd come across an article about it when I was scouring the pages of my parents' *National Geographics* for pics of naked boobies. These rats have wrinkled hairless pink skin and featureless faces, except for two sets of enormous yellow teeth sticking out of the mouth. If this thing in the hallway didn't have patches of fur—and wasn't the size of a cat—you'd swear it was a naked mole rat dragging that goopy rodent corpse up the hall. I guess the skin was different, too. It was more mottled, like it had been burned, but still saggy; it rippled with every tug it made on its dinner.

"Here and carry this," Mr. Lush said from behind me.

"Mr. Lush."

"Jesus, here!" He was close enough to look over my shoulder, holding the pump sprayer out for me to take. I pointed up the hall. "What in the jittering Christ?" he boomed.

The flesh creature froze. It dropped its food and raised its head. Its face was swollen and disfigured so that it was impossible to know if it had eyes, or if they were just lost inside one of the fleshy folds. Its nose (probably a nose, because it didn't have two nostrils, just one pea-sized hole) twitched.

Mr. Lush snatched the shovel from the floor and took off down the hall with a war cry. The creature let loose a rumbling growl. It reared up on its hind legs, back hunched, extending its front legs with long ragged claws. The first swing of the shovel missed the creature by more than a foot when the animal swiftly darted to the side. The clang of metal-on-concrete rattled in the inside of my skull. As quick as the shovel was down, it was up again for a second attempt. The mole-rat thing dodged again, this time darting between Mr. Lush's legs. It rose to its full height and, quick as a cobra strike, sank its yellowed fangs into the back of the custodian's thigh, and sprang away.

Mr. Lush's roar was pure rage. The hallway vibrated with it. The shovel fell to the floor as his hands clamped on his thigh. Blood squeezed between his fingers. By this time heads were poking out of open doorways, but they all retracted like turtles into shells when the creature tore down the hall. It took a corner and was out of sight.

A woman in a maid's uniform rushed up to us and helped me get Mr. Lush to the chair in his office. A small trail of blood specked the floor behind us.

"Goddamn thing probably gave me rabies," he said.

Seeing what bit him, I figured rabies was the least of his infection concerns.

He put his finger in the coin-sized hole in his overalls and tore it open enough to see the flap of skin hanging off the back of his thigh. Blood flowed out of it, making an ever-increasing pool under the chair.

Finally, a job I could do right! I went into Boy Scouts mode. Ignoring the maid's fluttering hands and Mr. Lush's protests and questions, I gathered clean rags and a bottle of isopropyl alcohol from the nearby supply shelves. I tore the rags into long strips. Mr. Lush was rambling by the time I'd cleaned and bound his wound; his skin was pale and glistening and his breathing fast and shallow. He was going into shock.

"Best call an ambulance," I said to the maid and Mr. Lush. "I'll go find someone to help."

"No," he got out weakly. "Can't…let it upstairs. Ruin it…"

It was a galvanizing thought. I imagined my father standing in the lobby in his crisp uniform, proud of the hotel he helped maintain, anxious to make a great impression on the CN managers this afternoon, his pride turning to horror as he watched a mottled flesh demon leap onto the reception counter and sink its teeth into the neck of the nearest clerk.

"You...skinny. Hippy...but maybe. Kill." His eyes rolled up and his head fell back. I checked his pulse. It was quick but strong.

Not much of a cheerleader, Mr. Lush. Maybe it would be best if I got his custodial crew down here to deal with it. They'd know the basement better, all the hiding places. But how long would it take to round them up and get them up to speed? Would they even believe me? If that thing got upstairs, what would that mean for my father and mother? Like everyone said about CN: they were always looking to make a case to sell or shut down the hotel. Their visit today was a make-or-break not just for my father's job, but also for dozens of his friends and colleagues.

His words from earlier rang in my ears, *If Mr. Lush tells you to fish a turd out of a toilet like bobbing an apple out of a barrel, you do it.* Thankfully it hadn't come to that. But taking on this creature could turn out to be worse. As I thought about it, I scanned Mr. Lush's desk. A yellow floral-print cleaning rag I'd torn up earlier lay there in a tangle. I picked it up. The strip of fabric covered my forehead like a band as I knotted it tightly around my head.

I could do this.

The hallway was peppered with people in groups of

two or three, some whispering, others gesturing wildly. All were equally ignorant of what had happened—was continuing to happen—in the bowels of the building. I picked up the shovel Mr. Lush had dropped and slung it over my shoulder. Some people stopped talking when I passed, others snickered. Everyone's head turned when the screaming started. I took off at a run.

I turned the corner, and my feet pounded on the concrete as I zeroed in on the sound. The shrieks were ear-splitting by the time I got to the open laundry room door. Marge and I did a full chest bump as I turned into the room, and I bounced across the hall into the wall opposite. Holding her ground, she turned and shouted back into the room, "Iris! Come on! Before it gets out of the bag!"

My lungs expanded to catch the breath the wall had knocked out of me, and I pushed past Marge into the laundry room. Iris was standing on the washing machine, shrieking in pulses. Pure terror froze her face in a wide-eyed stare at the writhing canvas bag nearby on the floor.

I took off running. The tiles were too slippery to come to a complete stop, so I slid the last two feet toward the washing machine and swung the shovel at the bag as I skidded. The tool connected with the solid mass inside like a hockey stick striking a puck and sent the bag flying between the shelves of stacked linens. Iris didn't stop screaming but jumped off the washing machine with the grace of a drunken foal and shot across the room so quickly she ricocheted off the doorframe when she hit it on her way out. Marge grabbed her arm and pulled her out of the room.

"Weirdest thing I ever saw," Marge said. "A cat or

something, all burned up! Came right at—"

"Get out and close the door!" I shouted. "Don't let anyone in unless they have a blowtorch. And tell them to give Mr. Lush a rabies shot. And tetanus. All the shots they have."

"*Rabies*? Tell who?" Iris panted.

Marge, as sensible a woman as there ever was, nodded, pushed Irish up the hall, and closed the heavy wooden door.

A guttural growl had my head swinging back to the bag I'd whacked across the room. It was empty. A streak of pink sped along the back wall and disappeared behind the stack of canvas bags Iris had been filling earlier. I raised the shovel and moved slowly toward it.

The laundry room was at melting temperature. In the minute I'd been in there, my headband was soaked with sweat and beads were starting to drip into my eyes. I wiped my face with my arm. The tumble of the lone dryer made it seem like the room's heart was beating around me. The stack of bags shifted, and I stopped when the top bag tumbled to the floor. The sound of too-long nails skittering across tile made the hair stand up on the back of my neck just as the animal streaked along the wall again and stopped behind a rolling bin stacked with more canvas bags. It stuck its raw pink head around the side, nose-hole twitching furiously. I took a step forward and it froze. Then it came slowly from behind the bin, its body slouched close to the floor as it inched toward the linen-folding table between us.

I held the shovel in a death grip, ready to deliver a blow and made my own creeping prowl toward the creature, keeping the table between us. I realized my mistake when it darted forward, and I lost sight of it under the table edge. I rolled myself across the table on my back and came down on my feet on the other side as I heard the ugly yellow fangs of the creature snap shut behind me. I lost my footing with the momentum of the roll and stumbled backward into the pile of laundry bags. They fell around me, pinning my legs. Quick as I could get the shovel up, the creature was on me. I choked up on the handle and swatted at its face, but it kept an arm's length from me. Close up, I could see the sprinkle of short, crinkled whiskers on its snub snout and recognized the remnants of stubby round ears. The tail, though pinkened and knobby, had a rough-scaled texture. Thickened and distorted, but unmistakably a rat's tail.

I changed my grip on the shovel and held it like a bar in front of me. The rat-creature made darts toward my face and throat, fangs clicking. It reached for my eyes with its claws. The smell of Mr. Lush's miracle herbicide invaded my nostrils with every move it made. I thought I was doing a great job fending him off until his teeth sank into the ring and pinky finger of my left hand. The scratch of teeth on bone and the crunch that followed pumped every last bit of adrenaline into my body.

I reared up. The laundry bags shifted, and the animal slipped backward with my two fingers sticking out of its mouth. In the second of respite, I dug my heels into the floor and stood. Powered by fury, I swung the shovel in a mighty arc that sent blood spray from my finger stubs across the white bags around me. Struck, the rat-thing flew back against the edge of the metal shelving with a sharp crack. It landed on the floor and came at me again. It dragged itself with its front claws, hind quarters twisted and still. I kicked the laundry bags out of the way and stood over it. It hissed like an enraged cat. As I raised the shovel, it lunged and sank its teeth into the tough leather of my workbook. I brought the tip of the spade down into its body, severing it in half. The front end twitched, its fangs still fastened to my boot.

The ruptured gut and intestines spilled out. They were full of soft goopy masses and an assortment of small bones. I wasn't a biologist by any means, but it did cross my mind that the absence of rats and their carcasses in the hotel basement could be explained by the appetites of this creature. A creature that seemed to me had been a rat itself before "Jimmy's little liquid helper" got a hold of it.

That's where it ended for me. The ambulance they called for Mr. Lush took me to the hospital, too. Back in those days, nobody reattached fingers. I don't mind. Maybe I'm getting soft in my old age—or maybe I've become the hippy Mr. Lush thought I was—but these days I feel sorrier for that rat than I do for myself. Wasn't its fault it got turned into a psychotic cannibal skin sack.

Oh, and the CN visit was a success. After it was done and the hotel management had smilingly shuffled the inspectors off to the airport, they shut the hotel down one area at a time and conducted the most aggressive rat hunt in the history of the city. They didn't find one rat, alive or dead, normal or deformed. But they did find Mr. Lush's orange-striped barrel of poison. Turned out he hadn't told the management about it, and they were *pissed*. I wonder how they all felt a few years later when pictures of barrels like that one started turning up on the evening news in stories about Agent Orange and the Vietnam War? I'll never know how Mr. Lush felt about it. While he was in the hospital, they found out he was riddled with cancer. He never made it to Christmas that year.

12

David stepped up behind Sarah, putting a gentle hand on her shoulder. She tensed as it slotted into place over the already bruised flesh that Barry had left but seeing him across the room reinforced that it was David's hand, and she relaxed, trusting his touch.

Barry had made it into a corner while speaking, as though he had been put there by some vengeful school-marm, and now he turned to them. There was another brief flash of change, and, for an instant, he was pale. He was so pale as to barely be seen. So pale that light almost passed through him.

There were only the three of them now, David, Sarah, and Barry. Bernice was gone, and now so were the two staff who had followed them through their entire journey.

They had stepped into a new room during the story. This room, Sarah found, was the most haunting yet. It was about crime, the history of Newfoundland crime. She knew on some level that the people in all the portraits they'd seen, all the histories, to this point were all dead. But these were different. There was a difference between being *dead* and being *murdered*.

She thought of what Barry had said about taking stories from the young, it was the stories left untold when a life was cut short.

In the centre was a jacket, pinned open to a display. Next to it was a portrait of the missing person it had belonged to; the jacket was all the police had found. She looked young, and reading the dates beneath the photo, Sarah realized she had been younger than her when whatever happened to her had happened.

"Yes, you see her?" Barry said, smiling the sinister smile of a man who had been hiding his grin for too long, and no longer felt the need to. "That's what I was talking about, yes? That's what makes this *special*. There's something about items like these; they're *imbued* with story. You know that word, *imbue*?"

Sarah nodded.

"Of course you do. You're a bright girl. A *smart* girl." He put his fingers along the picture frame. "So was she," he paused, holding the comma to bring about a horrifying implication, "I'm told."

"Come here, child. Come here, finally, and I shall tell you her tale."

Sarah turned back to David. Slowly, he nodded and released his grip on her.

FAMILY AFFAIRS
Taylor Barrett

Being one of the keenest detectives in St. John's is not an easy job. My interest in crime began as a nine-year-old, when my best friend, Ellen, and I buddy-read the worn, wrinkled copies of Sherlock Holmes that were housed in our elementary school's library. Twenty years later, I can still easily remember the crumbling covers of the books, and how their cracked spines felt against my fingers as I held them under my bed sheets, reading them with a flashlight in the middle of the night.

Sherlock and Watson's adventures were so captivating to my pre-teen brain that I immediately progressed to researching local crimes on my family's computer and watching whichever documentaries I could find on the television. It wasn't the crime itself that interested me, but the mystery surrounding it. I enjoyed trying to piece together evidence myself, and the pride I felt whenever my hypotheses were proven correct was unmatched. Ellen would often accompany me on my made-up endeavours, so much so that, by high school, we were certain that we wanted to become detectives ourselves, just like Sherlock and Watson, but without the trench coats, and with matching tattoos. We were even lucky enough to become partners once we began working.

But being a detective sometimes means being called to investigate a house that has not been touched in decades to find something of utmost importance. Of course, as Ellen and I make our way up the driveway, there is no doubt in my mind that we will find something substantial, but the case we're working on today has been closed since the '70s. Why are we only investigating the house thirty years later?

"Well, Clara, this is creepy, right?" Ellen remarks, nudging me with her elbow. We look up at the house from the front steps, shuddering synchronously.

The old Anderson family house is white with a rust-coloured door, roof, and shutters. The bushes around the house are overgrown, and a silver mailbox, dented and dangling on its stand, stands amidst them. November fog wraps its arms around the house, holding it in a damp, grey embrace.

"Definitely," I confirm.

"Let's get on with it, then."

Ellen takes a step forward, and I follow. She knocks three times, though we both know not to expect an answer, and when our hypothesis is proven correct, I turn the doorknob and let us into the house. Inside, the air is colder, and I sigh, my breath forming a puff of air like smoke in front of my face.

"I'm going to check the kitchen," Ellen says. "Do you want to check somewhere else, or help me out?"

"I'm going to go upstairs. You look around down here. Call me if you find anything."

"You too."

I nod and watch Ellen turn the corner before starting up a flight of creaky stairs. They groan loudly, protesting my every step. I flick the light switch at the top of the staircase, but it doesn't do a thing, and, instead, I turn on my flashlight and point it around the top floor of the house.

The first door I push open houses the bathroom. Its walls are painted a patchy green, and the floor is covered in chipped black and white tiles. Mould borders almost every tile. A Monet print hangs on the wall closest to the bathtub, which is also decorated with mould spores and mildew. The shelves above the tub are empty, without a single bottle or soap bar, and the ceiling above it is water-damaged and cracked. I raise my camera and take a photo of the water damage, then another of the bare shelves, and turn to face the sink.

The sink is built into a counter. Each of its drawers is empty, aside from one, full of moth-eaten face cloths and hand towels. A dirty mirror hangs above the sink, framed with rusted gold metal. I frown and run my fingers across a long crack down the center of the mirror, then take another photograph, before exiting the room.

The second room I enter is a bedroom, probably belonging to Mr. and Mrs. Anderson. The king-sized mattress in the center of the room rests upon a brown wooden bed frame with a square headboard. There are two nightstands, one on each side of the bed. On the right side is a white nightstand with an old Tiffany lamp and a rotary telephone, a ceramic dish full of mismatched earrings and metal earring backs, and a framed photograph of the Anderson family: the two parents and their son. I pick it up and turn it around, squinting at the writing on the back of the frame.

James and family, October 13, 1965.

I take photos of the picture frame and make my way over to the second nightstand. This one is the same brown wood as the bed frame. Sitting on top of it are three hardcover books, a lamp with a yellow shade, and a folded orange and blue tie. The nightstand has two drawers. The first is loose and opens with ease, revealing an impressive tie collection, all folded neatly and stacked together. I poke around between them and unfold them in search of clues but come up empty all the same. Finally, I pull on the second drawer, but, to my surprise, it doesn't budge. I drop to the floor and rattle it, trying once again to open it. When it stays in place, I huff and roll up my sleeves, yanking as hard as I can until the drawer comes flying out of the nightstand, sending me stumbling back onto the heels of my hands.

"Woah," I sigh to myself as I rise onto my knees and peer down at the contents of the drawer. Inside are at least fifty letters, several black-and-white photographs, and a multi-tool.

"Detective Byrn!" I shout, pulling myself up to sit cross-legged on the bed with the drawer in front of me. Ellen's footsteps thunder up the stairs and she appears in the doorway, eyeing the drawer skeptically. "This could be something."

Ellen comes to sit next to me and reaches into the drawer, pulling out a stack of envelopes. "They're all Mr. Anderson's?"

"Yes. Look," I hold one up, shining my flashlight over

the return address. "This one says it's from a Ms. Betty Wilcox."

"Why does that name sound so familiar?" Ellen wonders, skimming through the envelopes.

"She was murdered in '67. Stabbed to death and found behind the Grace Hospital, but her murder was never solved," I explain. "Why do you think Betty Wilcox was writing to Cooper Anderson?"

"Maybe Cooper Anderson was the one writing to Betty Wilcox. Take a picture and read the letter."

While I'm taking the photo, Ellen gasps and sits up straight, grasping my arm tightly.

"This one is from Richard Wilcox. Didn't he die, too? Drowning, I think."

"In '67, right after Betty," I nod, feeling my eyes widen. "They found his body at the bottom of Signal Hill. He had significant head trauma, right? There were rumours that he'd been pushed."

"But they ruled it as a suicide," Ellen finishes, handing me the letter to photograph. My heartbeat quickens, pieces slotting together in my brain.

Ellen begins to read Betty's letter. *"My dearest Cooper, I'm so sorry for not responding to your last letter sooner. Unfortunately, Richard has found my letters from you and has asked me not to write to you from now on. I wanted to write one last time, simply to let you know what has happened. Our correspondence has been life-changing. I believe that I have found love with you. I ask you not to write me back. I know that you loved me, too. Forever yours, Betty."*

"Cooper Anderson was having an affair with Betty Wilcox, and Richard found out. Do you think this has anything to do with the disappearance of the Andersons?"

"I don't know," Ellen says. "But it's still a big piece of missing information. Read the one from Richard."

"Mr. Anderson," I read. *"Does Laura know about your infidelity? I can't help but think that your wife would not approve."*

"That's it?" Ellen leans over my shoulder to read the letter.

"That's it."

"Richard knew about the affair and threatened to tell Mrs. Anderson. This was November 10th, 1970. When did Richard die?"

"December 8th..." I pull a Polaroid from the bottom of the drawer and hold it up in front of the both of us, staring at it until the grainy image registers in my brain. "Look. He had photos of Betty sleeping. Isn't that creepy?"

Ellen grabs the Polaroid from my hand and bites her bottom lip. "What makes it even creepier is that I don't think she's asleep. Look at the background, Clara. Those are bushes."

"Wait," I point to Betty's body, my heart pounding in my ears. "That's a wound on her neck, right? I could be reaching, but I think it is."

"A stab wound," Ellen confirms, nodding slowly. "Hand me the rest of the letters. I'll read them while you go through the photos."

"Hang on, we should check the multitool, too." I pass Ellen a stack of letters and pick up the old multitool, opening it carefully. My gloves make it difficult, but once I've successfully pried it open, I begin to look through the blades. The screwdriver head is blunt but looks normal, aside from rusting around its edges. The first saw is, similarly, in decent condition. However, I drop the multitool into the drawer when I pull out the first knife.

The blade is caked in a flaky brown substance, too dark to be rust, but not dark enough to be mould.

"Oh my god," Ellen gasps, abandoning her letters. "That's blood."

"It is. Call in the Sheriff and photograph this. I need to check the kid's bedroom."

The room next to Mr. and Mrs. Anderson's belongs to James. His bedroom looks just like any other child's—a twin-sized bed with dinosaur-printed pillowcases and a toy train track on the floor—but alarm bells are going off in the back of my brain. Frantically, I flip through water-damaged chapter books and a stack of crayon drawings. I lift picture frames off of the walls in search of something hidden behind them. All I find are peeling wallpaper and cracks near the baseboards.

Finally, I decide to check under the bed. The bed frame is so high off the ground that two cardboard boxes, stacked on top of each other, fit underneath it. James must have had to use a step stool to get into bed because a white one sits next to his footboard. I pull the boxes out and open them up, but I'm faced with baby clothes and blankets instead of any real evidence. Sighing, I begin to take the baby clothes out of one of the boxes: a sleeper with an embroidered lion on it, a blue fleece coat, and baby socks.

As I'm pushing the boxes back underneath the bed, my flashlight catches something toward the back of the bed, behind where the boxes would have been. My brows furrow, and I reach underneath the bed to slide it out. It's a miniature dollhouse, about a foot and a half tall, with four rooms and a roof. This should not be unusual for a child's bedroom, except for the contents of the rooms.

Inside the bottom right room are two figurines sitting at a wooden table, one man and one woman. Beside them is a room with a face cloth folded up to look like a bed, where a figurine of a woman lays. I pick up the doll to inspect it closer and notice that the stomach, back, and neck have been coloured red, possibly with a marker. Chills break out across the back of my neck and crawl down my spine. Laying underneath the doll is a miniature kitchen knife, cut from white paper and coloured with waxy crayons. I lay the doll back down and move the knife so it's next to it, then take a photo.

Directly above this room is one which is empty except for a paper sofa and rug. Next door, another face-cloth bed has been made. A figurine of a man is lying on the floor next to it. Looking closer, I notice faint red marks, similar to the woman's, have been made on the figurine's face and head.

"The Sheriff is on his way. Did you find anything else?" Ellen asks from the doorway, startling me into dropping the figurine.

"Yes," I nod as I pick it up and hold it out to her. "Take a look at this."

Ellen comes to kneel on the floor beside me, taking the figurine from my hand and holding it up to the light of my flashlight.

"That's disturbing," she observes. "Anything else?"

"There's another one. A woman." I hand her the figurine of the woman, and she grimaces. "There's a knife, too."

"You don't think this could be Betty, do you?"

"Who else would it be?"

Ellen frowns and turns the figurines over in her hands. "The markings are definitely similar to Betty's stab wounds. But how would the child know where the stab wounds were?"

"He couldn't have seen the Polaroid, could he?"

She bites her bottom lip and lays the figurines back down. "Let's wait for the Sheriff to get here. We can take it from there."

"Ellen, I really think that this is a big piece of evidence. These three cases have been unsolved for years, and now we know that Cooper Anderson was in contact with Betty and Richard Wilcox."

There's no way this is a coincidence. In my time as a detective, I've come to realize just how rare coincidences really are. These murders have to be linked to the missing Anderson family in some way, even if that way is a small one. It's undeniable.

"We've just spoken to an old witness regarding the Richard Wilcox murder," Sheriff Fudge announces two days later. Ellen and I look up from the computer document we've been reading, so quickly that I hear my neck snap. "He had the exact same story as in our last interview. He was a friend of Wilcox's but lived down the road from the Andersons. Says he was near Cabot Tower just after eleven at night, trying to get pictures of the Christmas lights on the tower for the newspaper, when he heard two men yelling. He turned around and saw Anderson push Wilcox over the ledge near the water."

"Why wasn't Anderson charged when this witness first told the cops?" Ellen asks, incredulous.

"The file notes say it's because he was the only witness. There were no other signs of anything happening, no fingerprints on Wilcox's body, and Anderson had a solid alibi for where he was that night. It seemed like a suicide attempt, like he tried to jump into the harbour without realizing he wouldn't go straight down," Sheriff Fudge explains. "The autopsy reports his cause of death to be head trauma and a snapped neck, most likely from hitting rocks on the way down. It didn't seem like a murder. We tried to look for security footage from that night, but we haven't been able to find any."

"But, now we know that it probably was," I say. "And it was probably linked to Clara Wilcox's death."

"It was most definitely linked to Clara Wilcox's death," Sheriff Fudge confirms. "After confirming the witness's story, reading Anderson's letters, and seeing the photo evidence, I'm certain the reason the Andersons fled is because Cooper Anderson was guilty."

"I still don't understand how the child knew everything about the murders," Ellen comments. "Unless he saw the Polaroid of Clara and just made an assumption with the male figurine."

"We think he overheard his father telling his mother the details of the murders. I've been speaking with Dr. Murphy, and he says that it seems like this was the only way James could find to cope with the information he was hearing. His parents likely told him not to tell anybody about it, so he used his figurines to depict everything, instead."

"Does this mean that the Wilcox cases are solved?" Ellen asks.

"I still have to speak with a few people," Sheriff Fudge sighs, running a hand through his grey hair. "But it looks like they will be."

BREAKING: MAY 28, 2003 - MISSING ANDERSON FAMILY FOUND?

Six months of desperate research and spotty communication later, James Anderson shows up in St. John's for the first time since 1971. We find out that he's been living in Toronto as John Andrews this whole time. He's brought into the police station from the airport by an escort and spends the next two days sitting in an interview room. When I see him, I'm taken aback by how similar he looks to the little boy in the Anderson family photo I found in the house. His eyes are the same, his nose is the same, and even his hair is the same as it was as a child. He has dark bags underneath his eyes and a long scar across his right cheek, which he tells Ellen is from a dirt biking accident in the '90s.

"What have you been up to?" I ask when it's my turn to interview him.

He sits back in his chair, eyebrows raised. "That's what you're asking me?"

"Well, you and your family have been missing for thirty years. I'd like to know what you've been doing since then."

"Trying to find a good job." James shrugs. "I don't know if the others told you, but my father died three years ago. My mother moved in with me last year, so we're doing some home projects."

"Pneumonia, right?"

"What?"

"That's how he died. Your father."

"Oh. Yeah," he nods, looking at his hands. "The last detective told me that you found my old dollhouse."

"I did," I confirm. "That's why I wanted to speak with you, actually. We know about the murders, and how your family changed names and moved away, but I'm curious as to how you knew so much about the murders at such a young age. Our forensic psychologist thinks that you might have heard about the details from your parents, and you expressed what you were hearing through your dollhouse. Is he right?"

"Not exactly."

"Do you want to tell me what really happened, then?" I prod.

He sighs heavily. "I know so much because I was there. I was there when the murders happened."

"You were there?" I sit up straighter, looking out the window of the interrogation room to meet Sheriff Fudge's eyes.

"The first time, with Betty, my dad and I were driving back home from supper at my grandparents' house. My grandfather had just given me a new book. It was late and dark, and my dad just pulled over near the Grace Hospital and told me to read my book. Then, he took his camera and left, all stressed out. I started reading, but it was too dark to see properly, so I was looking out the window. I heard a woman screaming, and I turned around to see who it was, but I ended up seeing my father stabbing Betty."

I wince. "Did you know her?"

"I didn't know who she was at the time, but when my dad got back in the car, he was calmer than when he left. I don't think he realized I had seen it happen because he told me that he just had to meet up with a friend for a minute. It wasn't until we left, and my mother told me he'd been having an affair, that I found out who she was."

"That must have been a lot to handle," I say, looking up from my notepad.

"It was," he admits. "But he confessed to my mom as soon as we got home. She told him that he couldn't tell anybody else, and I knew that meant I couldn't, either. That's why I started colouring the figurines."

"What about Richard Wilcox?"

"My father and I used to go on long drives through the city to look at the Christmas lights. We'd been driving for an hour or two because we stopped at Lar's in between. I remember we were driving downtown when he spotted a car and started following it until it went up Signal Hill. It was a clear night, so you could see the lights on Cabot Tower well, and he told me that was where we were going. But he parked and waited a few minutes until another man was near the tower. Then, he got out and started talking to him, just having what looked like a friendly conversation. It was almost out of nowhere, but my dad just pushed him down the hill near the harbour."

"Did he tell your mother about that, too?"

"Yeah. That's how I knew more about his injuries. He told my mom that he split his head open."

"James, would you happen to know why he did it?"

James sighs again. "He told my mother that he killed Betty because he was angry at her for letting them get caught. He wanted her to himself. Then, he killed Richard because Richard was the one who wanted them to stop seeing each other in the first place. He begged my mother not to tell anyone and said that he would never do anything like it again. And, I guess, he didn't. But it was still awful."

I huff out a long breath and clasp my hands on the table in front of me.

"Is it okay with you if I bring the Sheriff in? I think he needs to know about this."

"Go ahead," James says.

I motion for Sheriff Fudge to come in. He opens the door and makes his way over to the table, arms crossed.

"Any new information?" he asks lowly, though I suspect James can still hear him. I turn back to James and stand, letting the Sheriff sit where I had been sitting.

"Tell him exactly what you told me."

BREAKING: JANUARY 1, 2004 - JAMES AND LAURA ANDERSON FOUND NOT GUILTY FOR MURDERS OF RICHARD AND ELIZABETH WILCOX.

13

David clapped his hands, and the sound echoed throughout the room.

Rooms devoid of people in old museums always echoed like that.

It was just the two of them now, just David Hunter of Snook's Arm and Barry of the museum. The two of them were alone in a mostly empty exhibit towards the back of the building.

In the centre of the room was an empty display case.

Atop a wooden pedestal was a glass case covering a felt mat and nothing else.

There were lights inside the rim of the glass, tiny string lights that aimed up at the nothingness on display and held on to it.

"Quite a story," David said, stepping forward as he spoke.

Barry looked from one side of the room to the other. Nothing flashed within him. He wasn't something else for a moment, he was what he was: an old man who was small even by the standards of old men, made smaller still by a debilitating hunch. "It was, wasn't it?"

"Oh yes, I think so. I think you could get lost in it."

Barry nodded. He tried to step forward, stumbled, then braced himself on the empty display and apologized as he tried to compose himself.

"Oh, that's okay, old timer. Telling stories, well, you'd know, it takes a lot out of you, see?" David stepped around to the back of Barry and put a heavy hand on either of his shoulders as the old man had done to so many.

He clenched them and the old man buckled to the pressure, as David whispered into his ear, "Would you like me to tell one now?"

Barry smiled and, already, some colour returned to his cheeks. "Oh, yes. Yes *please*."

David squeezed.

"This is the tale of a man unlike any other," David said, pressing his fingers into Barry's clavicle and walking with him. "This man, he was great. But in that old way of saying someone was great, you know? That way people used to say it with the implication that great men usually came about their greatness by doing the things others couldn't bring themselves to, y'know? Back in the day, people knew that to call a man great was to also call him *terrible*."

"And Brutus was an honourable man," Barry croaked.

David ignored Barry's attempt at participating in the storytelling as he continued.

THE BOWTIE
Matthew LeDrew &
Mike Hickey

This man was a great man.

At some point, when the man was a boy at the cusp of becoming a man, he discovered that food held no worth or sway to him. Growing up in a place where food, especially good food, was a currency, this made the man, then a boy, particularly peculiar. Sure, he'd feel hungry but when he ate the food didn't satiate the feeling.

The man's, then boy's, mother would compel him to eat with the pleas that he needed the food for the utilitarian function of consuming the calories he needed for energy and if that didn't work, she'd use the motherly tactic of guilt, begging him to eat out of respect for the starving children in the world.

It was the stories of the starving children that worked.

Not to get him to eat, but to satisfy his hunger.

It was then that he discovered what he was truly hungry for.

He hid this from his mother and anyone else who would take note of his peculiarities. Once he learned what he actually needed for sustenance, it was easy enough to eat food just to stop the inquiries into why he wasn't eating.

The only problem with this makeshift solution is that it never allowed him to properly consume what he needed in the quantities he needed. It made him small, physically, and the resentment it fostered for those around him made him small, emotionally.

What he lacked in stomach, he also lacked in heart.

He didn't know why he was what he was. His mother and father weren't like him, his brothers and sisters weren't like him, at least not in so much as he was able to tell, and he was sure that he would be able to tell, that he would be able to smell it in them. It was him, alone, who was like it.

He didn't know what he was either. He tried to find out. He spent hours scouring science texts trying to decipher if there was some name for him or his condition, but he found nothing.

Having exhausted the scientific books, he looked to folklore trying to find a creature that sustained itself the way he did, but he didn't find anything.

He came closer there than he had in the science books. There were stories of fae that aligned with some of his experiences, but not quite all.

The closest thing he could find to describe his affliction was to call himself *a vampire*.

But even that didn't hold right for him. It wasn't the literal lifeblood of humanity he consumed, but the figurative lifeblood; he fed on stories.

He fed on the stories of those in pain. The stories of those who struggle. The starving children his mother would plead for him to show respect for as he pushed his uneaten food around on his plate.

This man, this vampire, he fed on the stories of rich and poor, young and old.

Of the old, he would drink deep of their experience, the wealth of what they had to offer.

Of the young he would drink deep on what they had left, the stories yet to be told.

"I think that was how he discovered it," David said, still clamped onto Barry's neck.

"Discovered what?" the diminutive man returned.

"Far back and away, away from these shores and her people, I think he cut a young life short. Years of consuming in short doses of the same old stories told around the hearth, the recitations he had heard of and over again left him starving. His hunger got so that he would try anything—*anything*¬—to sate it, and only at the tip of a blade did he discover what he truly salivated for."

He discovered that he could feed on stories and leave the victims frail but alive, if only for a limited time. That was when the man, now a man, became a hunter who does not kill what he eats but lets his prey wander the world, already consumed, to wither. A fate worse than death.

But he didn't care. He had felt alone so long that he didn't see himself as human. The people he fed on weren't equals to him; they existed so they could sate his hunger.

He travelled. Moving from place to place, feeding on

stories. Feeding on *histories*. Feeding on what makes a life worth living.

Soon, he discovered that a person was a meal, but a people were a feast.

And if he was able to get an entire people to feed him, he could feed on them forever.

Then he found it: a fresh, virgin country.

An island, all on its own and he drank deep from it.

Yes, a person and their stories were a meal, but a people and its culture were a feast. A banquet to gorge on.

But he never filled. He never grew tall, he never grew fat, and his hunger never subsided. Whatever hole was inside him to be filled by those stories stretched on forever and he kept eating.

Until he couldn't.

He was, of course, not a vampire as we know them from myth and legend. He was his own kind of vampire, so eventually, finally, the man did die.

But his hunger did not.

It kept travelling from space to space, still feeding on that island.

Still drinking up her culture and her people until there was nothing left to be had, and the people would become like ghosts, and then the community, they would become like ghosts, and finally the town itself would be a ghost town.

Abandoned.

Resettled.

And sometimes it would feed until there was nothing left but amber, and that amber would become an artifact of what had been there.

Then, unable to just let the culture he and his hunger had sucked dry wither away like his human victims, the remnants of the places, those artifacts, would be put on display for all to see so that those that had escaped, had made it out of those towns, would come from miles around to see the last shards of the place they had called home. They would reminisce. They would tell stories.

And the man, he would feed anew.

Until the descendants of his victims had told enough of the stories so that the man, unlike the places, could be resurrected.

David opened a door at the end of a long hallway, revealing a dark room that Barry had never seen before.

The staff were there. Silent.

In the middle of the room was a large circle, marked on the floor with salt distilled from the sea. Along its edge were thirteen markers, spaced equally apart, for today was the day, as Erin had professed, when thirteen held much power.

At twelve of the thirteen markers were the people from the tour, each of them holding an artifact encased in amber in one outstretched hand, and a candle in the other.

"What is this?" Barry squelched.

"Bruce Goodard from Three Arms," David said, pointing to him. When he did, Bruce nodded.

"Clive Burr from Aaron Cove. Freeda Smith, Bear Cove. Alphonsus Buck, Bear Cove, but not the same Bear Cove. Creed Dunford, Rencontre West. Rowe Saunders, Current Island. Gary Linehan, Oderin Island. John Barker, Harbour Buffett. Derek Rose, King's Cove, District of Fortune Bay and Hermitage. Charles Henry, Mosquito. Bernice Fletcher, Little Harbour Deep. Sarah Childs, Tickles."

He stepped out from behind Barry, arms outstretched.

"David Hunter, Snook's Arm."

Sarah handed him his own piece of amber, and he took it, stepping back into his place on the circle as the others shuffled and made way for him.

"What *is* this?" Barry demanded.

"Snook's Arm is the most recent. Bernice said that we shouldn't tell you where we were from. She said you'd remember and that we'd give it away. She thought that no beast could be so evil as to not remember the communities he'd devoured. Destroyed. Scattered and resettled and unearthed," David said and looked at Sarah.

She nodded, and he turned back to Barry, who had turned to see that the circle of salt and those around it had closed around him.

David waggled his amber artifact at him. "But we knew different, Sarah and me. We knew and we convinced the others. It's nice to think that you'd remember the people you consumed or even the towns you destroyed. But even if we named every pig we ate, would we remember all their names at the end of a lifetime of gluttony?"

Barry stepped back to the edge of the barrier and tried to step beyond it but found he could not. He screamed, but the sound that came from him was unlike a scream and more like a hiss or a growl, or both. He turned back to David and Sarah, and as he did, he became pale. His eyes became sunken and dark, his fingers long knitting needles. His teeth became sharp and yellow.

Beyond the circle, Sophia looked away, burying her face into Erin's sweater. Erin, on the other hand, could not turn from what she saw. She couldn't bring herself to blink for fear of missing something.

"Snook's Arm was the latest," David continued, as though no change had occurred. "And I was its mayor when it went, her last mayor. And I told those people, as we packed up the last of our things and buried our town, I told them I would live up to my family name. That I would hunt down the thing that did this, and that he would do it no more."

He gestured to those around him.

"And those living descendants of the communities you ate, they said the same in kind." He turned to Sarah. "Start the words."

Sarah pulled a thick, leather-bound book from her satchel.

"You wanted so many of my stories," she said to Barry. "But never once did you ask what I was a student *of*." She began to chant, and the others joined in, each in turns around the circle, each starting the first verse when the speaker before was starting their second, in canon.

By the time it reached back to Sarah, and she was finishing the thirteenth verse and beginning again, the sound was a cacophony of white noise, one word almost indistinguishable from the next. And then a wall shot up from the ring of salt, a yellow translucent wall that went from the floor to the ceiling.

And as they continued, that wall began to close on the creature trapped within it.

"No!" Barry tried to scream but his words lost their form, devolving into a guttural hiss that seemed to mimic the same dead language of the chanting until only Sarah could understand the deal he was trying to strike.

The bargain that he tried to sweeten, again and again, as the walls of amber closed in around him, foot by foot.

Only Sarah understood, but she did not heed them, and she didn't tell the other twelve what he had said. "It would curdle you," she had told David, in a moment of weakness, some years later. "It would curdle you to the bone, the things he said he could give. The things he said he would do to just keep going as he was, stuck between life and death."

The walls closed in until they squeezed at him. They squeezed until his skin ruptured and popped, but just as the vampire didn't consume blood, that wasn't what evacuated him as his body collapsed in on itself. It was air, like steam from a kettle, and on those streams of hot air were the voices of the stories he'd told and been told.

And he shrank as they left him, until his already small form was almost nothing at all.

And when it was over, when his screams and negotiations in a language long dead had ceased, there was only one small object left of him, the only thing of his charade that had substance, and it was coated in hardened amber.

In the back room of the museum, past all the other displays and artifacts and runes, there lies a display that few have ever seen, not open, and not yet complete. There is a large room with nothing in it except in the very center.

In the centre of the room is a single display.

Atop a wooden pedestal is a glass case covering a felt mat.

There are lights inside the rim of the glass, tiny string lights that aim up at the display.

And displayed by those lights, on that mat, under that glass and atop that pedestal, there lies a bowtie, too large for the man that wore it, tattered and frayed, encased in amber.

And if you sat in that room with that single old bowtie for long enough you'd swear you heard the whispers of the most incredible stories of people and places and their histories.

And then the screams.

THE END

AFTERWORD

It's incredible to see what Terror Nova has become since we launched the first book in 2020. Honestly, looking back it's wild to imagine that this all started *that* year.

The first book was born very simply. I sat down with Matt at a coffee shop that no longer exists, and we discussed what a project between me and Engen could look like. We settled on an anthology with a mix of authors selected from his world and mine coming together to write short stories that were actually closer to novella length with me framing them up; taking inspiration from *Tales from the Crypt* and *Are You Afraid of the Dark?* to have the stories wrapped within another story that's just as important to the narrative.

The timing of that first book gave me a few months with not much else to do but write it, and as the stories from the other authors trickled in things started to find their shape.

I'm what other writers call a "pantser," meaning I don't do much plotting in advance and tend to let things just flow – fly by the seat of my pants, as it were. That can prove problematic when it comes to collaborating, but that first Terror Nova clicked in a surprising way, with *The Town That Tore Itself Down*, a concept I had been picking at for years without much direction, getting dusted off to serve as the final story in the book only for it to weave into the framing story set aboard a Dublin-inspired double decker bus tour with minimal effort.

The second book proved harder. Once something is out there, it stops being yours and becomes open to interpretation. Other people consume that work, take it their particular way, and then have their own ideas about what it is. That sort of became a theme of the book as I struggled writing about the fictionalized author of the first book struggling to write the second book, only to have unsolicited manuscripts mysteriously appearing. *Writers Retreat* with its deliberate exclusion of a possessive apostrophe, was intended to be a sequel in name and format only, with the references to the first book being the tenuous tie. It was only as I was in the process of working an unfinished short story *No Candy* in to serve as the end story that Simon arrived, uninvited, and the book became not only a true sequel to the first, but the cliff-hanging middle of a trilogy.

Going into *Lurking in Darkness* knowing it's the 3/3 was a new experience for me as a writer. I mean, most of the experiences around Terror Nova have been new experiences for me as a writer, but concluding something like this and finding a satisfying way to do it brought a pressure I hadn't experienced before.

Unlike the previous two resolving stories, *The Desert Island* wasn't already out there when I started. It wasn't a collection of notes and thoughts, or even pages of prose waiting for an ending. The book was hanging there, waiting for me to figure out what was going to tie it all up, and I ended up on a work trip to Quirpon Island (pronounced Car-poon). After hearing the stories and legends of the so-called "Isle of Demons," I found myself conjuring the story of the archeology team on the deserted island of the coast that borrowed a lot from where I was staying, and hours later had most of it complete. I think I turned the manuscript in two weeks later.

But that left us in a bit of a limbo. We had seen through a Terror Nova trilogy and now had to figure out what to do with things moving forward.

Luckily, by the time that the third book was dropping, we had confirmed that my television series, which was sharing the name, would be premiering in time for Halloween 2024. This meant Terror Nova was expanding beyond this initial trilogy and wouldn't conclude with these three books.

And you have no idea just where we're heading.

With this new installment, we're moving the books into a new framing narrative while keeping things decidedly "Terror Nova." We're also working on bringing the stories to life with a comic book series, a non-fiction companion to the television series that will look at the paranormal investigations of the show along with how Buddha and I accidentally became TV ghost hunters, and other initiatives partnering with the province's tourism industry.

There's so much Terror Nova coming for you, and I can't wait to share it all!

Mike Hickey, February 2025

TERROR NOVA

THE THIRTEENTH EXHIBIT

Hunger. It's something that can stretch beyond the want for mere food, the need for nutrition. Hunger can be a craving only satiated by consumption.

When two tour guides managing Newfoundland's most haunted museum on the most haunted day of the year must contend with a group of tourists looking to take advantage of their services, they find their roles usurped by a mysterious man whose descriptions and explanations of the exhibits carry with them a sinister tone.

Following the bestselling trilogy that spawned the hit unscripted NTV television series that shares its name, TERROR NOVA returns with a bold new direction featuring thirteen terrifying short stories from Newfoundland's top talents, including returning favourites ALEX MCINTOSH & NICOLE LITTLE, along with series newcomers AINSLEY HAWTHORN (*Land of Many Shores*), TAYLOR BARRETT (*Cover My Eyes*), & ANDREW HAWTHORN (*Teenage Mutant Ninja Turtles*).